TO WEAR A FAE CROWN

THE FAIR ISLE TRILOGY BOOK TWO

TESSONJA ODETTE

D1453301

FEB - - 2022

Copyright © 2020 by Tessonja Odette

All rights reserved.

No part of this book may be reproduced in any form or by any electronic or mechanical means, including information storage and retrieval systems, without written permission from the author, except for the use of brief quotations in a book review.

THE FAIR ISLE
FAERWYVAE
WINTER
STAR
Lunar Court
SUMMER
SOLAR
FIRE
Autumn Court
BIRCHARBOR PALACE
EARTHEN
WIND
Sea Court
SPRING
LUNAR AXIS
SPRING AXIS
AUTUMN AXIS
THE AXIS LINE
for interaxis travel
THE FAEWALL
Sableton
THE SPIRE
Grenneith
EISLEIGH
MAINLAND
BRETTON

1

Every young woman dreams of wearing a crown.

Well, I never held such a frivolous desire, but I've finally come to understand the appeal. Not so much the crown itself but what comes with it. Influence. Power. Responsibility. A king at my side.

For me, it's not just any king.

It's a mate I care for, one who ignites my anger as often as he sparks my desire. And I would have been his queen.

Would have been being the operative phrase here, as that is now completely and utterly wrecked.

A hollow ringing reverberates in my ears as I stand in the dining room at Bircharbor Palace, eyes unfocused as I rock on my feet. An explosion has come and gone, one of several that have occurred this hour, but this time I don't react. It isn't that I've grown used to the work the fae soldiers are doing on the beach below the palace, sealing the coral caves with detrimental blasts of explosives. It's more that I'm too numb to care. Too shocked to do anything but stand here wishing the last minute of my life could be reversed.

A minute ago, Aspen was in my arms.

A minute ago, we still had plans to get married.

A minute ago, our alliance would have protected both the humans and fae from certain doom.

But now...

"We're going to war." It's my voice that utters the words, but it sounds distant, strange.

King Aspen and Ambassador Foxglove stand before me, but I can't bring them into focus. My eyes glaze over, the dining room shrinking until it's nothing more than a pinprick of light. The summer heat wafting in through the open expanse in the wall behind me sends waves of dizziness to my head. I take in a deep breath, then another, but I can't seem to get enough air. I'd give anything for a cool breeze. For the usual Autumn Court weather to return and dry the sweat beading my brow.

The sound of paper crinkling pulls my attention back to the present, like an anchor in my whirlpool of thoughts. I realize the sound belongs to the letter in Aspen's hand, now crushed into a ball within his fist. The letter bears the words that announced the invalidation of our pairing. The end of the treaty. Of everything I've been fighting for.

The end of me and Aspen.

My lungs constrict, and I feel like my thoughts will swallow me whole, but I refocus on that piece of paper, on the shape of Aspen's fingers curled around it. Finally, the room ceases spinning, and my breathing begins to ease. My eyes lock on my mate, taking in every curve and angle of his beautiful face as if doing so can further root me into this moment. With my study of him comes a sudden awareness of the anger written in the rigid set of his shoulders, the tick in his jaw. The sight of his rage snaps me further out of my stupor, and I feel my own fury rise to meet his. A willing partner in a fiery dance.

My anger invigorates me at once.

"No," I say through my teeth, "this isn't happening. Not after everything we've been through, after everything we've done."

"Are you honestly surprised?" Aspen mutters.

"Yes, I'm surprised. We did everything the treaty called for. Our wedding is set for three days from now—the exact date the human council gave us. We met every deadline."

"Apparently the council doesn't care about deadlines. They'll use any excuse to keep us from solidifying the pact."

"How can you say that? They can't want war any more than we do. Besides, every suspicion you had about the human council being a threat to you has proven to be misguided. Cobalt was behind every action that kept you from securing the treaty thus far."

"If that were the case, they wouldn't have sent this." He lifts his hand and the paper crumpled in his fist.

"What exactly does it say?" I look from Aspen to Foxglove. While Foxglove verbally relayed the general message of the letter, I haven't read it word for word myself. "They must have given a reason to invalidate our alliance."

"Well, they—" Foxglove cuts off abruptly at a sharp look from Aspen.

A chill crawls up my spine. "What is it? What aren't you telling me?"

Foxglove looks to Aspen in deference, lips pressed tight as if he's fighting to keep from blurting some dangerous truth.

I step closer to my mate. "Tell me what it said or let me read it myself."

He doesn't meet my eyes. "I'll take care of it."

Fury roars through me, arguments storming from my mind to my lips. Before I can utter a single one, the ground rocks beneath my feet again, forcing me off balance. From the corner of my eye, I see water shooting into the sky from the explosion.

The rumbling calms, but before I can properly right myself, another blast shakes the palace. Aspen pulls me close to keep my feet beneath me. I lean into him, and it's for more than just support. His closeness reminds me yet again how badly I wish I could erase the moment where Foxglove came in with the letter. If only we could go back to where we were moments before that, enveloped in each other's arms with tender words on our lips.

But that moment was shattered, and even this slight reprieve is stolen away as the sound from the explosion is replaced with shouts. Screams of terror.

I reluctantly part from Aspen and turn toward the rail along the open wall. Several figures limp away from the site of the most recent explosion. I can't see much else through the spray of sand and water, but I'm almost certain there are dark patches covering the beach. Blood.

My heart pounds at the sight, echoed by footsteps

tearing down the hall and growing nearer with every beat. I can hardly move, can hardly tear my eyes from the scene below as I wait for the rubble to clear.

"Your Majesty."

I whirl toward the panting guard entering the dining room.

Aspen storms over to him. "What in the name of oak and ivy just happened?"

The guard's youthful face is pale, eyes wide as he explains, "It was Prince Cobalt's fae, Your Majesty. They were spotted in the caves, trying to thwart our efforts. I was sent to tell you—"

Aspen brushes past him into the hall. His voice is almost a roar. "I knew he'd be back. Where is he?"

The guard follows hard on the heels of the king, as do Foxglove and I. "The prince hasn't been spotted," the guard says, "but the fae were clearly his. They ambushed the detonation team, but your soldiers were able to keep Cobalt's fae back while they set off the explosion. Only two caves remained uncollapsed at that point, and detonation teams were sent in at once. That's when I was ordered to come to you."

Aspen's jaw shifts back and forth. "I take it from the shouts, there have been casualties."

The guard goes a shade paler, and we descend a set of stairs. "I was already on my way here when I heard the last two explosions go off, Your Majesty, but the second blast shouldn't have happened so close to the previous. Not unless..."

"Not unless it were necessary to set it off early," Aspen says through his teeth. "Have any of Cobalt's fae emerged from the caves? What about the caves leading to the tunnels in the palace?"

"Those tunnels were the first we collapsed, and I didn't see any of the prince's fae make it to the beach before I left."

Aspen is nearly running as we descend farther and farther down the palace. We must be near the bottom floor.

I quicken my pace and address the guard. "Where will the injured be taken?"

He opens his mouth, but Aspen stops in his tracks, spinning to face me. "Why are you following me? It isn't safe."

"I came to help."

He faces the guard. "Take Miss Fairfield somewhere secure."

The guard steps toward me, but I freeze him with an icy glare before turning it on Aspen. "No, I'm going to help the injured."

"You need to remain—"

"I'm going to help the injured," I repeat, louder, slower, each word pointed as my eyes burn into his. "It's what I'm trained to do."

"Fae can heal without your help."

I raise a brow, eyes roving over his torso before narrowing on the site of his former wound. A wound that would have been the death of him if it hadn't been for my intervention. I cross my arms over my chest. "Oh, can they?"

He lets out a frustrated sigh. "Fine." He returns his attention to the guard. "Take her to the east wing. That's where the injured will be. If you so much as sense a breach in the palace, take Miss Fairfield to safety."

The guard nods, and I don't dare argue with the order. Aspen's eyes find mine as his fingers grasp my palm, giving it a soft squeeze. The gesture says more than his words can, cutting through his temper to soften my heart. I can only enjoy the touch for a single breath before Aspen releases me and starts off down the hall again. As I move to follow him, the guard puts a hand on my shoulder. "This way is faster to get to the east wing." He nods toward another set of stairs. We take off, but I realize Foxglove has remained on the landing, wringing his hands as he stares at me with an open mouth. Like he wants to say something.

"Foxglove, with me." Aspen's voice echoes from down the staircase.

The bespectacled fae closes his mouth and gives me an apologetic smile. I don't want to read into what it means. But I'm sure it has to do with the letter.

I STEEL MYSELF AS I ENTER A FAMILIAR ROOM. THREE STONE tables are lined up in the center, and upon each lies a writhing fae guard: two male, one female. They've each sustained several wounds of varying severity, blood pooling on the tabletops beneath them as uninjured guards assist in removing their bronze armor.

I shudder, remembering the last time I was here. There was but one table then and Aspen was its occupant. It's hard to believe that was less than two weeks ago. Back then I wouldn't have cared if Aspen died.

I shake the morbid thought from my mind and join Gildmar, a tiny fae with bark-like skin and leafy hair, at the far end of the room. Her small hands fly over the table as she lays out her tools—shards of shell, sharp bone, pointed sticks, swaths of spider silk, bowls of water, herbs, and wine. I'm grateful I don't have to demand wine this time.

"Are these the only survivors?" I ask Gildmar.

She nods. "The last explosion went off while they were still prepping the keg inside the cave. These three were standing nearby. All inside the cave and near its opening didn't make it."

I swallow hard, wondering if she's been informed of the true cause for the early explosion. "What can I do to help?"

"First, ease their pain." She hands me a vial. I don't need to ask to know it contains extract of honey pyrus, a psychoactive fae fruit. Its extract works like laudanum, easing pain and allowing a patient's mind and body to slip into euphoric stillness.

I move from one injured fae to the other, administering a dropperful to each while Gildmar cleans one of the male fae's wounds with an herb-infused liquid. Once all three patients have fallen beneath the honey pyrus' spell, I take one of the bowls of wine and approach the unconscious fae female. I cleanse my hands with the wine and inspect her wounds. The fae's skin is pocked with bloody gouges from shards of coral spearing her flesh where the armor hadn't covered. I peel back the linen tunic from her torso, finding severe bruising blooming over her chest, likely crushed by her breastplate. I pour the wine over her wounds. "Are they in mortal danger?"

Gildmar shakes her head, though her face remains grave. "So long as we can staunch any bleeding and keep them calm, their bodies should heal on their own. There was no ash or iron involved, so their natural abilities will remain strong. However, if they lose too much blood, their bodies won't be able to keep up with healing."

I'm relieved to hear their prognosis is good, although it's hard to believe any creature could recover after being so close to an explosion. The concussive force alone would be enough to kill a human. "What were the explosives made from? Gunpowder?"

"Marsh gas, most likely," she says, her voice like the creak of an old branch. "Most often found in the marshes where Fire and Wind courts meet. A beastly practice, if you ask me. We shouldn't be bottling up nature the way humans do, using the elements for harm. My kind didn't do that before your people came to the Fair Isle."

Her tone is more resigned than accusatory, but my stomach sinks with guilt just the same. "How long will it take for them to recover?"

"Their wounds are grave, but it won't be like it was with the king."

Again, the memory floods my mind, of Aspen near death, veins of black trailing across his skin to show how deep the iron had poisoned his blood. I had been concerned about his recovery, but only because he was my patient; I'd been nowhere near as distraught as I'd be if something like that were to happen now. Not after how close we've become.

My heart squeezes. We were growing closer even still

before that letter arrived. I finally got him to express his anger over me using his name against him. We were making amends. I was so close to telling him that I...

I shake the memories from my head. Thoughts of Aspen and the mysterious contents of the letter will have to wait. For now, I have work to do.

2

It's midday by the time I finish helping Gildmar, my body heavy with exhaustion as I make my way from the east wing, Aspen's guard trailing behind me. Being this tired isn't a bad feeling, considering it's the result of a job well done. The three patients' wounds have been cleaned, stitched, and bandaged, and their bodies have been moved to a more comfortable room with actual beds where they can recover. All were dozing peacefully when I left them to rest in the recovery room, but before that I sat with each, resting my hands over their torsos for several minutes at a time.

Luckily, my guard remained outside the door during my visit. If anyone would have seen what I was doing, my cheeks would have blazed with embarrassment, no matter how benign my actions would have appeared to onlookers. For inside me burned the hope that my hands were doing more than just providing comfort. I'm still not positive I had anything to do with healing Lorelei's wounded leg or in aiding Aspen's sudden recovery from iron poisoning. I don't know if it was by some power of my own that helped me perform Aspen's surgery without the tools I'm used to.

If I'd considered such a notion two months ago, I would have laughed, deeming myself delirious. But now, after everything I've seen and done and experienced...

I believe in possibilities. Especially if they allow me to help others.

As we near the end of the east wing hall, a second guard awaits. She looks hesitant as she approaches us. My heart leaps into my throat as I begin to fear the worst. "Has Aspen returned?"

"No, he's involved in a skirmish with Cobalt's fae not too far from here," she says, "which is why I'm coming to you. Queen Melusine is on the beach, surrounded by our guards. She's demanding to speak with you."

"What does she want to speak with me about?"

"She wouldn't say. Only that she'd make a binding promise not to harm you and called upon the protection of *a peaceful exchange of words*. This means violence would be forbidden during your talk. If she were to attack you, each attack could be met blow for blow."

I bite the inside of my cheek. "What did you tell her?"

"Nothing. It is up to you whether to hold an audience with her. With King Aspen absent, you're in charge."

My head rushes from the weight of her words. *I'm in charge.*

The guard Aspen left to watch me clears his throat and faces me. "King Aspen wouldn't want you to meet with her without him present. He wouldn't deem it safe."

"Then you better see that no harm comes to me." I turn to face the fae female. "Take me to Queen Melusine. I want to know what she's up to."

It might not be the smartest move, but Melusine could know something about today's attack. She may have information about Cobalt, about Amelie, about the letter and the treaty—no, I'm getting ahead of myself. If she knows anything at all, she'll hide it behind a web of deception and weave it to her advantage. I should harbor no false hopes regarding her whatsoever.

I inhale a heavy breath to steady my racing thoughts and follow the guards to the beach. With the caves beneath the palace closed off, we take the long way down, skirting around the palace to a steep staircase cut into the cliff wall. When we reach the bottom, I find my unwelcome guest. Like the first time I spoke alone with the Sea Queen, Melusine perches on the shore, chin held high with a confident smirk. This time, however, she's surrounded by a circle of Aspen's guards. Luckily, she appears to be alone. Her beauty is as prominent as ever, with her dazzling stormy eyes, coral-red lips, and her long, indigo hair that flows in waves over her bare human-like upper body. Her blue-green serpent's tail props her up from her waist to where human feet should be, while the rest of her tail undulates behind her in anxious ripples across the sand.

"My, my, don't you look dreadful," she says in her melodic voice before flashing her sharp teeth in a semblance of a smile. My two guards flank me as I stop several feet away from her. Only now do I consider my state of dress. Foxglove and Lorelei always had me primped and preened with the utmost care before meeting with the queen. Now I come to her wearing a bloodstained robe and hair still mussed from sleep.

I narrow my eyes as if my appearance is the least of my concerns. That much, at least, is true. There are far more pressing matters at hand. "Why are you here, Your Majesty?"

"I wanted to know what my dear son was doing to my beautiful caves," she says with a pout.

"Your son doesn't want to speak with you." I hope she can't sense the omission in my voice—that my words obscure the fact that Aspen isn't currently here. That is, if she doesn't already know as much.

"It's clear he doesn't want to speak with me. I've tried making contact every day since the incident with his brother."

The incident. I bristle. That's a mild way to refer to Cobalt's attempt to steal Aspen's throne. "So, you decided to speak with me instead?"

She shrugs a bare shoulder. "It worked, didn't it?"

I hate that she's right. Aspen had the sense to ignore her, yet here I am giving in at her first request. My curiosity always does get the better of me. "Cut the iron-laced kelpie crap and get to the point," I say with a sweet smile. "Why are you *really* here?"

She rolls her eyes and lets out a huff. "I want you to speak to Aspen for me."

"And tell him what?"

"Tell him I want to form an alliance."

My mouth hangs on its hinge before I can speak. "An alliance? Isn't that what the council is for? Weren't you already supposed to be his ally when you sought to replace him with Cobalt?"

Her cheeks redden, lips pressing into a tight line, looking flustered for the first time. "I was wrong. I never should have supported Cobalt's claim."

I let out a bitter laugh. "Why, because he turned on you? Lied? Because you realized he was never going to be your unseelie puppet?"

"Cobalt stole lies from a human and turned them on me," she hisses through her teeth. "That is unforgivable. More than that, I respect the decision of the All of All, which he did not and will not abide by. The All of All should not be questioned. The unseelie know this in our blood."

"I'm sure Aspen will appreciate your acceptance of the All of All's verdict," I say without warmth. "Why do you seek an additional alliance?"

Again, she purses her lips as if her next words pain her to say. "I seek his protection."

"His protection? From what?"

"From my other son." Each word is punctuated with her growing rage. "He's all but taken over my court. Half my soldiers think they serve him, and that wretched human pet of his struts around in her selkie skin like she's the Queen of the Sea."

I narrow my eyes. "That wretched human is my sister."

She meets my gaze with a glower. "Then you know just how wretched she is."

My nails dig into my palms, irritation growing hotter inside me. "Melusine, you're one of the most powerful fae alive. You have the entire sea at your beck and call. What protection do you need from Aspen that you can't provide yourself?"

"I can't defend myself against my son when he can meet my powers underwater. I need somewhere on land to stay until he can be dealt with." Her shoulders tremble visibly.

I'm caught off guard by how truly shaken she seems. How can Queen Melusine fear Cobalt, her own son? He may have power over the water element, but he can't be anywhere near as fearsome as she is. Right?

As if she can sense my question, she adds, "I can't trust Cobalt now that he's ceased to be bound by fae rules. He can lie like a human and betray his allies without so much as blinking. Now that he's won over so many of my soldiers, I don't know what he's going to do next. I'd rather not wait around and find out."

My heart sinks. Unless she too has stolen the power to lie, she's serious.

She slithers closer, but Aspen's guards stop her from closing the distance between us. With a grumble, she says, "Speak to Aspen on my behalf. Please."

"You've already told him all this yourself?"

"He won't listen."

"What makes you think he'll listen to me?"

Her expression hardens. "You hold sway over him like no one ever has before."

Is she referring to my ability to use his name...or something else? She must know I'd never use Aspen's name on her behalf. It was hard enough using it to save his life. "I'll see what I can do."

"Is that a promise?"

"No."

Her lips pull into a smirk that looks close to admiration, then she nods in a semblance of a bow. "Very well." With that, she faces the ocean and slithers toward it. The guards maintain a tight circle around her, careful not to stumble over the shards of coral littering the beach. I don't take my eyes off the queen until the last flick of her tail glides beneath the water.

WHEN I RETURN TO THE PALACE, THERE'S STILL NO WORD on Aspen's current status. My heart races as I consider the myriad of concerns plaguing me—the skirmish Aspen's involved in, Melusine's fear of Cobalt, the letter. *The letter.* My stomach turns every time I think about it. I wish he'd left it for me to read. I need to know what it says, what it means, why the treaty has been broken, why our pairing has been invalidated. I need to pull it apart and analyze every sentence, every word, every loop and curve of the pen that wrote it to understand it. I must know...what does it mean for me and Aspen?

With nothing to do but wait for Aspen's return, I make my way to his bedroom to change out of my bloody clothes. Behind the dressing screen, I exchange my ruined nightdress and robe for a gauzy blue gown with a multi-layered, flowing skirt. When I come out from behind the screen, Lorelei enters the room. Her smile is warm as she approaches me, a shimmering swath of opalescent silk hanging over her brown arm, her petite frame swaying with every step.

"I was told you'd returned from surgery," the wood nymph says. "Did everything go all right?"

"It went well," I say, although I can't bring myself to feign a grin. "The patients are recovering."

She furrows her brow, clearly reading into my lack of enthusiasm. Still, she doesn't pry and holds out the luxurious fabric instead. "Your wedding gown is ready for its final fitting."

My eyes lock on the dress, and a shock of pain sears my heart. My emotions threaten to overwhelm me, but I force them down, force my voice to remain level as I say, "I don't know if there's going to be a wedding, Lorelei."

She lays the dress over the arm of the nearby couch and takes me by the shoulders. "Why would you say that? Did something happen between you and Aspen?"

I open my mouth and snap it shut. "I...I don't know."

"Whatever he said or did, you'll get through it. You know he loves you, right?"

That word—*love*—unravels me. Tears spring to my eyes, a sob building in my chest. "No, I don't know and I might never know."

"What do you mean?"

I squeeze my eyes shut, fingers clenching into fists as I swallow my tears and let anger replace my pain. "I'm so tired," I say through my teeth.

She takes a step away. "Then I'll leave you to rest—"

"I'm tired of living in fear of this treaty."

I open my eyes to find her nibbling her bottom lip, expression brimming with concern. "It's been hard, I know."

"It's been more than hard," I say, my anger growing, burning the anxiety from my mind, the sorrow that tugs at my heart. "We've done everything we were supposed to. We had the mate ceremony. We performed the Bonding ritual by midnight on the required date. We won Aspen's throne back from Cobalt. Our wedding is scheduled. Now we get a letter from Eisleigh's council saying our pairing has been invalidated."

Her eyes bulge as she processes my words. "Invalidated? But that would mean..."

I nod. "That would mean the treaty is broken. That we're going to war."

She shakes her head. "No, there must be a misunderstanding. King Aspen will take care of it." She takes my hand in hers. "You *must* believe he will."

I wish I could say I agree with her, but there's only so much he can do. Besides, what if Aspen was right? What if the human council *wants* war? What if they fabricated this invalidation to give them what they wanted all along? "I feel like everything is working against me and Aspen. Maybe we aren't meant to be together. Maybe there's a reason things keep coming between us."

"Don't say that. There's a genuine connection between the two of you. I can sense it with more than just my eyes. Whatever comes, you and the king will face it together."

Her words manage to stabilize some of the rage and anxiety writhing within. Yet they don't comfort me completely. There's a much darker cloud hanging behind all of this—the possibility of war. If war comes to the Fair Isle, it won't be as simple as facing the challenge at Aspen's side. At least not for me. Not when my people—my mother included—will be suffering on the other side of the wall. They'll be facing death and destruction because of a broken treaty my marriage was supposed to keep intact.

Anger returns to me in a rush. “There must be something I can do to fix this.”

“There might be.” Foxglove stands in my doorway, wringing his hands. “But you aren’t going to like it.”

3

I jump to my feet as Foxglove enters the room. "What do you mean I'm not going to like it? Where is Aspen? Is he all right?"

"He's fine," Foxglove says. "The threat has been dealt with, and the king is uninjured."

I let out a sigh of relief. "Where is he now?"

"He's in his study, but that's not why I came here. I came to talk to you myself. There are...things I think you have the right to know *before* you speak with the king."

"What does that mean? Is he hiding something from me?"

"I wouldn't say that, it's just..." He sighs. "We should all sit down for this. Trust me."

I feel like my legs will give out as I lead us to the couch. I can't bring myself to sit next to the silky wedding dress strewn over the arm, so I take a seat in the chair across from it. Lorelei and Foxglove lower onto the couch.

Foxglove adjusts his spectacles, lips pulled into a grimace. "Oh, I just hate being the bearer of—"

"Just tell me."

"Very well. As you know, the human council has sent a letter invalidating your pairing with King Aspen."

I nod, leaning forward in anticipation. "Did the letter say why?"

He swallows hard. "My dear, might I ask you something? Are you of fae heritage?"

I whip my head back in surprise. "No, of course not. I'm obviously human."

He raises a brow. "Is there not the slightest chance you could have fae blood?"

I open my mouth, but too many arguments fight for dominance, making it impossible to utter a coherent word. Why would he ask me such a thing? There's no way I could be...I could be...

"I would know if I were," I finally say.

"Would you, though?" His face is full of apology.

"Yes. How else would you explain my ability to touch iron? The fact that I don't possess the sort of rapid healing the fae do? That rowan protects me from glamour?" My hand moves reflexively to my neck, seeking the feel of the red beads. I somehow managed not to lose this strand, even after being captured by Cobalt and journeying through the sea with the kelpie. However, it is by far the worse for wear, with fraying thread where beads have broken off, and haggard, lopsided berries. I can't seem to bring myself to take it off, and it isn't just because it protects me from being put under a glamour. It also reminds me of Mother. Amelie, too, for better or worse.

"The differences between the fae and part-fae are not well known," Foxglove says. "We've always assumed human-fae offspring had all the fae weaknesses and very little power. But when would they have had the need or opportunity to find out? I doubt any of the previous Chosen's children have been tested with iron. For all we know, they could be exactly like you."

"But my—" I stop myself. *My mother is human,* I want to say. She would have told me if I wasn't. Right?

But she isn't my only parent.

I shake the thought from my head. "Why are you asking me this? What does it have to do with the letter?"

"The human council is under the impression that you aren't fully human. That you and your sister are part-fae. Since the treaty requires a pair of human girls be sent to Faerwyvae..."

"Then a part-fae girl can't validate the treaty," I say under my breath, shoulders sagging. "But why do they think I'm part-fae to begin with?"

"The letter says they have proof."

"What proof?"

Foxglove shakes his head. "That they didn't say. Can you think of any way it might be true?"

I can hardly believe I'm entertaining this possibility, but I force myself to voice it. "My father, I suppose, but that's highly unlikely. Mother never gave any indication that their relationship was unusual. She never said a cryptic word about him, always said he was a decent man."

Lorelei squints as if pondering. "You never knew him?"

"I was still a baby when they separated."

"Where is he now?" Foxglove asks.

I shrug. "Still on mainland Bretton, I assume. Mother said they parted ways because he wouldn't move to Eisleigh with us. That's what doesn't make sense about this ridiculous suggestion. How could a fae, or part-fae, or whatever we're hypothesizing my father was, sire me on the mainland? Isn't being so far from Faerwyvae certain death for the fae?"

I remember the story Cobalt had told me, about the exile of the Fire King at the end of the war. They sent him to the mainland to die as punishment for being the first to engage humans in organized violence. In return, the humans agreed to the tradition of the Hundred Year Reaping. The very thing that got me into this mess.

"It is indeed death for fae to leave the Fair Isle," Foxglove says, expression grave. "Even being on the human side of the wall creates a drain on our magic. Without that magic, our lengthy lifespans are forfeit."

"So, the exiled Fire King definitely died, then?" My stomach churns. I don't want to admit the ludicrous train of thought that prompted the question.

Foxglove nods. "The exiled king lived out a mortal lifespan after arriving on the mainland. Ambassadors were sent to confirm his death when he passed."

I let out a sigh. That removes one absurd possibility. "Have there been others? Any other fae who've been exiled this century?"

Foxglove and Lorelei exchange a glance. "Not that anyone knows of," Foxglove says. "And no fae would go to the mainland willingly."

"Then it makes no sense. Either their proof is false and the human council is fabricating this excuse to break the treaty, or there's been a misunderstanding."

"I'm going to find out which of those possibilities is the case tonight," Foxglove says. "King Aspen is sending me to meet with Sableton's mayor and get to the bottom of this at once. If it is a simple misunderstanding, I'll take care of it. I'll offer whatever compensation they desire to make up for the error that led them to believe this. Then your wedding to the king will continue as planned."

Lorelei slowly turns to Foxglove. "What if it isn't a misunderstanding? Or if there's no way to dissuade them from believing their accusations?"

"Then the treaty is broken," I say, "and we go to war. Right?"

The grimace returns to Foxglove's lips, and he adjusts the bridge of his spectacles with trembling fingers. "Not necessarily."

His words should bring relief, but his expression is not one of hope. "What is it?"

"This is the part—one of many, I should say—that you won't like," he says. "The human council offered the king one final option to secure the treaty. If their suspicions about you prove correct, he'll have to accept two new Chosen and perform all three parts of the alliance at once. The mate ceremony, the ritual, and the human wedding. All of it. They've gone so far as to confirm the names of the potential new Chosen. Some Maddie and Marie Coleman. And the council insists Aspen be the one to marry, no minor cousin or other relative as has often been the practice during previous Reapings."

My stomach sinks as his words cleave my heart in two. Not only will Aspen have to marry someone else, but he'll have to marry *Maddie Coleman*. The girl I despise more than any other in my village. "Of course it's her," I mutter, a bitter smile on my lips. I remember how jealous she'd been when we met outside the Holstrom farm, how she'd boasted about being selected as backup Chosen if the Holstrom girls didn't work out. She was livid when she realized Aspen had requested me by name. Of course, I was livid too. Still...could this somehow be her doing? Her jealousy might be believable, but I can't imagine her having the power to orchestrate this new development, even with her uncle being Sableton's mayor. No, there's something much bigger behind this.

With a deep breath, I curl my fingers into fists, nails biting into my palms. "This is the only way to avoid war?"

Foxglove nods. "The mayor wants me to agree to this new arrangement when we meet tonight. If I do, I'll be leaving Sableton with the new Chosen by midnight."

I don't know what to say, so I remain quiet, eyes shifting out of focus as they fall on the wedding gown hanging near Lorelei's arm.

Foxglove wrings his hands. "King Aspen, however, has ordered me to refuse."

My eyes snap to his. "What?"

"If it comes down to breaking the treaty or accepting the new Chosen, he'll take the former."

"And bring war to us all?"

"He has his reasons," Foxglove says, "and many of them are sound. Even as an ambassador, I understand there's only so much one can take before fighting back."

I rise to my feet with every intention of storming to Aspen's study and breaking down his door. But Foxglove rises as well, palms held up facing me, as if to keep me in place. "I didn't tell you this to use as fuel in a fight with the king."

I let out a bitter laugh. "Well, I'm using it anyway."

"I told you this because it's far more personal to you than you know. The mayor has your mother. She's being detained by order of the human council. If Aspen refuses to accept the new Chosen, not only will there be war, but your mother will be executed."

4

The blood leaves my face. "They're going to execute my mother? What does she have to do with any of this?"

Foxglove's brows knit together. "She's being imprisoned, charged with treason for hiding your supposed fae heritage. It's illegal for any fae to live on the Eisleigh side of the wall, much less pose as a human. She's being held responsible for jeopardizing the treaty. While Aspen's decision to accept the new Chosen should have no impact on your mother's life, I'm guessing they wanted to make it harder for him—or you—to refuse."

Rage heats my core, and it takes all my effort not to strike the nearest piece of furniture. "When are you leaving to meet with the mayor?" I say through my teeth.

"Mid-afternoon."

I'm about to say more when a shadow darkens my doorway. I don't need to face it to know it belongs to Aspen.

Lorelei comes up beside Foxglove, shoulders tense.

"We should give you some privacy," she says, then pulls him toward the door. Their heads bow low as they approach the king, but his eyes burn into Foxglove.

"You told her," he says with a snarl.

Foxglove, to his credit, meets his gaze without so much as a tremble. "I'm sorry, Your Majesty. She deserved to know."

Aspen steps aside, allowing the two fae to pass, then slowly meets my furious gaze.

"Were you just going to let my mother die without telling me her life was at risk?"

He closes the distance between us. "I came to tell you everything."

"Everything? *Everything*, everything? Or just the parts you wanted me to know?"

"I wasn't going to let them execute your mother."

The fact that he didn't fully answer my question tells me plenty. I put my hands on my hips. "Oh, and what were you going to do about it?"

"I don't know yet." He throws his hands in the air. "I would have come up with something. Break her from imprisonment. Steal her to Faerwyvae. Slaughter everyone in my path until I had her safely away."

I'm surprised that he'd be willing to go so far for my mother, yet terrified at how easily he can consider taking lives to save her. Even so, it would only solve one problem, not all of them. "That still wouldn't save the treaty, Aspen. They gave you another option, and you told Foxglove to refuse."

"Yes," he admits without shame.

"Why?"

"Because I'm not going to lose you." The hurt in his

eyes takes my breath away. My heart threatens to crumble at the vulnerability on his face, the fear in his eyes. But then I remember what it means, what his dedication to me would cost.

"Don't make this about us." My words come out with a tremor. "We are nothing compared to the importance of saving the isle from war."

His vulnerability fades, retreating beneath the steely mask he wears so well. When he speaks, his voice is barely above a whisper. "Nothing? Is that really what you think we amount to?"

No, we're so much more than nothing. You *are so much more.* "Yes."

He shakes his head, narrowing his eyes at me as his lips pull into a bitter smirk. "I don't believe you."

I take a step toward him, meeting his smirk with a glare. I know my next words will sting, but they're the only weapon I have. My only defense against his fierce dedication, even though I know it will kill me to use. "Why? You think you know me so well just because you took me to bed once?"

His expression hardly falters. "I do know you."

"If you did, you'd know I'd want to do anything to keep the treaty from being broken."

"Even if it means giving me to another woman?"

My stomach churns at his words, at the images they conjure. I swallow the word I really want to say and replace it with a lie. "Yes."

He turns away from me and storms over to the decanter of wine on the bedside table. "I'm not going to do it," he says, then knocks back a glass of the deep red liquid.

"Yes, you are. If that's what it takes to save the treaty—"

"Maybe the treaty isn't worth saving."

My eyes go wide. "How can you say that? If the treaty protects our people from war, then of course it's worth saving."

He lets out a shaking breath, running his hands through the blue-black hair between his antlers. "This isn't a treaty, Evie. It's a blade our councils toss from one side to the other, waiting to see who gets cut first. I'm tired of playing the game. I'm tired of watching both sides point that blade at me."

His words send a chill down my spine. I can't let myself consider whether he's right. Didn't I say nearly the same to Lorelei? *I'm tired of living in fear of this treaty.* I shake my head. "If maintaining the treaty means lives can be saved, then it is worth saving in return. So long as there's a choice that means peace, then that's the choice we have to make."

"It isn't a choice if I *have* to make it."

For the love of iron, he's stubborn. "Even if you're right about the corruption of the treaty, do you think war is going to make things better? Can you honestly live with yourself, knowing you're the cause of the destruction that will follow?"

"If it's in the name of freedom, then yes."

Heat rises to my cheeks. "Well, I can't."

Aspen pours another glass of wine and knocks it back, chest heaving as his eyes remain locked on me. "What are you saying?"

"I'm saying I can't be the reason my people suffer. You know this."

"*Your people*. You do realize war would affect both humans and fae, don't you?"

"Of course I do."

"But it's the humans you care about more."

I cross my arms over my chest. "I'm trying to protect your throne too. I didn't face Cobalt for nothing. If you refuse the human council's offer to maintain the treaty, the fae council will finish what Cobalt started."

"The All of All chose me. The council will honor that."

"The All of All chose *me*," I argue. "If the Council of Eleven Courts thinks the treaty has broken because of me, the ruling of the All of All won't matter. They'll turn on both of us."

He presses his lips tight but makes no argument. Probably because he knows I'm right. "There must be another way."

I uncross my arms, letting some of my rage drain out with a sigh. "I hope there is too. That's why I'm going with Foxglove tonight, to see if I can prove I'm not what they think I am."

"Like hell you are. It isn't safe. If the humans consider your mother a traitor, you could be in danger as well."

"I'm not going to sit here while my mother suffers, not if there's something I can do about it."

"If anything can be done, then Foxglove will do it. There's nothing you could do that he cannot."

"I could prove they're wrong."

"And if they aren't?"

I can't consider that possibility right now. I *can't*. Not when it means...

"If they aren't," I say, "then I face the consequences."

He sets the wine glass down, shoulders slumped in defeat. His voice comes out like a growl. "I don't want to lose you."

I force my words past the lump in my throat. "If Foxglove can sort out this madness, then you won't have to. My mother will be released, the treaty will be secured, and I'll return to you."

"Promise me."

I shake my head. "I need a promise from *you*. Promise me if I don't come back, you'll marry your new Chosen."

His fingers curl into fists at his side, but he remains silent.

I burn him with a glare. "Promise me you'll do what needs to be done for the good of both our people. Promise me you'll save the treaty. If you can't do it for the sake of the isle, then do it for me."

He glares right back. "I promise."

"What are you promising to? All of it?"

"I promise if everything goes to hell, I'm going to make a decision neither of us is going to like," he says through his teeth.

It isn't the promise I asked for, but at least it's one he can keep, considering there's no solution I like. I hate all of it. The dissolution of the treaty. Aspen marrying Maddie Coleman. My mother being imprisoned and threatened with execution. Where do I stand in all of this? What happens to me?

"Fine," I say as I turn toward the door.

"Wait."

I shouldn't stop, but I do. Not daring to look back at him, I focus on his slow footsteps drawing near. A thousand heartbeats seem to pass as I hold my breath in anticipation of him. My pulse races even faster as his body presses into my back, hands wrapping gently around my waist, fingers splayed over my stomach. My body responds to his touch, a wave of desire blooming inside my chest as I breathe in the rosemary and cinnamon scent of his skin.

"Don't leave yet." His voice is deep, pleading, heavy with emotion as he nuzzles into my neck.

I close my eyes and angle my head, allowing him closer, his lips grazing the skin at my collarbone.

"We have time," he whispers. "We should make the most of it, just in case..."

He doesn't need to finish the sentence for me to know what he means. If everything goes terribly, this could be our last moment together. Ever. I might never see him again.

The thought is so crippling, tears spring to my eyes, and I feel my knees buckling beneath me.

With one hand warm on my stomach, the other brushes along my jaw, turning my face toward his. Our lips are just a breath away. "Evie."

I want nothing more than to close the distance, to feel his lips on mine. With one move, I could fold myself into him, feel the comfort of his arms, the heat of his body. What if this really is our last moment, our last memory together? My breaths are shallow as I fight the searing desire pulsing through me. I know I must fight it. Because if I give in now, I don't know if I'll ever have the strength to leave again.

I turn my lips from his and step out of his grasp. "I have to go."

This time, he doesn't stop me as I make my way to the

door. But as I reach the threshold, he says, "Come back to me, Evie."

I pause for only a second. "I can't promise that." Then my feet fly beneath me, taking me as fast from Aspen's room as they can go while sobs tear from my throat.

I may not be able to promise Aspen I'll return, but I can vow that every step I take away from him feels like a knife twisting in my heart.

5

I'm almost to the sanctity of my parlor when my feet are forced to slow.

A figure glides toward me, one with golden-brown skin, honey-colored hair, and yellow butterfly wings. Queen Dahlia is the last person I want to see right now. I'm in no state to entertain a guest, and her cheery smile is an infuriating contrast to my pain. I quickly wipe my cheeks dry before I pause outside my parlor door and offer the Summer Queen a curtsy. Hoping beyond hope that she'll ignore me and pass me by, I avoid meeting her gaze.

"My dear Miss Fairfield. Is everything all right? You look positively wretched."

I clench my jaw, letting my irritation overpower my anguish. Luckily, the lies flow from my tongue with ease. "There was an accident this morning, Queen Dahlia. I attended the wounded but am overcome with grief over those who perished in the caves."

"So I heard," she says with a scoff. "Serves them right, using explosives in such a manner."

I bristle at that, even though I agree that using them had been reckless. All I want is for her to leave so I can be alone, but I can't resist my urge to use words against her now that she's sparked my ire. "How much longer are we to be graced with your company? You were quite generous in lending Bircharbor your weather, but I must say it's dry now. And there is such a thing as too much sun."

She gives me a simpering smile. "Perhaps a few days more, Miss Fairfield, just to be sure. I do hope we can spend more time together. I think the sun is starting to do you good. One would almost say you don't look so drab."

I force an exaggerated grin. "Almost."

She takes a step closer, lowering her voice, although her expression remains unchanged. "I do hope nothing is amiss. I heard the king received a vexing correspondence."

The grin falls from my lips, and I don't try to remedy it. "The king's correspondences are his business, and he will attend to them appropriately."

"Oh, I know he will." She lifts a dainty hand and lights it on my shoulder. "It's just...I worry about him. He is a very, very dear friend of mine. We've known each other for many hundreds of years. I'm not much younger than he is, you know. You could say we grew up together."

I purse my lips, wondering if I'm reading too much into her words, into the purr in her tone. "Your care will warm his heart, Queen Dahlia. I'll pass it along to him."

"Oh, don't worry, Miss Fairfield. I'm sure I'll tell him

myself before then." With that, she gives my shoulder a final squeeze and brushes past.

Heat blazes my cheeks as I stand frozen in place, lips immobile no matter how many clever retorts surface in my head. I know it's too late; I can barely hear her buzzing wings behind me anymore. Still, I can't shake my irritation. What was she suggesting? That she has a greater chance of seeing my mate before I do? That she...*has* been seeing him more than I do? Or does she know I'm leaving and might never return?

I might never return...

The thought extinguishes my rage, reopening the wound left by my conversation with Aspen. His pleading voice fills my mind, his beckoning touch. *Come back to me, Evie.*

My chest heaves with a sob as I dart inside my parlor and slam the door behind me.

LORELEI FINDS ME INSIDE. I'M PERCHED ON THE GROUND IN front of my couch, knees pulled to my chest as I weep into my hands. She crouches at my side and lays a soft hand on my back. "You're all right," she whispers, her voice a soothing hum. "Just breathe."

I gasp a shaking breath, forcing my sobs to recede. I haven't broken down like this since...since I thought my sister had died.

"I brought some of your things from Aspen's room," she says.

The sound of his name sends a shard of glass through my heart, and it takes me a moment to comprehend what she means by *my things*. That's right. For my journey. I inhale deeply to steady my breathing, a sense of urgency clearing my mind. It must be mid-afternoon by now, and I'm not sure how much time I've already wasted. I rise slowly to my feet. "Did you talk to him?"

She nods, expression grave. "We should get you cleaned up and packed."

I let out a sigh of resignation and reach for one of the bags she brought, plopping it on the couch. I freeze when I see what's been laid at the top of the pile of clothing within—a crown of gold shaped into a circlet of swaying leaves. I reach for it but stop myself. "Why did you bring this?"

Lorelei shrugs. "King Aspen told me to."

"Why?"

"Perhaps he wants you to wear it to meet with the mayor. It wouldn't be a bad idea. Let the human council see you as the Autumn Queen. Let them see you aren't someone to be trifled with."

I shake my head. "I don't think posturing as fae royalty will do me any good in this instance. Not when it plays so well into their accusations about my heritage."

"Then perhaps just take it with you."

"No." My throat tightens. "It doesn't belong to me. I won it as Aspen's champion. I won it for *him*, for Autumn."

"And he gave it to you."

I take the crown in my hands, gingerly, as if it could burn me. Without so much as looking at it, I place it on the tea table in front of the couch. "If it's meant to be mine, it will still be here if I make it back." *If*. The word crushes my lungs.

I refocus on the bags of clothing, removing their contents and setting aside the most practical dresses I can find. The weather will be cool in Eisleigh, October in the human realm being nowhere near as mild as it is in the Autumn Court. Most of the fae dresses are light, flimsy, and entirely inappropriate for the human realm. The fabrics are too sheer and reveal far too much skin.

I toss the dresses on the ground with frustration until I see a familiar sight at the very bottom of the last bag—stiff, starchy, cream-colored linen. I retrieve the corset and find a pair of trousers and a blouse lying beneath. The latter two are wrinkled but they are the only undamaged human clothing I have.

"I will return to my people the same way I left," I say, smoothing a wrinkle in the blue cotton blouse. My fingers brush a pearl-like button. There was a time when I rebelled against wearing anything but the clothes I now hold in my hands. I hated dresses. I hated corsets too, but they were a price I knew I had to pay to get away with wearing trousers in a society that frowns upon such unfeminine ways.

I stare at the clothes, expecting sentimentality to wash over me at any moment. Instead, I feel a sense of foreboding. Restraint. I've come to appreciate the freedom of a flowing chiffon skirt as it swishes around my legs, in the lightness of an unbound chest beneath nothing but gauzy spider silk.

Now I might never wear such things again.

With my corset, trousers, and blouse in hand, I make my way behind the dressing screen and peel off my silky gown.

Lorelei approaches the other side of the screen. "Do you need my help?"

I'm about to say no, but stop myself as I pick up the stiff corset. "I do, actually."

She rounds the corner of the screen, eyes widening as she stares at the undergarment. "What in the name of oak and ivy is that thing?"

"A mandatory article of clothing for women," I say through my teeth as I turn my back toward her. "I need you to tighten the laces and tie them off."

She takes up the ends of the laces, grimacing as if she expects them to bite. "Why is this necessary for human women?"

"To support our figures," I say in a mocking tone. Lorelei pulls the laces tight at the top, eliciting a gasp from me.

"Did I hurt you?" she asks with alarm.

"No, I just...forgot how uncomfortable these are."

"Is this really necessary? You could wear something else and cover your clothing with a cloak if you're worried—"

"Just do it," I say, though there's no bite in my tone. More an eagerness to get this over with. "I need them to see me as one of them."

She releases a sigh, then returns to tightening the laces. "Do I have to wear one of these too?"

I turn my head to the side to eye her from my periphery. "No, of course not. Why would you?"

"Because I'm going with you, obviously."

I'm taken aback. "Did Aspen order you to come with me?"

"I asked *him* if I could accompany you."

I sigh. "Lorelei, I appreciate your dedication, but I'll have no need for a lady's maid while I'm in Sableton."

She pauses her tightening and shifts to my side until our eyes meet. "You may not need a lady's maid, but you might need a friend."

I want to argue, to tell her Foxglove will be there, but I can't bring words over the lump in my throat. Instead, I nod and return to facing straight ahead, eyes unfocused as they well with tears. Lorelei resumes her work, and I grit my teeth against every pull.

By the time I'm finished dressing, outfitted in human clothing and my most unassuming fae cloak, I feel the same way I did when I first left home for Faerwyvae.

Like a lamb being led to slaughter.

My heart is heavy as Lorelei and I leave my parlor. Every shadow in the hall pulls my attention, and my eyes dart to each one, expecting Aspen at every turn, around every corner. But he doesn't appear, neither to try and stop me from leaving nor to offer me a heart-wrenching farewell. I am both disappointed and relieved.

Foxglove awaits outside the palace, standing beside the carriage led by two dark puca. The puca aren't nearly as terrifying to behold as they were when I first saw them, especially now that I've become so well-acquainted with the far more menacing kelpie. Then again, the kelpie helped me during my trial in the Twelfth Court when I fought to win back Aspen's throne from Cobalt. But had any of that surreal experience been true? Or had it only occurred inside my imagination? The crown I returned with was my only proof.

And now it sits on my parlor table. Belonging to no one.

I climb inside the carriage, taking a seat on one of the long benches while Foxglove and Lorelei take the one across from me. As the carriage begins to move, I don't dare look out the window. I don't think I can handle the sight of Bircharbor fading from view. Not because it's become dear to me—it was only just beginning to feel like home—but because I'm afraid I'll see an antlered silhouette watching me from one of the windows. The thought alone strips the air from my lungs.

It isn't until we've been traveling in silence for what feels like an hour that I finally lean forward and stare at the scenery. We're surrounded by oaks and maples with deep red leaves twinkling like rubies overhead, falling like stars to the ground where they coat the earth like a blood-red sea. I take in each crimson hue, memorizing the shape of every leaf like it's the last time I'll ever see it.

I settle back into my seat and face Foxglove, seeking a less emotional conduit for my thoughts. There's always one thing I can count on to do just that. Logic. "How are we getting to Sableton? I'm assuming we aren't taking the long way."

"Right you are," he says. "We're nearing the Autumn axis. Once we reach it, we'll be transported to the axis line along the wall. From there, we'll make our way to the Spring axis where we'll cross the wall into Sableton."

Aspen once explained interaxis travel to me briefly, but there's still so much I don't understand. "Where exactly is the Autumn axis within the court? I know where the axes are along the wall, but I've never left Autumn but by sea."

"The axis encompasses a portion of land in the forest on the southern end of Autumn near the perimeter where Autumn meets Wind."

"And it will automatically transport us to the Autumn axis along the wall?"

"If by automatically you mean as a result of me using my magic to get there, then yes."

"You have to use magic?"

"Of course." Foxglove scoffs. "We must have the option to bypass the axis and proceed the long way, must we not? So, to communicate our intentions with the axis, we must have a sort of key."

"A key."

"That's what you can imagine the magic we use to utilize the axis is."

I blink at him a few times, wishing I could make logical sense of his words. I've come to allow some suspension of disbelief when it comes to the fae and their magic. Before I came to Faerwyvae, I would have laughed at such a notion. Now that I've seen what I've seen, done what I've done...I admit there are things far beyond rational explanation. Yet, it still doesn't stop me from seeking to understand it.

"How do you use this *magic key?* Do you say some sort of incantation?"

Foxglove and Lorelei exchange a look, one that tells me they think my line of questioning is quite simple-minded. "I merely use it, my dear," Foxglove says. "It is more about intent than it is about tangible action. All magic is."

I lean back in my seat, brows furrowed as I try to pair his words with reason.

Lorelei seems entertained by my obvious struggle, lips tight to suppress a grin. "Didn't you learn about magic in the Twelfth Court?"

"I wouldn't say I learned anything," I say. Sure, it opened my mind to new possibilities, made me feel like I was drunk on honey pyrus. But if my journey to the All of All is supposed to be any indication of how magic works, I have no hope of making sense of it any time soon.

"We're entering the axis," Foxglove says.

I return to looking out the window, trying to discern any change, any flicker of magic. The forest looks the same as it did the last time I looked out at the scenery. More oaks, maples. More red leaves. I continue watching as the carriage rolls along, but there's no change.

My attention then shifts back to Foxglove. I study his face, his eyes. "Are you using your magic right now?"

He lets out a light giggle. "When am I not using my magic?"

"Are you using it for the axis?"

"I already have. We're on the other side now, nearing the wall."

I look back out the window. Still, nothing has changed. Another magical occurrence I can't decipher. It is both a frustration and an invigorating challenge to be so utterly perplexed. I shake my head, about to retreat to my seat once again, when movement catches my eye. There in the distance between the trees is a dark shape, hidden in shadows. A hulking creature with massive antlers.

My breath hitches as I study the silhouette, seeking

recognition. I've seen Aspen in his stag form before. Could this be...

I can't let myself wonder. I can't.

I watch the figure until it's lost from view, swallowed by shadows beneath the setting sun. Only then do I question whether I saw the stag at all.

6

The fog that envelops the carriage tells me we're approaching the wall. We've already traveled through the Autumn and Summer axes, and when we reached Spring, the carriage turned south. Now the towering stones of the faewall emerge from the fog. We pass between two stones into a familiar forest.

Unlike the smooth transition from Autumn to its axis, the shift from Faerwyvae to Eisleigh is jarring. Night has fallen as it had over Spring, but there's a dullness to the light of the moon. The leaves don't shimmer as they drop from the trees, and unlike the Autumn Court, fall has already stripped half the branches bare. Gone are the nectar-like aromas wafting through the air, replaced with the pungent smell of decay. The sound of the wheels rolling over brown, mushy leaves brings an odd sense of nostalgia mixed with a sinking feeling.

Home. I'm home.

Less comforting thoughts chase away any sense of relief, reminding me of the confrontation I'm approaching. I don't know what to expect from my meeting with the mayor. A minuscule spark of hope whispers the possibility that I'll arrive, state my case, solve this outrageous misunderstanding, and set everything to rights. The mayor will order my mother released and I'll secure the treaty with my marriage to Aspen.

If that hope has any chance of coming about, then why does my stomach plummet when I entertain it? Because it hurts too much to hope? Or because deep down I know the hope is futile?

I grit my teeth as we continue the journey in silence.

When the carriage rolls to a stop, my heart leaps into my throat.

"We've arrived at the mayor's house," Foxglove says. His expression reflects the anxiety I feel. He opens the carriage door but hesitates, his gaze falling on Lorelei. "I think you should wait here while Evelyn and I speak with the mayor."

She meets his eyes, something like relief flickering over her face as she nods.

Foxglove's attention moves to me. "You may wait here as well, if you like. I could speak with him first and glean more information before involving you."

There's no way I'll let this situation unfold without being front and center. I want every piece of information I can possibly get handed directly to me. Forcing confidence, I lift my chin. "I'm coming."

With a sigh, Foxglove exits the carriage and extends his hand to help me out. The mayor's house looms on the other side of the carriage, an elegant manor framed with neat hedges and a manicured lawn. This is my first time seeing Mayor Coleman's house, although I've walked by his drive many times growing up. Back when my sister was friends with Maddie Coleman, we often walked with her here, leaving her at the top of the drive for visits with her uncle.

Of course, thoughts of Maddie Coleman only fill me with contempt, but at least it feels better than fear.

Foxglove and I approach the front door, where a smug doorman greets us. After a brief statement of our business from Foxglove, the doorman leads us inside the manor and into a parlor. It's clear he means to take us swiftly through to the door at the other side, but I find my feet rooted as a familiar face snags my attention.

Maddie Coleman sits on the couch in the middle of the parlor next to her younger sister, Marie. Overstuffed bags and luggage litter the ground at their feet. With a haughty grin, Maddie looks up from her needlework and meets my eyes, blonde curls bouncing with the movement. She assesses me from head to toe, although she doesn't seem surprised to see me. Her gaze moves to Foxglove. "Have you come to take me to my new husband?"

A violent heat floods me, boiling my blood as I fight the urge to lash out at her. Even my hands are hot, as if each palm holds a flame.

Foxglove inspects the girls on the couch, nose wrinkled in distaste. Without so much as a word, he turns up his chin and meets the doorman at the other side of the parlor. I burn Maddie with a scowl before joining him, but she doesn't so much as flinch. Marie, on the other hand, goes a shade paler, mouth hanging open as if she wishes to speak.

I'm shaking with suppressed rage as we move down

the hall; I only begin to sober once we stop at the end of the corridor. The doorman knocks on a door, then opens it.

Inside the room, Mayor Coleman sits at a desk with two armed guards standing on each side. It never occurred to me that the mayor employed guards, but I suppose the extra protection is a comfort when meeting with the fae, even if it's with a peaceful ambassador.

The mayor is a well-dressed man, but he looks nothing like his slim, blonde niece. He has a heavy-set build, a bushy mustache that hides his upper lip, and shrewd eyes beneath thick, caterpillar-like brows. He wears a brown jacket and waistcoat over a white shirt and cravat.

He lifts his eyes from his desk as we enter, his gaze flicking toward Foxglove before resting on me. "Miss Fairfield," he says with a reserved smile. "I wasn't expecting you, but I must admit, this makes things much easier for us all." He motions to one of the guards to lean forward, and the mayor whispers an order too soft for me to hear. Then the guard crosses the room. Toward me.

I flinch, hands flying to my thigh, my hip, but the automatic response to danger is fruitless; my iron dagger was lost when Cobalt captured me, and I've yet to replace it. A moment too late, I realize my reaction was unfounded. The guard isn't coming for me. Instead, he skirts behind Foxglove and rushes out the door.

Heat floods my cheeks in embarrassment as I release a breath and return my attention to the mayor.

Mayor Coleman eyes me through slitted lids and motions for Foxglove and me to sit. "Your king has made his decision regarding the correspondence the council sent, I presume?"

"King Aspen has considered the contents of the letter, yes," Foxglove says. I'm surprised how collected he is. I've gotten used to his often-anxious ways when dealing with unfortunate circumstances—wringing his hands, nervously adjusting his spectacles—that I nearly forgot how calm and regal he can be. This is how I first saw him, posture erect, voice high and snobbish, expression smug.

"I take it he wasn't pleased."

"That's an understatement, Mayor Coleman. I can't say Miss Fairfield and I are pleased either, and we have many questions."

The mayor leans back in his chair. "I will answer what I can, but I assure you, nothing will alter the conclusions we've reached or the final olive branch we've extended."

I grip the arms of the chair to channel my rage, my anxiety. It's all I can do not to shout my questions at him, but I know it's best if Foxglove takes the lead. For now.

"The first issue we seek clarity on is the accusation over Miss Fairfield's heritage," Foxglove says. "The letter stated she has been deemed ineligible to secure the treaty due to being of fae blood. The king's mate has assured us she knows nothing about such a possibility. Will you explain what gave your council this outrageous idea?"

The mayor purses his lips, pulling them both beneath the cliff of his mustache. "We have evidence that Evelyn and Amelie Fairfield are of fae blood and that their mother, Maven Fairfield, knew this and withheld the truth even after they were selected as Chosen. She deliberately put the treaty in danger with her omission."

I can keep quiet no longer, my body trembling from head to toe. "What evidence do you have?"

The mayor slides his gaze to me, and a flash of hatred crosses his face. "The proof we have is not up for debate and will be more thoroughly discussed at your mother's trial."

"My mother's trial," I echo. "When will that be?"

"It will be held in two weeks' time, when Eisleigh's council gathers at the Spire."

The Spire. That's the name for the prison in Grenneith, the capital city of Eisleigh. Only the most serious crimes in Eisleigh are tried at the Spire. The only thing worse would be if her trial were being held at Fort Merren on the mainland, involving the entire kingdom of Bretton as well as the king. At least her accusation of treason is being considered a territorial threat and not a national one. The thought doesn't give me much comfort.

The mayor continues. "Even though the proof we have is irrefutable, we are giving your mother a fair trial as well as allowing you and your sister plenty of time to get your affairs in order beforehand. Your presence today tells me it won't be as difficult as we'd thought to get you to comply."

"I'm here to prove my mother's innocence. My sister and I aren't fae."

"If there is innocence to prove, you may present it at Maven Fairfield's trial, as both you and your sister will be required to attend."

"That's in two weeks!" I'm nearly shouting. "You won't divulge whatever proof you have to support your claims, nor will you allow me to argue on my mother's behalf for *two weeks*?"

"Exactly," he says without remorse. "Considering your mother is being held under charges of treason, any conversations we have outside of an official trial are of no use. We are both better off waiting until then to speak more on the matter."

Foxglove puts his hand on mine for a moment, a silent request for me to regather my composure. "If the trial isn't held for two more weeks," he says, "we should delay all actions regarding the treaty until then."

Mayor Coleman shakes his head. "That won't do. Eisleigh's council has already given your king ample allowances to secure the treaty, and numerous times he's failed. This is the last chance we're giving him."

"But this most recent setback is not King Aspen's making," Foxglove argues.

"Isn't it, though?" The mayor scoffs. "Your king requested Evelyn Fairfield by name after the Holstrom girls were executed. He bypassed our selection of my nieces and received the Fairfield girls in their stead. For all we know, he could have selected them on purpose, knowing their fae heritage. He could have done it to compromise the treaty."

Foxglove doesn't argue. Even though I know the mayor's theory is wrong, I also know how the humans—and many of the fae too, for that matter—view Aspen. They see him as cruel, volatile, and reckless. They don't realize everything he does is meant to maintain balance in Faerwyvae.

But there's something else tugging at my mind. Something that doesn't quite add up. "If Eisleigh's council thinks Aspen is responsible for this newest complication, then why are you giving him a final chance at all? Why not consider it a breaking of the treaty?"

Foxglove throws me a sharp look, one I ignore as I keep my eyes fixed on the mayor.

"We don't want war, Miss Fairfield. Giving King Aspen a final offer to maintain peace is mutually beneficial to both humans and fae. We have every right to withhold this generous proposition, but we are giving him the benefit of the doubt one last time." He says this with confidence, but there's a flicker of uncertainty that crosses his face, so subtle I almost miss it.

My eyes lock on his, seeking what he's leaving unsaid. I hold his gaze, and it feels like I have his eyes in a cage of my own making, a bird trapped between my fingers. I see it in my mind's eye; his attention is that bird, and the cage is my will. The longer I hold both, the more pliant the mayor becomes. "There's something you aren't telling me," I say, my words rolling with a calm yet deadly fire. "Tell me why you're really doing this."

The mayor's face seems to have gone slack, but his eyes are still locked on mine, pupils dilated like enormous black saucers. "King Ustrin demanded our compliance. He's put us in an exceedingly difficult place."

My mouth falls open, and with it goes the image of the bird held within the cage of my hands.

The mayor blinks several times, cheeks burning crimson. He leans back in his chair, a subtle move, but it's like he wants to put space between us. Like he's...scared.

I'm keenly aware of Foxglove's stare. I meet it, but I'm not sure what it means. He seems flustered.

But why? I can't help but wonder at the strange imagery that flooded my mind moments ago when I met the mayor's eyes. One word comes to mind. Glamour. I glamoured the mayor.

Of course I didn't. All this nonsense is just getting to my head.

I focus instead on what Mayor Coleman said. That King Ustrin demanded compliance. I ponder the name and try to match a face to it. Then I recall the fae who approached me in the hall after Aspen won back his throne from Cobalt. Orange scales, lipless mouth, slitted nostrils—the King of Fire. I shudder. I don't know much about the lizard king, but our first encounter left me nothing but unsettled.

I furrow my brow. "What does King Ustrin have to do with anything?"

The mayor pins me with a chilling glare. "That is not up for discussion either."

"Mayor Coleman," Foxglove says, his light tone in stark contrast against the tension building in the room, "if the human council is willing to allow King Aspen a final chance to secure the treaty, then I don't see why another two weeks will matter. He and Evelyn Fairfield have done all but the final step in securing the treaty. If there is even the slightest chance they can finish what they've already begun, I think it's worth waiting for."

"No," the mayor says. "If your king wants to secure the treaty and prevent Maven Fairfield's execution, then he will accept my nieces as his new Chosen. You will bring them to the Autumn Court tonight. King Aspen will take the eldest as his wife and perform all acts required by the treaty in a single day by the end of one week."

"King Aspen has already made Evelyn his mate," Foxglove argues.

"That doesn't make her his wife."

"They have performed the Bonding ritual." He says *bonding* in a half-whisper, like it pains him to utter the word aloud. Considering his reluctance to tell me about it before the mate ceremony, I assume it isn't discussed with humans often.

Mayor Coleman, however, shows no sign of reverence as he says, "If Miss Fairfield never sees King Aspen again, the Bond is of no consequence between them."

His words send anger and nausea swirling inside me, a volatile mix that makes my head spin. *No consequence. Never see King Aspen again.*

The study door opens, pulling me from my thoughts. My mind sharpens as two figures enter the room. One is the guard who left earlier. The other I recognize as Sheriff Bronson, Sableton's law enforcer. There's no doubt he's here for me.

"Evelyn Fairfield," the mayor says, "you are sentenced to imprisonment."

7

Sheriff Bronson takes a step toward me, and the mayor's two guards follow suit. I stand, knocking my chair over in the process. Foxglove springs to his feet a moment later, blocking my body with his. He holds his palms before him, as if they stand a chance against the swords at the guards' waists or the sheriff's revolver—*a gun!* Such a rare weapon to see in my village, or on the isle at all, for that matter. At least no weapon has been drawn yet.

"Wait," Foxglove says. "Until a trial proves otherwise, Evelyn Fairfield is a subject of the Autumn Court. You cannot harm her or hold her captive."

"Miss Fairfield is suspected of treason alongside her mother," Mayor Coleman says through his teeth. "She will be escorted to Sableton's jail tonight, and tomorrow she and her mother will be transported to the Spire to be held until the trial."

"It will be easier if you come willingly." Sheriff Bronson extends his hand, expression apologetic. I'm sure this is awkward for him. It's not that we know each other well, but he's been Sableton's sheriff since I was a little girl.

"Besides, wouldn't you rather be with your mother?" The mayor's voice is mocking, grating on my ears. But his words meet their mark, taking the fight from me as my mind fills with images of Mother alone in a dark cell.

"She's being kept comfortable, as will you," Bronson says, his tone far more placating than the mayor's. "That comfort will be extended during your stay, and I've been assured it will be maintained at the Spire."

The mayor clears his throat. "When we hear word from your sister, she will join you as well."

I lay a gentle hand on Foxglove's shoulder, wordlessly asking him to stand down. "What will happen to us after the trial?"

"Afterward," the mayor says, "the three of you will be exiled to mainland Bretton."

"Only if your suspicions prove correct," Foxglove says.

The mayor nods.

Exiled to the mainland. At least it isn't execution.

There was a time not long ago when I would have given anything to move to the mainland. But that was before the Reaping. Before Faerwyvae. Before Aspen. Now it's all over. Even if Mother is proven innocent at her trial, it will be too late for me and him. He'll already be married by then.

But my mother will live. She'll live and we'll be together. It's all I can focus on if I'm to prevent another emotional breakdown.

"I'll go to my imprisonment willingly." My voice

comes out with a tremor. "Foxglove will take the new Chosen to the Autumn Court."

"A wise choice," the mayor says.

I face Sheriff Bronson as frantic footsteps sound in the hall, followed by a much slower set farther down. The familiar figure that emerges through the threshold catches me off guard.

"Do not imprison her," Mr. Meeks says through panting breaths. The aging surgeon doesn't so much as look at me as he approaches the mayor's desk. "I will host her until the trial."

Mayor Coleman shakes his head. "She must be held behind bars."

"She's just a girl," Mr. Meeks says. "She cannot be subjected to the indignity of prison."

I bristle at being called *just a girl*, but the sentiment softens my heart. My former mentor, who I apprenticed under for two years, is the one human I respect above all others. And he's here fighting on my behalf.

He continues. "Even if proven guilty of having fae blood, the fault will not lie with her but with her mother. I've known Miss Fairfield since she was a child, and can attest that she knew of no secret heritage. Do not punish her for her ignorance."

The second set of footsteps crosses the threshold, revealing an unfamiliar man. He appears to be in his thirties, wearing cream trousers and a navy-blue jacket and waistcoat. He's tall with neatly trimmed dark-blond hair, a slim mustache, and pale blue eyes that match his silk cravat.

Mayor Coleman lets out a grumble of relief. "Councilman Duveau, please speak some sense into Mr. Meeks."

Mr. Duveau scans the room, gaze roving from the mayor to Mr. Meeks, then gliding to Foxglove. Finally, it settles on me, although he doesn't meet my eyes.

Mr. Meeks faces the newcomer. "Henry, please allow Miss Fairfield this comfort. Let her stay with me while she awaits her mother's trial. I will escort her to the Spire myself when the time comes."

The mayor opens his mouth to argue, but Henry Duveau speaks first. "I don't see the problem, Mayor Coleman. Miss Fairfield can do what she pleases. She can return to the Autumn Court for all I care, so long as she and her sister attend the trial and submit to their sentence."

The mayor looks taken aback, cheeks burning. "If we don't lock her up now, what is to keep her from going into hiding?"

"She'll have ample incentive," Mr. Duveau says. "More than she has now, in fact."

I shudder as he faces me. "What do you mean?"

When he looks at me, there's no malice in his expression, no teasing. He's stoic. Confident. "You and your sister will present yourselves at the Spire by the twenty-fourth of October. If you fail to do so, your mother will be executed and a bounty will be placed on your heads."

I'm reeling from his statement, so much that I can't utter a word.

He returns to face the mayor. "See? Let her do what she will between now and then. Either way, the threat will be eliminated in the end."

What threat? I want to ask, but I still can't find my words.

"Fine," Mayor Coleman says with a sneer. "You heard Councilman Duveau. The choice is yours."

I swallow hard. "I already told you my choice. I'll stay with my mother."

Mr. Meeks faces me. "No, Miss Fairfield. Please allow me to spare you such humiliation."

"If it's humiliating for me, it can't be any better for my mother."

"But she wouldn't want this for you, dear girl," he argues. "I couldn't live with myself if I didn't do my best to protect you when she cannot."

The tender look in his eyes crushes me. I always knew he was fond of me as his apprentice, but I never expected him to care so deeply. To seek to protect me like the father figure I always wished he were. My eyes move to Mr. Duveau. "My mother will be cared for? She won't be harmed in prison if I stay with Mr. Meeks?"

"I'll even make you a bargain," he says, "that no harm will come to your mother while she's imprisoned, so long as you promise to attend her trial. Do you accept this bargain?"

I'm caught off guard by his choice of words until I realize he thinks he's making a *fae* bargain. Because for some crazy reason no one will tell me, he thinks I'm fae. "Yes, I accept."

"Where will you choose to await her trial?"

Before I can respond, Foxglove puts a hand on my shoulder, a weak smile tugging his lips. He lowers his voice to a whisper. "There's the other option he mentioned. You could return to Autumn with me."

Autumn. I could return to Bircharbor, spend two more weeks with Aspen. A distant trill of laughter falls on my ears, muffled through the hall that stands between here and the parlor. I know who it belongs to. Aspen's new Chosen. His soon-to-be-wife. If I return to Bircharbor, it won't be to a respite. Being there for two weeks means I'll have to witness his wedding to Maddie Coleman. The thought alone sends bile rising to my throat.

"I'll go with Mr. Meeks," I say, "if I will be allowed to speak with my mother before she's taken to the Spire."

"No," the mayor says at the same time as Mr. Meeks says, "Of course."

Mr. Duveau rolls his eyes. "Let her see her mother."

"You can visit her first thing in the morning," Mr. Meeks says.

"Very well." The mayor leans back in his chair, shoulders slumped in defeat. "Then it's settled. My nieces are ready for their travels, ambassador."

Foxglove's face goes pale as he nods to the mayor.

Mr. Duveau turns on his heel, followed by Sheriff Bronson. Mr. Meeks gives me a warm smile, extending his arm to allow me to pass into the hall ahead of him. "I'm so glad I got here in time," he whispers, walking by my side. "I don't know what I would have done if I found my dear apprentice had been locked up before I arrived." Again, his care surprises me. Even after these allegations, he still considers me his dear apprentice. However, the tenseness in his posture isn't lost on me. He may be doing me a kindness, but he isn't fully comfortable about it.

"How did you know I was here?"

"I was meeting with Henry—Mr. Duveau, that is—when the mayor's guard came to inform him of your presence. Thank the stars we got here before Bronson took you away."

We enter the parlor, and Maddie and Marie rise to their feet. "Are we leaving now?" Maddie asks with a haughty grin.

"Yes." Foxglove's answer is curt as he comes up behind me. He says nothing more as he brushes past the girls and out the door, not even bothering to help them with their things.

Maddie gapes after him, then snaps her fingers at a maid. "My bags. Now."

A whimper draws my attention to the girl behind Maddie—her sister, Marie. The girl is a few inches shorter than Maddie, her hair a mousy brown, her dress far more modest and subdued than her companion. She was always the more studious of the two, kind where her sister is sharp. Practical, save for a naive sense of dreaminess about her. I've never seen her so flustered. Marie's voice comes out small. "I don't want to go."

"Grow up," Maddie mutters. "You know this is your duty."

"But I...I'm not ready." Her eyes fill with tears.

"We've been ready for this all day. All our lives, if we're being honest. You always knew this would be a possibility."

"I'm not ready to get married."

Maddie shrugs. "Perhaps a marriage won't be required of you. I'll gladly fulfill my duty for the both of us." There's more mocking than warmth in her tone.

I find myself frozen as Marie's eyes lock on mine, silently pleading. I don't know what she expects me to do.

I've never been close to the younger girl, not even when our older sisters were friends. She's three years younger...

A shiver crawls up my spine. That's when I remember Marie Coleman is only fifteen years old. My stomach churns. No wonder the girl is terrified.

She may be old enough for the Reaping, but the terms of the treaty were crafted a thousand years ago. Since then, girls rarely get married that young in Eisleigh. Despite my personal pains, an ache of sympathy tugs at my heart.

But there's nothing I can do. In this—in this entire situation—I'm powerless.

I tear my gaze away from the girl and rush out the door.

Outside, Mr. Duveau enters a sleek black coach pulled by two enormous brown Clydesdales. My stomach sinks as Mr. Meeks guides me toward the door held open by the councilman's driver. "Mr. Duveau can take us to my house on his way back to his hotel. I figure you'd prefer that over riding with Sheriff Bronson."

My eyes flash toward the prison wagon parked behind Mr. Duveau. The enclosed end of the wagon is designed for transporting prisoners, not casual passengers. Yet, my stomach lurches when I consider sitting in a carriage with the brusque councilman.

"Evelyn!" Lorelei's voice has me whirling to face her as she jogs toward me. I almost forgot I left her waiting in the carriage. Her eyes are wide as she approaches me, sparing a hesitant glance at my human companion. Mr. Meeks takes a step away, giving us some privacy, and she lowers her voice to a whisper. "What happened?"

I don't have the energy to explain. I've hardly

processed it myself. "It...it went the way we feared it would. There's no swaying the council. Aspen will take the new Chosen and I...I will await my mother's trial."

"When will that be?"

"Two weeks from now. After that..." Exile at worst. But what happens at best? If we can prove the council is wrong about my heritage, where do we go from there? Will we be able to return to our old lives, with Mother running her apothecary, and me acting as apprentice to Mr. Meeks, and Amelie...

My blood goes cold. For the first time, I consider a chilling possibility. What if Amelie doesn't come? What if Cobalt receives the summons for her to attend the trial but keeps the information to himself? What if he tells her about it but won't let her leave? What if...what if Amelie refuses to come?

My knees go weak, lungs constricting.

"Where are you going?" Lorelei asks.

I focus on her words to reel in my frazzled thoughts. "I'll be staying with my mentor, Mr. Meeks, until the trial. He's taking me to his home."

She visibly shudders, swallowing hard before saying, "I'll stay with you."

My shoulders slump. "No, Lorelei. They nearly imprisoned me on the grounds that I might be part-fae. There's no way you'll be allowed to remain here. Besides, why would you want to?"

"I'm not going to let you face this alone."

I'm not alone, I want to say. *I have Mr. Meeks.* But I know it isn't the same. She and Foxglove are my final tethers to the world I left behind. Proof that everything I experienced in Faerwyvae was real. Her presence is both a comfort and a painful reminder, and there's a selfish part of me that wants her to stay. But I know it isn't possible.

I open my mouth to say as much when Mr. Meeks draws near with slow, hesitant steps. "If your friend would like to keep you company, I will allow her to stay at my residence as well," he says. "Mr. Duveau will give his permission. He's a reasonable man. So long as she returns after the trial, he could have no argument against it. She can serve as an honorary ambassador until your name is either cleared or condemned."

I'm surprised at his willingness to let a fae into his house, in addition to a supposed criminal. Mr. Meeks never hated the fae as much as I did, but I never got the impression he liked them either.

"I'm staying," Lorelei says. The set of her jaw tells me there's no arguing with her.

I nod, and we follow Mr. Meeks to the black coach. Before I climb inside, my eyes snag on the other carriage, the one of gold and pearl and lustrous wood. Foxglove stands outside it and offers me a sad smile, one that makes my heart plummet. That is, until Maddie Coleman obscures my view of my friend as she saunters to the carriage door. She meets my gaze and gives me an exaggerated smile. "Looks like I get to be queen after all."

Fury roars through me, and I let it burn away my hurt, my anxieties. I shape it into a smirk, eyes burning into the girl. "Just beware of the king's antlers," I say sweetly. "He has no patience for easy prey."

8

Inside the carriage, I sit next to Lorelei while the two men sit across from us. Mr. Duveau seems unperturbed by the presence of my fae companion, his attention taken by the dark scenery outside the window. I, on the other hand, can't suppress the creeping feeling of being so near Councilman Duveau. I never met the man before tonight and only vaguely recall his name from conversation. From what I know, he's a member of Eisleigh's council, alongside Mayor Coleman and all the other mayors that oversee Eisleigh's villages. I don't think Mr. Duveau is a mayor, though, so perhaps he's one of the council's heads. Whatever the case, I find even his silence and inattention oddly domineering.

The only person who seems more uncomfortable than me is Lorelei. She watches the two men, posture stiff at my side. Considering what happened with the last human male she encountered, her suspicion is understandable. I just can't fathom why she chose to stay.

Mr. Meeks' house isn't too far from the mayor's, and

before the ride grows too tense, we roll to a halt. The driver opens the door, announcing our arrival. Mr. Meeks gets out and offers his hand to assist my exit. Before I can accept, Mr. Duveau leans forward and blocks the door with his arm. A flash of red peeking from under his cuff catches my eye—a strand of rowan berries wrapped around his wrist. I reach for the strand around my neck, seeking comfort in their feel.

"Your friend may exit first," Mr. Duveau says. "I'd like a word with you."

"I'm not leaving her," Lorelei says with a snarl.

His face flashes with irritation as he assesses my companion for the first time.

My words come out calm but firm, as if I can cut the tension with them. "Mr. Meeks assured me you would accept Lorelei as honorary Autumn ambassador until the trial. If that is so, then she may be present for whatever you must say to me."

He looks at me through narrowed eyes, but he doesn't meet my gaze for long. Slowly, he leans back and straightens his silk cravat. "Very well, Miss Fairfield. I want to impress upon you what is at stake. Despite the comforts and freedoms we are allowing you, what I said holds true; if you and your sister fail to present yourselves at Maven Fairfield's trial, your mother will be executed."

I clench my teeth. It's an effort to keep my voice level as I say, "I assure you, Mr. Duveau, that my mother's life is of the utmost importance to me."

"And to your sister? Why is it you are here when your sister is not?"

I wonder if the humans know anything about what has happened with Amelie. Aspen refused to send word when I thought she'd died; I doubt anything has been communicated about her allegiance to Cobalt or even Cobalt's treachery. "My sister feels the same as I do."

"Is that a promise?"

I open my mouth but consider my words carefully before I speak. "I'll leave that promise for her to make." I shift my weight to rise from the seat, but again Mr. Duveau blocks the door with his arm.

"The council has heard nothing regarding your sister since the announcement was made that you would be marrying the Stag King and not she. Why is that?"

"Why have you not heard from my sister or why did I get paired with King Aspen?"

"Both."

I meet his eyes, holding his gaze with a glare. Shoulders square, I adopt the bearing of a fae royal. "Mr. Duveau, your curiosity flatters me, but it is getting late. I am vexed by today's news and my companion and I are tired. You will excuse us and allow us our rest."

A muscle ticks at the corner of his jaw, expression darkening. "Don't toy with me, Miss Fairfield."

"Is that a threat?"

"If I were threatening you, you'd know it."

My chest heaves as rage and terror flood me. Something in his tone, slithering beneath his words, has my skin crawling. Never would I have imagined being so terrified of one of my kind—a human. Especially after being thrust into the fae world where I was attacked by a kelpie, the Sea Queen, and Cobalt. I can't put my finger on why, but this man is far more dangerous than any creature I've ever met.

Still, I hold his gaze, my words like a growl. "Goodnight, Mr. Duveau."

He returns to his seat with a curt nod.

Lorelei and I all but tumble through the door in our rush to get away from the man. Mr. Meeks greets us with an apologetic smile. "Let's get you girls to bed."

We turn away from the carriage, but before the driver closes the door, I hear Mr. Duveau's voice. "If you're in contact with your sister, I implore you to pass along what I've said."

I refuse to turn around, refuse to do anything but dart into the safety of Mr. Meeks' house.

Lorelei and I are given a guest room to share, even though he offered us two separate accommodations. With Mr. Meeks being a widower and his son once again on holiday in the mainland, he has ample space. However, Lorelei wouldn't be persuaded to leave my side, although I get the feeling she needs the comfort of my presence more than I need her protection. It's clear she's shaken by the events of this evening, her face paling from its usual rich umber to an ashen brown, a slight tremble with every move.

"Are you all right?" I ask her as we climb into the small bed piled with an assortment of quilts and blankets.

She winces as she tries to settle into the pillows, as if they pain her. "I'm fine," she says, although her tone implies otherwise. "I've just never been on this side of the wall before. Never slept in a human house, in a human bed. It's...uncomfortable for me."

"Physically? Or emotionally?"

"Both. Also, I can already feel a drain on my magic. It makes me feel unwell."

A flash of panic tenses my shoulders. "Unwell? Is the drain on your magic a danger to you?"

"Not an immediate danger," she says. "My magic won't be as strong here, but I'll get through it. It feels like when I was healing from my iron injury."

My heart squeezes. I can't imagine why she would put herself through this for me. In fact, I have a feeling there's more to her motives than she's letting on. "Why are you really doing this, Lorelei?"

"I told you. I won't let you face this alone."

"But why? I appreciate your company, but this goes above and beyond the duties of friendship, and I can tell you're uncomfortable about all of it. What aren't you telling me?"

She lets out a heavy sigh. "When you asked me if Aspen ordered me to stay with you, I answered by telling you I'd asked him if I could come. That is true, but he asked more from me. He asked me to watch over you so long as you're here and until the situation with your mother is settled."

My breath hitches at the mention of Aspen. "Why?"

"For the same reason I agreed. Because neither of us trust the humans."

"But you trust me and I'm one of them."

"You're more than just a human. You're my queen. You may not wear the crown and you may never hold the position, but until Aspen forces me to kneel before another female in your place, I will serve you."

I'm at a loss for words. It's strange to think Lorelei and I disliked each other so much when we first met. Even she and Amelie became friends before she and I began to make amends.

She continues. "If anyone tries to hurt you here, I'll protect you however I can. I've protected myself once from them before, although I failed to protect another. I won't make that mistake again with you. Aspen will have my head if I do." The last words are said in jest, but her tone can't hide the sorrow beneath.

I can't imagine how deep her pain must go, the death of her lover still recent. Now here we are in the home of the man who helped save her lover's murderer. Where *I* helped save him too. I aided Mr. Osterman's amputation, eased his pain with laudanum, comforted him. It's still difficult for me to reconcile the man I knew growing up with the man Lorelei despises, but I believe her now.

"How did it happen anyway?" I ask, my voice barely above a whisper. "Why were you at the Spring axis when Mr. Osterman found you?"

"Malan invited me to meet her parents in Spring," she says. "I'd taken a week's leave from King Aspen's court and was on my way back to Autumn. Malan had decided to walk with me from the Spring axis to the Autumn axis, but we didn't get very far. I was being careless, so caught up in our love that I didn't smell the iron until the teeth of the trap were in my leg. That's when the Butcher of Stone Ninety-Four came out from behind one of the trees near the wall. He'd been waiting for prey."

My stomach churns. "I'm so sorry, Lorelei. I hate that

you've suffered at the hands of my people. I don't know how you can handle being here."

"If I didn't know there were humans like you, it would be impossible to be here. But you—and even Amelie, before everything with Cobalt—taught me that not all humans are to be feared."

"I learned the same from you about the fae."

From the light of the moon peering into the window, I see a smile form on her lips. "He won't make her queen, you know."

I wrinkle my brow. "Excuse me?"

"The new Chosen. I told you I'll serve you until the king puts another in your place. But he's never going to put her in your place. You know that, right?"

A lump rises in my throat. "It shouldn't matter to me. It isn't likely I'll ever see him again."

"It shouldn't matter, yet it does, doesn't it?"

I nod. "It does."

We fall into silence, and exhaustion quickly sweeps all thought from my mind. But as tired as I am, I can't seem to fall asleep. Even Lorelei finds slumber before I do. What she said about Aspen weaves its way into my consciousness, tickling my mind each time I'm about to slip into sleep. I toss and turn, but nothing seems to rid me of it.

So instead, I give in.

I open my heart and dig into the gaping wound where my mate should be. *Aspen.* I think his name, let it fill my mind. Like a bell, it reverberates through me and clears the fog from my head. In place of the fog lies a bridge—one I've seen before, spanning between two jagged cliffs. Last time I crossed it, the results were detrimental. What happens if I cross it now?

With hesitant steps, I make my way over the bridge, feet balancing on each precarious plank that lines the way. I don't bother looking down, for I know what's there —sharp rocks, pointed spikes. When I reach the other side of the bridge, I see not the cliff I'd been heading to but a dark room. A familiar room.

In the middle of it sits the bed I awoke from just this morning. *Was it really just this morning?* Beneath the covers lies a slumbering figure.

I approach the edge of the bed and look down at my mate. His lips are parted, face slack, making him appear more youthful than ever. His blue-black hair lies in disarray, waves curling at his neck and over his bronze pillow. His antlers make deep impressions in the pillow where they touch it, but the bulk of them hangs past the back of the mattress.

Everything inside me yearns to crawl in next to him. We've never spent the night in the same bed. We slept in the same room when he was recovering from his injury, but he had the bed while I dozed on the couch. The only other time we spent the night together was in the cave where we finally gave in to our desires. In the days leading up to now, he stayed away from our bed, either working on repairing the palace or avoiding me.

I reach out to touch his cheek, the warmth of his skin kissing my fingers. There's something about the touch that feels wrong, though, some tenuous barrier that keeps him from feeling real.

It's because I'm dreaming.

That's when I notice the violet haze that covers my

vision. I'm only just now seeing it, but in the mysterious way of dreams, I know it was here all along. Even Aspen glows with a violet aura, one that pulses with every breath.

My heart sinks with disappointment. I'm about to pull my hand away when Aspen's eyelids flutter open. With a start, his eyes lock on mine and his fingers curl around my wrist. My breath catches, remembering what happened last time he woke to me standing over him. Of course, that time had been real, not a figment of my imagination.

He pulls my hand to his lips, pressing a kiss to my wrist. I close my eyes and sink to the edge of the bed, sitting at his side. "You aren't really here, are you?" he asks, voice sounding both close and far away at the same time.

"No," I say, opening my eyes to find his face. "Neither are you."

His lips pull into a crooked grin as his hand moves to my cheek. "I never knew I could dream something so beautiful."

Heat stirs inside me as his eyes drink me in, but all potential desire is crushed by the logic that permeates my thoughts. Not even my dreams are a respite from the brutal realism I hold so dear when I'm awake. "This hurts too much," I say, lip trembling. "By tomorrow, your new Chosen will arrive. You'll see that carriage and you'll have no idea whether I or they will emerge from it. I don't even want to imagine what your reaction will be."

His eyes widen, jaw clenching at my words, but he says nothing.

"I can't even warn you. I can't even say goodbye." I let

out a bitter laugh. "Perhaps that's what this is. My mind's way of letting me pretend I can."

"Then pretend with me." His words come out low, and I swear there's a hint of a tremor to them. He beckons me forward. "Lay with me."

My face crumples, and I fold myself into him, burrowing into his bare chest. He pulls the blanket over us, arms wrapping around me as I breathe in his rosemary and cinnamon scent. I'm surprised I can conjure the scent within this dream, yet the certainty that this is a dream remains. Aspen's arms don't feel as heavy as they should, the blankets not nearly as warm. Yet, I enjoy it all the same.

"I'm sorry," he whispers into my hair. "I should have been with you every night like this. I never should have let my pride keep us apart."

"It wouldn't have changed anything," I say, the beating of his heart pulsing against my ear. "All of this still would have happened."

"But we would have had *this*."

"It only would have made things harder."

"Perhaps it should have been harder." His tone deepens. "Maybe I should have fought harder to keep you here."

"I would have fought back even more." We fall into silence, and I know that means the dream is coming to an end. With that knowledge, I cling tighter, willing this moment to remain frozen in time. My heart races as I wait for the dream to fizzle into nothing, for my body to jolt awake in Mr. Meeks' guest room. But the dream remains, and all I can do is revel in the sound of Aspen's heart, in the feel of his breath stirring my hair.

9

The dream is the first thing I remember when I wake. I feel hollow in its absence, wishing it had been real. I can hardly shake it, not even as Lorelei and I get dressed and prepare for our day. It isn't until the two of us are in Mr. Meeks' carriage that I finally manage to tuck the dream away. That's when more pressing concerns flood my mind.

I'm about to see my mother. I'm about to see her *in jail*.

It's a comfort that Mr. Meeks loaned his carriage and driver to me, allowing me and Lorelei privacy for our visit. The fewer witnesses to my anxious state the better. It's still perplexing to consider everything that has happened, and I'm not sure what to expect from my conversation with my mother. At least I'll know the truth once and for all—whether she truly hid my heritage or if the human council is as devious as Aspen suspects.

I'm shaking by the time the carriage comes to a stop outside the jail. The small justice building is in the village plaza on the south end of Etting's street, several blocks from the apothecary. The morning is cool with a light drizzle of rain greeting us as Lorelei and I exit the carriage. The driver gives me a nod. "I'll wait here for you, Miss Fairfield."

"Thank you." With my attention fixed on the building ahead, I hurry through the rain, forcing myself not to look around the plaza. I don't want to see any familiar faces or curious stares. By now, I'm sure half the town knows everything that occurred last night.

Sheriff Bronson meets us by the back door to the jail, expression hard. He's a rugged-looking man in his sixties with graying hair, long sideburns, and a frizzy mustache. His sheriff's jacket looks a bit the worse for wear, his dress not nearly as refined as the mayor, Mr. Duveau, or even Mr. Meeks. I suppose such a gruff appearance comes with the job.

"Your mother is inside," he says, opening the door. His gaze finds Lorelei for only a moment, but he doesn't seem surprised. Good. Lorelei donned a glamour before we left, disguising herself as a human to prevent as much undue attention as possible. I can't see the glamour myself, but at least it seems others can despite her fears that her magic wouldn't be strong enough here to hold it. In addition to the glamour, she wears one of my most modest fae dresses I'd brought, one of pink chiffon with several layers to the skirt.

We follow Sheriff Bronson through the doorway. Inside, I find a small, dimly lit room with a bench near the door and cells lining the walls. There appear to be four cells total, each smaller than an average bedroom. Only one is occupied.

I run to the bars, finding my mother huddled on a narrow cot, a thick wool blanket over her shoulders. "Ma!"

Her eyes widen when she sees me, and she rises to her feet. She's dressed in rough, gray homespun, skin pale, hair a tangle of copper waves. Gone are her colorful scarves, her whimsical shawls and jewelry. Gone is the brightness in her eyes and the color in her cheeks. "Evelyn, what are you doing here?"

Bronson clears his throat. "I'll give you some privacy and wait right outside the door." He exits the jail but doesn't close the door behind him.

Lorelei squeezes my shoulder. "I'll give you some space as well."

"Thank you," I say. Lorelei takes a seat on the bench at the other side of the room, and I return my attention to my mother. I want to hug her through the bars, to make sure she's hale and whole, but my words are already tumbling from my lips. "What in the name of iron is going on? Why does the human council think I'm fae?"

She presses her lips tight, and I hold my breath for the answer. "Because it's true," she finally says.

There it is. Her confession. My blood feels like it's rushing from my head, and I think I might be sick. "How is this possible?" I say with a gasp. "Who is my father?"

Her brow furrows. "Your father? I told you who he was. His name was Howard, he was a good man—"

"You never told me he was fae."

She shakes her head. "He wasn't."

"Then how the bloody..." My words dry in my throat as logic pieces itself together in my mind.

"I'm the one who's fae, Evelyn."

This time, the blood really does leave my head, and I slide to my knees at the base of the cell. "I don't understand."

Mother joins me, kneeling down and reaching her hands through the bars to grasp mine. "I'm half-fae. My mother was human but my father was originally from Faerwyvae."

"So, Amelie and I...we're a quarter fae." My heart races to admit it out loud. Mother confirms my understanding with a nod. "Who was *your* father then? You told us you were born on the mainland. How did a fae male from Faerwyvae sire you?"

"I was conceived on the Fair Isle, but my mother gave birth to me on the mainland."

"She left your father?"

"I suppose you can say that, although it wasn't her choice."

"But...I remember you mentioning your father. You loved him, he was kind and strong. If your mother left him, who is the father you spoke to me and Amelie about?"

"My father didn't stay on the isle. He was exiled to the mainland."

"Foxglove said no fae has been exiled this century."

She gives me a sad smile. "Evie, I'm over a thousand years old."

Her words send me reeling, blood turning to ice. "A thousand years old," I echo.

"My father was King Caleos." She says it like it should mean something to me, but the name doesn't spark recognition. A sigh escapes her lips. "No, I suppose you wouldn't have heard of him. They consider his name taboo in Faerwyvae. You'll know him as—"

"The exiled Fire King."

She nods. "Before King Ustrin, my father ruled the Fire Court."

I close my eyes, trying to recall everything I've learned about the war, about Faerwyvae. Most of what I know, I learned from either Foxglove or Cobalt. "The Fire King had an affair with a human woman. The humans executed her when they found she was pregnant with the child of a fae."

"And he burned down her village in retribution, killing everyone who didn't flee in time."

"That sparked the war," I say.

"Yes. The war went on for decades, and my father was exiled at the end of it. That's when he was reunited with me and my mother."

"Reunited...are you saying...but his lover was killed. You just said so yourself."

"My mother was executed, burned at the stake, but she didn't die. Can you imagine why?"

"No, it's impossible."

"She didn't die because she was pregnant with me. As daughter of the Fire King, I am strengthened by fire. It was my life inside her that kept her heart beating when her flesh was scorched. It was my life that helped her slowly heal from her wounds."

My breath hitches as I look at my mother under a new light. All this time...she's been the Fire King's daughter. She's been fae.

She continues. "My maternal grandmother prayed over

my mother's corpse late into the night, long after all the spectators left. It was she who discovered the healing begin to take place. That's when she sought the first fae she could find—a lunar fae—and bargained her life for a promise that my mother and I would be taken to safety. The lunar fae took my grandmother's life and burned her body, leaving it in my mother's place for the humans to find the next day."

I've seen a lot of blood and gore during surgery, but the images in my head are somehow far more grim. The willing sacrifice of a life to save one's child is more than I can imagine. "The lunar fae kept their end of the bargain, I assume."

"Yes. The fae took my mother to the Lunar Court, where Queen Nessina offered her sanctuary until she healed. Not even my father knew she lived, which was why he sought to avenge her death. Once Mother recovered, the queen secured safe passage for her to the mainland. I was born shortly after."

"Queen Nessina..." The name isn't familiar to me. The current ruler of the Lunar Court is Queen Nyxia, a vampire fae. "Is she Queen Nyxia's mother?"

"Yes, and she was the one who convinced the council to exile my father as his punishment at the end of the war. Very few fae know the truth, that his penance was a mercy far more than it was a death sentence. Because it reunited him with us, let him live and die at my mother's side after a human lifespan. But before the end of his life, my father took a promise from me."

"What promise?"

"That I would refuse the punishment he'd been given. That I would return to the Fair Isle and live the immortal lifespan that was my blood right."

"That's how you've been alive so long?"

She nods. "Being near Faerwyvae's magic slows my aging, but it's never been safe for me to stay in any one place for an extended period, not when my agelessness could arouse suspicion. Sometimes I returned to the mainland, living there for years or decades, which is how I met your father. There were many times I thought I would stay away from the isle for good. When I met your father, I thought I was ready to do just that, to grow old with him. But then you and Amelie were born."

Tears glaze her eyes, and I feel mine swimming in response.

She continues. "There was a light missing from the two of you, apparent from birth, and I felt it reflected inside me as well. Being on the mainland meant I was in a constant state of mental fog, of unease and illness. I had no connection to magic or healing. My existence was a flicker of life compared to the vitality I felt on the isle, and I could see my daughters were suffering the same. Amelie was a quiet, sallow, unhappy child. You were sickly and hardly did anything but cry. I realized then why my father had taken that promise from me, and why my grandmother had sacrificed her life for my mother and me; it's one thing to suffer yourself, but it's another to watch a child languish. That's when I left your father to live in Eisleigh."

"Why didn't you ever tell us?"

"I knew I'd have to tell you eventually, and perhaps I was wrong to keep the truth from you so long. You'd stop aging once you reached adulthood and we would need to move elsewhere. But the truth was dangerous. I wanted to keep the burden from you and Amelie as long as I could.

By the time you were Chosen, it was too late. I couldn't bring myself to further overwhelm the two of you."

I feel a flash of anger over her excuse for not explaining things before we were taken to Faerwyvae. If we'd known the truth, at least we would have been better prepared for complications such as this. But my attention is fixated on what she said before that.

"Why was the truth so dangerous?" I ask. "I know the fae aren't allowed to live on this side of the wall, and I understand our heritage compromised the treaty, but after how lenient the mayor has been with previous mishaps with the fae, why is this considered such a serious offense?"

"It isn't just that we have fae blood," Mother says, expression grave. "It's whose fae blood we have. My father wasn't the only one included in his exile. Any possible descendants were sentenced to the same fate. My return to the Fair Isle went directly against that. And it isn't just the humans you have to fear. There are fae who feel threatened by your very existence. It's why I tried to keep you and Amelie safe from the Reaping. It's always been a precarious balance, trying to stay close enough to the wall to benefit from Faerwyvae's magic while maintaining a low profile."

"Why are the fae threatened by us?" As soon as the words are out of my mouth, I know the answer. The mayor mentioned King Ustrin last night but never explained why. I recall what the Fire King said to me when I met him, that I felt like an old enemy. "King Ustrin is responsible for this, isn't he?"

She nods. "It was he I hoped you'd never meet, as he has benefited the most from my father's exile. I wouldn't be surprised if he orchestrated his demise in the first place. Someone caught my father with a human lover and convinced the humans to execute my mother. Now that I've seen firsthand what lengths he'll go to, I'm certain he's been against my father from the start."

"How did he turn the human council so firmly against us?"

"He came to the apothecary three days ago and attacked me. I should have known his attack was a ruse. I should have known to stand down. But instinct had me returning the attack, and he saw my fire powers unleashed. As soon as he realized what I could do, he set the kitchen ablaze and disappeared." She brings her hand to her heart, rubbing her palm over her chest as if the memory pains her.

"Is the apothecary..."

"It's gone, Evie." Her voice is a hoarse whisper. "I was still trying to smother the flames when the sheriff came. And the mayor. They took me into custody before the firefighters arrived. I've been told it is nothing but a charred husk."

My stomach churns at the impossibility of what she's saying. The apothecary, her life's passion, *our home*...it's gone. "Why did you come with them? Why didn't you fight them with these fire powers you have?"

"I didn't dare make any move against them, not when there was a chance I could convince them they were wrong. I knew King Ustrin would have given my identity away, but I underestimated how far he would go. He threatened the council, saying he would tell the fae that the humans broke the treaty by giving them a fae girl for the Reaping instead of a human like the treaty demands.

That's why the human council is so adamant about punishing me."

"That's the real reason they're giving Aspen a final chance with a new set of Chosen." I nearly choke on the name of my mate. "They're trying to shift the responsibility back to him."

Mother nods. "Still, I'd hoped I'd be able to sway them in the end, but I now know that was folly."

The defeat in her tone slashes at my heart, and I'm torn between guilt and sorrow. Guilt because the mayor was right. We are fae and Mother has been hiding our heritage. We've broken the law. But I feel sorrow too because I know what this is costing her. What this is costing all of us. It feels like that sorrow will open a chasm in the ground beneath me and swallow me whole. There's only one thing I can do to keep from losing my mind. Seek logic. Truth. "They say they have proof. What does that mean?"

Her face pales. "Yesterday, Henry Duveau paid me a visit."

"What is the significance of Mr. Duveau?"

"He's the descendant of the original councilman who exiled my father. I take it by now you know about the fae Bonding ritual?"

"I have some firsthand experience." I ignore the crushing pain in my chest at the confession.

"The councilman who exiled my father did so with the power of the Bond, but it wasn't just a regular Bond between them. It was a Legacy Bond, meaning it's passed on by bloodline instead of ending with the death of the bargainers. My father's Bond was extended to me, and I have passed it on to you and Amelie. Likewise, the original councilman passed it down through his family. Ever since the end of the war, Eisleigh's council always reserves a seat for a man of the councilman's blood. That's their guarantee against any of my father's descendants breaking the treaty with their return. All Mr. Duveau has to do is use my name—*all our names*—and we will be forced to obey our exile."

"So that's who Mr. Duveau is."

"Yes. He has the power of my name and can use it against me. He did just that when the mayor brought him to my cell yesterday. With the power of my name, he commanded me to take his knife and cut myself. I did. They watched me bleed. Then they witnessed my skin heal right before their eyes."

My shoulders slump, and I feel that chasm of sorrow widen, feel myself slipping into it. It's over. All of it. The council has irrefutable proof. Her trial will be nothing more than a farce. A mercy.

"There's no hope," I whisper.

Mother gives me a sad smile. "Not for me, no. But there may be hope for you."

10

"What do you mean, there's hope for me?" I search my mother's face for understanding. "There's nothing we can say to aid our case. We're going to be exiled."

She leans closer to the bars, lowering her voice to a whisper. "Not if you run."

My stomach takes a dive. "I'm not going to do that, Mother. If Amelie and I don't present ourselves at your trial, they are going to execute you."

"It's a sacrifice I'm willing to make."

"Well, I'm not."

Her eyes well with tears, but they crinkle at the edges as she forces a smile. "Everything I've done since you girls were born was to give you the best possible life. I'll gladly give mine if it means you get to live."

"Don't say that." My voice is a furious whisper. "You aren't giving your life for us, and that's the last I'll hear of it. Sure, it may be unfair that we're being punished for the crimes of our ancestor, but the law is the law. At least this way all three of us keep our lives. We'll be exiled, but we'll be together. We can live out the remainder of our days in peace. No compromising the treaty. No hiding from fae who feel threatened by us."

She shakes her head. "You don't know what you're giving up by leaving the isle. Life on the mainland is but a half-life for those with fae blood."

"But it's worth living. You said so yourself; you were willing to stay before we were born. And your father was given a merciful punishment by being allowed to live a mortal life with his loved ones. I'm willing to do the same." Despite my optimistic words, my throat constricts at the bitter taste of them. Deep down, a spark of rage threatens to ignite.

"You deserve so much more. You deserve to live a long life, to thrive on your own magic—"

"What magic, Mother?" I say with a glare. My anger burns brighter. Even though I know it's misdirected, it feels better than sorrow. My hands ball into fists. "Magic is nothing but trouble. Up until now, I lived without magic just fine. I was happy before I went to Faerwyvae. Amelie was happy. You were happy. I was going to go to medical school, and I would have if not for the idiotic Reaping. If not for a chance encounter while making a pointless offering at the wall."

Angry tears spring to my eyes as memories of that first time I met Aspen swim through my mind. I have yet to confess to Mother or Amelie that meeting him is what prompted all of this. My rage grows and grows, boiling inside me like a kettle ready to howl. I rise to my feet, gripping the bars of her cell.

"Evelyn—"

"It's my fault." The words burst from between my teeth and through my lips, hot tears streaming down my cheeks. "It's my fault for speaking to Aspen at the wall the night before the Reaping. And it's his fault for choosing me after he killed the Holstrom girls. It's your fault for endangering the treaty by bringing us here. And it's your father's fault for burning a village, and the villagers' fault for executing his lover. It's Queen Nessina's fault for spiriting your mother away and telling no one. It's everyone's fault including my own and it makes me so furious I feel like I'm going to explode."

Heat radiates from my core, down my arms, and into my palms. I let out a shout of frustration, and with it comes a flash of light followed by molten heat beneath my fingers. I spring away from the bars, my fury evaporating into shock as I stare at the glowing metal where my hands just were. In their place are two bright orange prints, as if the bars were partially melted by my hands.

Mother stands, eyes wide as she watches the glow slowly begin to cool.

"What was that?" I manage to gasp.

"Your magic. *Our* magic."

I grip my stomach, nausea turning inside me as I stare at the bars even after the glow dissipates. Then I return my attention to my mother. "How did I do that?"

"Rage is an element of fire," she says gently.

"Why am I only able to do this now?"

"This isn't new, my love. You've always been able to manipulate fire, although I must say, never in such a literal sense."

"What do you mean?"

"Why else do you think you have always been drawn

to the healing arts, Evelyn? The element of fire is more than physical flame. It's deeper. It encompasses pleasure, passion, anger, creativity. In healing, it's the life force energy that animates living beings. I channel that life force into every tonic I make, let it flow into every spell and charm, even when working with the earthen elements I favor as an herbalist. You work with the same life force too, my dear."

My eyes search hers, a chill of understanding crawling up my spine.

She continues. "You've always held the talent to heal, to weave someone's inner fire, to strengthen their life force. You used it long before you picked up a scalpel."

My mind spins with memories. Lorelei's leg. Aspen's surgery. The silly motions I performed when I was a child, laying my hands on Mother's shop patrons. "I wish you would have told me."

"I tried, Evie. You didn't believe me."

I want to argue, but she's right. When I stopped believing in magic, I stopped believing in *her*. Started ignoring everything she had to say about magic and her craft. "I had my reasons," I say. Despite my best efforts, I can't hide the note of condemnation in my tone.

As if she can read my mind, her shoulders slump. "I know, my love, and I don't blame you for it. Magic isn't infallible, and I will regret failing your sister every day for the rest of my life."

"Why did it happen? If you have these healing gifts, why didn't you know how to help Amelie when she almost died?"

"Do you remember what happened the morning before you and your sister left to play in the woods?"

"No. Nothing out of the ordinary."

"I was caught in a downpour on my way back from delivering Mrs. Collins her draught. I caught a terrible chill from it."

"What does that have to do with anything?"

"An attack by water weakens fire, Evelyn. That's an important factor you need to know for your own good."

I'm frozen with a sudden realization. I recall how weak I felt after my near drowning with the kelpie, how it took me three days to recover. I remember how awful I felt waking up with water in my lungs after Cobalt trapped me in the coral cage. Each time I've been injured underwater, I've suffered greatly from it.

"If I'd been at my full strength, I would have known there was no curse on your sister, that her discomfort was due to a physical ailment, not a magical one. I never should have tried to rely on my powers in such a state, and I should have taken her to Mr. Meeks at once. I'll live with that guilt always."

My throat feels tight as I take in the shame on her face. I sigh. "That doesn't matter anymore."

"It matters if you can learn from my mistake."

"What's there to learn?" I let out a bitter laugh. "In two weeks, we'll be going to the mainland and I'll never be bothered with magic again."

"Despite what you think now," Mother says, "being stripped from your magic is no laughing matter. When we get there, you'll see what I mean."

"Does that mean you're done fighting me on this?" I lift my brow. "You'll go peacefully to your trial and not try to convince me or Amelie to run?"

It's her turn to bark a cynical laugh. "I don't have

much of a choice, Evelyn. Mr. Duveau holds me in this cell by the power of my name. After he escorts me to the Spire, I'll no doubt be restrained with water. So, if by *go peacefully* you mean do what I'm forced to do, then yes."

"Mother, we have no right to be here." My rage threatens to return, to argue against my own statement, but I breathe it away. For good measure, I cross my arms and tuck my hands beneath my elbows. "If our presence on the isle means war, then this is a sacrifice we must make. We have to save the treaty."

I can tell she's resisting the urge to disagree. "I wish you'd reconsider," she whispers. "I won't force a promise from you, but I will implore you to take your sister and find allies who will protect you. Claim the life you deserve."

My inner fire begs to rise and meet her offer, but my good sense tamps it down. "I'm not a revolutionary, Mother. I'm a surgeon. And I'm going to stand at your side from now until death and make the sacrifice that saves the most lives."

She nods and lets out a heavy breath. "I know. This is who you are."

I lift my chin. "It is."

"What does your sister think?"

It's a struggle to maintain my composure at the mention of Amelie. Mother has no idea what has happened to her. Has no idea where she is or whose thumb she's under. The same questions from yesterday pound at my head. *What if she doesn't come to the trial?*

I force a look of nonchalance. "You know how she is, Mother. So long as a favorable marriage is an option, she'll be happy. I'm sure the sheer number of eligible bachelors on the mainland will be more than enough to keep her spirits from sinking too low."

Mother holds my gaze but gives no other sign that she can see through my ruse. "Perhaps you're right."

I approach the cell and take Mother's hands through the bars, entwining our arms. It's as close as we can get to a hug. "As long as we have you, we will get through this."

She nods.

We shed a few tears as we break apart, and I try not to crumble as Lorelei and I return to the carriage. Behind the closed doors, the two of us maintain silence, and the carriage rolls into motion. Lorelei says nothing about what I did to the bars or gives any indication she'd been listening to our conversation. But she had to have seen and heard everything. I can feel it in her silence, in her burning stare.

I lean back in my seat, analyzing the conversation with my mother forwards, sideways, and back again. No matter what conclusions I try to establish, one question repeats again and again.

Where in the blazing iron is my scientific explanation for all of this?

11

I have magic.

I have *fire* magic.

The concept isn't any easier to comprehend now than it was at my mother's cell. I stand at the window in Mr. Meeks' parlor, chewing a nail as I stare out at the trees surrounding Mr. Meeks' property.

Lorelei's soft footsteps come up behind me. "Are you all right?"

I shrug. "As all right as I can be."

"Do you want to talk about it?"

"What's there to talk about?" I turn to face her.

Her expression is hesitant, a look I've seen her wear around Aspen but rarely with me. "There's a lot to talk about. Your mother. Her trial." She nibbles her bottom lip. "What you did at her cell."

"You saw."

She nods. "If you want to talk—"

I skirt around her and walk to the middle of the room. "I don't want to talk."

"But I know about magic. I don't personally utilize fire, but I can help you make sense of it."

Part of me wants to smile. She's come to know me well if she understands that making sense of things is my primary aim. Still, I'm not ready to verbalize what I experienced. Not when it matters so little considering I'll be leaving the isle, magic, and these strange powers behind so soon.

I open my mouth to give her an excuse when the parlor door opens.

In walks Mr. Meeks with a tray of tea and cookies. He sets it on the tea table, then faces me with a warm smile. "I thought you might want some refreshments."

"Thank you kindly," I say, hoping my words don't carry the turmoil I'm hiding.

He nods, then turns to Lorelei. "I apologize, miss, but I admit I don't know what refreshments your kind desire."

She looks from him to the tea table. "Tea and cookies are fine." Her tone is brusque, reminding me of how she spoke to me when we first met. I bristle, hoping Mr. Meeks doesn't take offense, but he doesn't seem perturbed in the least.

He takes a few steps closer to her. "Are you implying the fae eat human food?"

"Seelie fae prefer human food, yes. We are also fond of fae fruit and wine, though, and that goes for the unseelie too."

His eyes are alight with wonder, as if her words are a gift. "That is very interesting indeed." He brings a finger to his chin, watching her with a querulous expression. Lorelei crosses her arms over her chest and narrows her eyes, but Mr. Meeks doesn't seem to get the hint.

"We thank you for your consideration, Mr. Meeks," I say to avert his unwanted attention from Lorelei.

He turns to face me, cheeks flushed. "Ah, yes, and do forgive me for my questions. It's a rare thing to chat so intimately with a fae."

"Rare indeed," I say. "I can't thank you enough for allowing us to stay."

"Of course," he says, drawing closer to me. The scrutiny returns to his face as he studies me now. "How was your mother, by the way?"

I tense, searching for words. "She seemed well-accommodated. For a prisoner, that is."

"It must pain you greatly to see her like that."

"It does."

He lowers his voice. "Did she reveal anything to you? Any explanation over these allegations?"

I consider lying to him, but what would be the point? It won't change anything. "Mother confirmed that I am of fae heritage." I watch his face, waiting for it to pale, for the fear to strike his features.

Surprisingly, he remains composed. In fact, his expression seems to brighten. "Really! Oh, that is extraordinary."

"Extraordinary is a...word for it, I suppose."

He clasps his hands together and looks me over as if seeing me for the first time. When his eyes meet mine, he blinks in rapid succession. Heat rises to my cheeks as I realize what the gesture means. I take a step back. "Mr. Meeks, I'm not going to glamour you. I don't even know if I can." My statement forces me to recall what happened with the mayor, the way I imagined holding his attention in a cage, how he spoke about King Ustrin without meaning to. So perhaps I *can*, but I most certainly *won't*. It's not like I meant to do it in the first place.

His face burns beet red, and he lets out a nervous laugh. "I know dear, I know. It was but an automatic response. However, that does pose an interesting question. How much fae blood do you have?"

"I am a quarter fae."

"I do have so many questions for you. Do you mind?"

"About..."

"About your heritage. You know how keen I am to understand the fae from a scientific perspective."

"Mr. Meeks, I only confirmed my heritage today. There's not much I can tell you."

"Still, you likely hold a great deal of answers inside you. Answers the scientific community can only guess at."

Normally, I'd be as excited as he is about such a learning opportunity. Not today. Not with mental exhaustion tugging at my mind.

Mr. Meeks flushes again as he presses his lips tight and takes a step back. "Forgive me, dear girl. I dare not press you when you are clearly in no state. However, can I request your assistance later? Would you be interested in running some...experiments of sorts?"

"Like I said, I don't know how much help I could possibly be."

He waves a dismissive hand. "You'll help me plenty. It will be like old times. Me and my dearest apprentice working side by side. You never know, we could discover something that could transform human understanding of the fae."

I let out a heavy sigh. His enthusiasm is impossible to ignore. Besides, perhaps he's right. Maybe we can learn something that will further my own understanding of myself. "I'll do what I can to help."

He turns his grin on Lorelei. "And you—"

"No." She burns him with a glare, then sidles up next to me, arms still crossed over her chest.

My shoulders tense, but again Mr. Meeks is unaffected by Lorelei's sharp edges. He lets out a nervous laugh. "Once more, I beg you to forgive my overeager excitement over your heritage. You know how I can get."

I force my lips into a smile. "I do."

"Very well. I'll leave you to it. Oh, but I have yet to mention..." He extends his arm toward the tea table. "The tea I brought is of a special nature. It's something I had from your mother's apothecary. When I bought it, she said it was a formula meant to ease the nerves. I've hardly had use for it since I much prefer laudanum, but now I find the perfect recipient of its cure."

My throat feels tight as I stare at the teapot. Only now do I recognize the aromas wafting from it. The blend is one of Mother's favorites—lavender, chamomile, vetiver, and lemon balm. Mine too, although I was always loathe to admit it before. My voice finds its way past the lump in my throat. "Thank you."

Mr. Meeks extends a hand and squeezes my shoulder, then nods at Lorelei with a warm smile. "I'll be in the surgery if you need anything."

Once he leaves, I make my way to the couch. My hands tremble as I pour the tea. Tears prick my eyes as the aroma grows stronger. I bring the cup to my nose and deeply inhale. Sipping slowly, the warm liquid dances over my tongue, soothing me with its comforting familiarity.

"I don't trust him." Lorelei's voice shatters my reverie. She walks toward me, eyes narrowed to slits. "This man is your beloved mentor?"

I furrow my brow as I look at her. "You should be kinder to him, Lorelei. He's our host. I would be sleeping in a prison if it weren't for Mr. Meeks."

"I don't like his talk of experimenting on you."

"He wasn't talking about experimenting *on* me. I'm sure he just wants to ask me some questions. Besides, of course it sounds odd to you. Healing in Faerwyvae is far different than it is here. In the human realm, we make breakthroughs in the medical arts by way of experimentation."

She shakes her head. "No. It's more than that. It's..." Her words dry on her lips, and for a moment she sways on her feet.

"What is it?"

She puts a hand over her forehead, then comes to sit next to me on the couch. "I'm not feeling well."

My stomach sinks. I haven't worried much over Lorelei's state of health since last night, but being this far from Faerwyvae can't be getting any easier for her. I set down my cup and reach for the other, then I fill it with tea and hand it to her. "Drink this. I doubt it will help much, but you'll feel calmer. It has lavender, chamomile, lemon balm—"

"Iron?" Her eyes are wide as she stares at the cup in her hands. She all but throws the cup on the table, rising to her feet. "Those cups are painted iron. That's what is making me feel ill right now."

I look at the two cups, both painted white. There's no sign that they're made from iron; before I examined them, I assumed they were porcelain. "Why would he serve us..." I can't bring myself to finish my train of thought.

Lorelei backs away from the table. "We need to get out of here."

My heart begins to race. "It can't be what we think this is. It was a mistake, an accident. An experiment, perhaps."

She darts toward the front door but pauses before it. "Someone's on the other side."

I run to her and take her hand in mine, then pull her toward the side door. It leads to the hallway and the kitchen, where we can leave out back. I fling the door open and freeze. Mr. Meeks stands on the other side, an apologetic smile on his face as I hear the front door swing open behind us.

I whirl to find Mr. Osterman in the doorway, a spear of ash and iron in his one remaining hand. His eyes burn into Lorelei. Spear aimed, he charges forward. I launch myself toward Lorelei, but an arm pulls me back.

"I'm sorry, my dear," Mr. Meeks whispers as something metal covers my nose and mouth. An inhalation cone. I recognize the familiar scent of chloroform.

Lorelei's scream is the last thing I hear.

12

A subtle sound creeps upon my awareness. *Evie. Evie.*

It's my name, I realize, although the voice sounds far away.

Evie. Evie.

"Evie." The voice becomes clear. It's Aspen's. I pry my eyes open and find myself lying on a bed in a dimly lit room. Aspen stands over me, face pale as his eyes take in his surroundings. "What in oak and ivy is this place?"

I push myself to sit, expecting to feel a head rush, but nothing more than an odd sense of mental fog comes over me. Like Aspen, I look around the room. It reminds me of Mr. Meeks' surgery, but it's far too small and cluttered, not to mention unfamiliar. Shelves line the walls full of bottles and boxes.

My heart leaps into my throat when I notice the operating tools laid out on a tray next to me. That's when I realize I'm not in a bed but on a table. An operating table.

Did something happen? Was I injured?

I try to recall the last thing I remember, but it's a blur. There was my visit with my mother. Was I hurt? No, I remember leaving. Then returning to Mr. Meeks' house. I remember the parlor, the tea, the arrival of Mr. Osterman...

Panic threatens to overwhelm me, but Aspen's presence and the violet aura around him tell me something important; this is a dream. Was my last memory a dream too? It must have been. Mr. Meeks would never...he'd never...

I refuse to consider it further until I have more proof. My anxiety lowers to a simmer, but I can't shake the wariness I feel in this unsettling environment.

"I liked the last dream better," I say, voice like a croak.

Aspen whirls back toward me, relief washing over him. "Where are you?"

I shrug. "I've never seen this place. I don't know why I'm dreaming about it."

"You need to get out of here," Aspen growls. "What happened?"

I ponder his question but can't seem to make sense of anything through the fog in my mind.

Aspen takes me by the shoulders. His touch feels the same as the last time I dreamed of him—warm but with something missing in our touch, like a barrier lies between us. "Evie, tell me what's going on."

I open my mouth, but a rumble of voices distracts me. The voices sound both near and far at the same time, but I recognize one of them. It's Mr. Meeks. I stagger to the other side of the room and through the doorway. To the right stand three shadowed figures at the end of a dingy hall, lit by the faint glow of a single light bulb overhead.

There isn't a window to be seen, and only one other door occupies the hall, just across from where I stand.

Fearing I've been spotted, I pull myself back into the room, then slowly peer out again. I see the faces of Mr. Meeks, Mr. Osterman and—I suppress a shudder—Mr. Duveau. None, however, appear to have noticed me.

Aspen tenses at my side as he stares daggers down the hall. He seems far less concerned about being seen and ignores my every attempt to pull him behind the threshold with me. When sudden movement catches my eye, I stop tugging Aspen's shirt. Instead, I watch Mr. Duveau pass a pouch into Mr. Meeks' hands, expression hard. "You have some nerve bringing the Fairfield girl here," Mr. Duveau says. "I can't have her dying before the trial."

"I'm not going to kill her, Henry," Mr. Meeks says. "The girl is dear to me, regardless of bloodline."

"I can't have her talking about this...*operation*...you and Mr. Osterman have here either."

Mr. Meeks waves a dismissive hand. "Why do you think I brought her in unconscious? She will leave the same way. She agreed to help me with my scientific research. I believe once the shock wears off, she will understand quite well what had to be done. She's a sensible girl, I promise you."

"You better be right. If anything goes awry, I'm holding you responsible. If she takes word of this to the Council of Eleven Courts, the fae would consider it a breach of treaty."

"I assure you," Mr. Meeks says, "she will know nothing of her whereabouts or what we do here aside from this being a place for scientific study."

Mr. Duveau gives a curt nod. "I'll be back for the wood nymph this evening when it's time to take Maven Fairfield to the Spire."

Mr. Osterman's face breaks into a dark grin. "Can I have fun with her first?"

Mr. Duveau fixes the large man with a glare. "The patrons of the Briar House have exotic tastes, but they don't like their merchandise damaged. Do what you will, but be sure she is whole and of sound mind by the time I return tonight. You have her in iron?"

Mr. Osterman nods.

"Good. Until this evening." Mr. Duveau turns from the men and ascends a narrow staircase behind them. Daylight flashes overhead for a moment before the hall is plunged back into semi-darkness.

Mr. Meeks faces Mr. Osterman, an exasperated look on his face. "Did you have to mention having fun with the wood nymph in front of Henry?"

Mr. Osterman grunts. "He didn't seem to mind."

"Well, I do. I don't like hearing you speak like that."

"You know what happens behind my door as well as I do."

Mr. Meeks brushes his hands on the apron he wears, wrinkling his nose in distaste. "Well, do be quiet about it. I won't have you frightening Miss Fairfield while we are at work."

"I can do quiet."

"No screams."

"I'll grab rope then."

"Rope?"

Mr. Osterman's mouth twists with a disgusting grin. "I like using rope when I don't get to make them scream."

Mr. Meeks shakes his head. "Your tastes are far beyond my means to understand."

Mr. Osterman chuckles, then heads toward the staircase while Mr. Meeks starts down the hall toward us. I spring back into the room, pressing myself against the wall, chest heaving as I process everything I just heard. Aspen stands in the doorway, eyes still locked on the hall as his body trembles with rage, his violet aura writhing to match.

That's right; this isn't happening. This is a dream.

With shaking steps, I return to Aspen's side and watch Mr. Meeks approach. The man shows no sign that he can see either of us. "Why am I dreaming this?" My words do nothing to snag his attention. Mr. Meeks opens the door across the hall and peeks inside. It's too dark for me to see what lies within. His expression is grim as he closes the door and faces this one instead. Now I know for certain we're invisible. He should be able to see us.

As he enters the room, he flips a switch and the buzz of electricity hums overhead, illuminating several bulbs hanging from the ceiling. The dim room comes into full view, and I see now what lines the shelves. A vibrant, ruby-red heart is preserved in a thick green liquid encased in glass. Bones, talons, and teeth fill countless jars. A pair of enormous blue wings like a dragonfly's rest on the topmost shelf. A set of smaller green wings are set upon it.

Aspen takes my face in his hands, his terrified eyes locked on mine. "Evie, it's time to wake up now."

I pull my face away, craning my neck to see Mr. Meeks nearing the table I had been lying on. A table I'm *still* lying on. As if standing outside myself, I see my unconscious form strapped to the table by metal cuffs locked around my wrists and ankles. I've been stripped down to my corset and knickers, sending a wave of nausea through me. Even my rowan berry necklace has been removed.

Mr. Meeks approaches his table of tools and selects a scalpel. With his free hand, he gently brushes a strand of my hair off my face as he looks down at me with his kind, fatherly smile.

Aspen forces my gaze back on him. "Wake up, Evie."

My entire body is racked with tremors.

Aspen's eyes are pleading, hands warm on my cheeks. His voice rises to a shout. "WAKE UP!"

I OPEN MY EYES AND FIND MYSELF IN THE SAME ROOM I WAS dreaming about. How can that be? My mind still feels cloudy, but it's slowly beginning to sharpen.

Mr. Meeks stands over me, just as he was in the dream. Only my perspective has changed. "Miss Fairfield, so good to see you awake."

"Where am I?" My throat feels like it's coated in cotton. Aspen is nowhere in sight.

"I'm so sorry to distress you, but this was the only way I could bring you here."

"Where. Am. I." I say it through my teeth.

"In my laboratory. It's a rare thing I get to do this kind of work, and I'm so grateful to have your assistance."

I try to sit but remember the metal cuffs around my wrists and ankles.

He follows my gaze and runs a finger over the cuff at

one of my wrists, brow furrowed. "Does the iron hurt you?"

I almost say no but stop myself, some instinct urging me to lie. So I wince. "Yes, the iron burns. It weakens me."

He nods and returns the scalpel to the tray, then faces the counter behind him. I lift my head and watch as he scribbles notes on a sheet of paper. "Interesting," he mutters.

I drop my head as he finishes his notations and turns back to me. "Where's Lorelei?"

"She's fine."

"She was stabbed with a spear." Even though I didn't see it, I know it's true.

Mr. Meeks offers a comforting smile. "I'm sure it appeared that way to you, but Mr. Osterman meant her no harm. She reacted violently when she saw him with the spear and may have been injured when Hank defended himself. But she has already recovered and returned to Faerwyvae."

Lies. That is, if my dream had any truth to it. Something tells me it was more than a dream. "What's the Briar House?"

He narrows his eyes for a moment. "Nothing you should be concerned with."

It was real. Aside from Aspen being there, of course. I must have been half-awake. I must have seen this room, heard the conversation in the hall, my mind constructing it into a dream. "What are you going to do to me?"

His eyes widen as he lets out a gasp. "How could you ask such a thing as if you're frightened of me? I'm not going to hurt you, Miss Fairfield. I'm only going to gather some data like we spoke of. You said you would help me."

"I didn't say you could knock me out and restrain me."

"I'm sorry you feel like I betrayed your trust, dear girl, but I couldn't have you knowing the location of my laboratory."

"And you couldn't have asked me to come willingly with my eyes closed?"

"I never said I was a patient man." His lips pull into a grin. "This kind of work simply cannot wait. Not when you'll only be here for two weeks."

"Does that mean you plan to experiment on me for two weeks?"

"If only we had years," he says. "If only I'd known what you were when we started working together. Just think how much more the humans would know about the fae by now."

"This isn't what I agreed to."

"Which is why I had to do what I did. I do hope you can forgive me someday." He lays a gentle hand on my arm. With the other, he retrieves his scalpel.

I shout as he drags the blade over the flesh of my forearm. Once he finishes the cut, I crane my neck to examine the wound, a red line of streaming blood. I bite back tears at the searing pain. My voice comes out strained, panicked. "I thought you said you weren't going to hurt me."

"Curious," is all he says in response, brow wrinkled as he studies the wound. "You aren't healing as quickly as a full-fae would."

"I told you, I'm only one-quarter fae," I hiss through my teeth. "I may not have rapid healing abilities at all, which means this experiment is pointless."

"Not pointless." His eyes glitter with excitement. "I'm desperate to know what kind of healing can be done. In fact..." He turns toward the counter and reaches for a stoppered vial on one of the shelves above it. As he brings it to me, I see it's a deep red color.

"Is that blood?"

He nods, grinning with pride. "This one is from a brownie. I'd like to see if the blood will heal your wound. So far, fae blood has yet to show any positive effect on a human wound."

"How many fae have you killed?"

He puts a hand to his heart. "I don't kill fae, Miss Fairfield."

My eyes rove from the vial of blood to the jar of hearts, then land on the two sets of wings. "But Mr. Osterman does. You simply experiment on the ones he captures."

His expression darkens.

"Is that before or after he has his way with them?" Heat burns my core and I do nothing to extinguish it. I let it burn, radiating from my chest to my—

Mr. Meeks plunges the scalpel into my bicep, and I shout as I feel the blade dig into muscle. "Perhaps we won't experiment with healing just yet. Perhaps we will experiment with pain tolerance first." He pulls the bloody scalpel from my arm and slams it onto the tray along with the vial of blood. With a frown, he takes up a much larger knife.

I let my anger and pain burn away my fear, let it fuel the fire that rages down my arms.

Mr. Meeks moves to my other side, the tip of the knife

pressed into the top of my shoulder. With a thrust, he cuts down my arm.

I scream, arching my back as the restraints hold me in place. My fire gathers hotter and hotter inside me, searing my wounds, flooding my hands.

Mr. Meeks takes a step away, eyes alight once again. "Now this is odd indeed. It seems you are beginning to heal—oh my."

The cuffs grow hot around my wrists, burning me. I close my eyes against the pain and feel the metal begin to warp. Once I can take it no longer, I lift my wrists through the molten metal, the force of my raging fire fueling me. With my wrists free, I reach for the scalpel as Mr. Meeks darts at me with the knife. I whirl toward him, thrusting the blade with a violent swipe. I don't see what happens through the blur of motion, but I feel the scalpel meet resistance. Mr. Meeks staggers back, dropping the knife and grasping his throat, ribbons of red streaming beneath his fingers.

I try not to focus on the gory sight, on the guilt that threatens to extinguish my fire. Instead, I focus on the pain of my open wounds, on the anger still burning inside me. I sit forward and press my hands over the ankle cuffs, vaguely noting that the burn marks on my wrists are beginning to heal. Once the cuffs reach a molten state, I pull my ankles from them, gasping at the pain from the blistering heat.

I push myself off the bed, landing with a cry as my ankles protest the motion. Hobbling toward the doorway, I'm suddenly aware of smoke filling my nostrils. I hazard a glance behind me to see the table linens have caught fire from the burning cuffs. Mr. Meeks still grasps his bleeding neck as he slides to the ground.

I feel another shock of guilt, but I burn it away, forcing myself out of the room, into the hall, and to the door on the other side. A soft whimper comes from within the room, and I throw the door open wide, letting the light from Mr. Meeks' laboratory wash inside. As my eyes adjust to the new environment, I see a figure against the far wall, iron shackles hanging from the ceiling, pulling Lorelei's arms overhead. A cloth gag is tied over her mouth.

I run to her and summon my rage, letting it burn through my palms as I place them over the cuffs. "I'm sorry, but this is going to hurt."

She lets out a muffled cry as the metal burns hot around her wrists. With a deep breath, I wrap my hands around the molten cuff, stifling a cry as the heat blisters my palm. Once free, she drops to the ground. I pull her up, dragging her to her feet. We cross the room just as the laboratory grows brighter, the fire blazing over the table, flames licking toward the shelves. Knowing what kind of chemicals Mr. Meeks must have in there, it's only a matter of time before the flames set off an explosion.

"We need to hurry," I say, pulling her down the hall toward the staircase. Once we reach it, I see a door at the top. "Can you climb?"

Eyes glazed, she pulls the gag from her mouth. "Yes. Let's get the bloody oak and ivy out of here."

Smoke chases us, filling our lungs as we climb to the top of the stairs and push open the door. We scramble outside and collapse onto the earthen floor, chests heaving as we struggle to catch our breath. My vision spins but I manage to make out dense trees all around us beneath a sunset sky. I lift my head toward the smoking building we emerged from. From this vantage point, it looks like nothing more than an old-fashioned outdoor toilet, revealing no evidence of the underground operation hiding beneath it.

I think of Mr. Meeks trapped inside, fire dancing around him while ribbons of blood spill down his throat from a wound I gave him. In contrast, I recall how he sliced the scalpel and then the dagger through my arm. I think of the way he sold Lorelei to Mr. Duveau and offered her body to Mr. Osterman with nothing more than a few minor qualms.

I scoot farther from the door and lift my leg. With a kick, I slam it shut. I lay my head back in the grass, willing it to cease its spinning.

I can't stay here. I know I can't. The fire will reach the stairs, then the door, and that's only if an explosion doesn't happen first. Despite knowing this, I can't find the strength in my limbs to stand.

"Evelyn." Lorelei's panicked voice beside me prompts a rush of adrenaline. I roll onto my side and follow her line of vision.

There, between two trees, stands Mr. Osterman.

13

Mr. Osterman's eyes bulge as he stares dumbfounded at me and Lorelei. A spool of rope hangs over his shoulder, spear in hand.

My body protests at the thought of moving, but I force myself to scramble to my knees, then my feet, pulling Lorelei up with me. "Run!"

As we take off, darting toward the trees, Mr. Osterman unshoulders the rope and charges after us. "Get back here!"

"We can't outrun him," I say through gasping breaths. My back tingles with the fear that any moment I'll feel the tip of his spear pierce my flesh.

"We don't have to outrun him," Lorelei says. Her voice sounds stronger now. "We're near the wall. I can feel it."

"Mr. Osterman can cross the wall, and he'll catch us before we find it."

"All we need to do is get closer to it. Just a little closer."

"Why, what will that do?" My voice is strained, the fire

of my rage smothered to ash beneath my fear. My muscles scream with every move, flesh pulling at the half-healed wounds on my arms, wrists, and ankles.

Lorelei, on the other hand, looks stronger, more vital with every step, her stride becoming more and more even. A look of euphoria crosses her face.

Her confidence is of little comfort when Mr. Osterman's pounding steps and heaving breaths draw nearer and nearer. "Forget the councilman's orders," he calls out, voice taunting. "I'm going to cut you both into a thousand pieces."

I pump my legs harder, faster, stumbling over the uneven ground, ignoring the sting of branches that whip my face and arms. My lungs burn, vision going bleary. I can hardly keep up with Lorelei as she whips between the trees. I try to feel what she must feel, the call of the wall, the magic of Faerwyvae drawing her closer, strengthening and healing her. But I feel nothing. Nothing but an internal weight dragging me down.

My legs nearly give out beneath me when Lorelei holds up her hand and skids to a halt. I stumble at her side, my momentum not nearly as gracefully controlled as hers. But why have we stopped? The wall is nowhere in sight and Mr. Osterman is within range to spear us.

Lorelei takes a step toward the man as he closes the distance. He lifts his spear, an angry snarl on his lips. Lorelei raises her hands, thrusting them outward. Mr. Osterman moves as if he's about to throw his weapon when the ground rocks beneath his feet, forcing him to stumble back. A root as thick as a man's arm shoots from the earth, its tip sharp like a blade. It rears back, then barrels into Mr. Osterman, piercing straight into his chest and coming out the other side. The man convulses, blood seeping from his lips.

My stomach heaves, but I can't look away. Not until he ceases moving. Only then do I whirl around, falling on my hands and knees, and retch onto the forest floor. I retch until my stomach is empty, until hot tears stream down my cheeks. When I feel Lorelei's hand on my shoulder, I realize I'm wailing.

"You're all right." Lorelei's voice is a soothing whisper but laced into her tone is a hidden truth. I'm *not* all right. None of this is all right. I see pink from the corner of my eye and realize Lorelei is handing me a bundle of filthy chiffon. As I turn to inspect it, I see she's torn one of the layers off the skirt of her dress. That's when I remember I've been stripped to my undergarments.

I accept the fabric and do my best to tie it around my waist. "I killed someone," I finally manage to say. "I killed Mr. Meeks. My mentor. My lifelong friend."

Lorelei hesitates before speaking. "There's nothing I can say to make that right for you. I can only share your burden."

A burden is exactly what this is. Will I ever be able to forgive myself? In the heat of my rage, I did what I thought I must do. I reacted. I saved myself and my friend and condemned a man to die. Of course, Mr. Meeks was by no means innocent. He may not have intended to kill me, but it was clear he had no reverence for Lorelei's life or my well-being.

But does that make it right?

"We both made difficult choices today." Lorelei's voice quavers.

I rise slowly to my feet, feeling every aching muscle in

the process. When I meet Lorelei's eyes, I see conflict in them. She too killed a man today.

As if she knows what I'm thinking, she shakes her head. "I've never killed a person. Not before today."

"Do you regret it? Even though he killed Malan?"

She looks at the body impaled upon the root. "I can't say I regret it, no, but I don't feel good about it either."

"Then we feel the same."

She takes my hand and gives it a squeeze. "Come. We're close to the wall. We'll both feel better once we cross it. Physically, that is."

IT'S A SLOW JOURNEY TO THE WALL, WITH NEITHER OF US pushing ourselves to the limit now that we're no longer being chased by a madman. However, we must put as much distance between us and the laboratory as we can. Mr. Duveau said he'd be back to fetch Lorelei on his way to take my mother to the Spire.

My mother.

My breath hitches. I hate to think that Mr. Duveau could punish her for what was done tonight. He warned Mr. Meeks that he'd hold the surgeon responsible if anything were to go awry. Well, awry it went, and then some. But will Mr. Duveau maintain that no harm will come to my mother until her trial? Had I allowed too much room for interpretation in that bargain? Do I even have enough fae blood to enforce a fae bargain, however that works to begin with?

The towering stones of the faewall come into view as the trees begin to thin. I don't know if it's simply relief or from our nearness to Faerwyvae, but my pains seem to lessen. My breaths come to me easier with every step we take closer. Lorelei appears to be back to full health despite her torn, bloodied dress and grave expression.

I rub my arms over my bare shoulders as we cross between two standing stones and enter the dense fog. Only when it fades to reveal a spring meadow do we stop. We fall to our knees and sink into the plush, dew-covered grass. Night has fully fallen and all is quiet around us. Pink blossoms sway in the trees at the edge of the meadow while opalescent moths flutter through the night sky.

Lorelei tilts her head to the stars, as if bathing in their radiance. My eyes rove her wrists, and I see nothing but the faintest marks where the cuffs had chafed and the molten metal had burned. A dark stain covers her torso, probably from where Mr. Osterman speared her when he and Mr. Meeks captured us.

I examine my wrists and see that my own wounds have faded, perhaps more so than Lorelei's. My eyes then move to my arms. Aside from being smeared with dirt and dried blood, it appears the cuts have sealed shut. Is that because of my heritage? Or because I used fire? Growing up, I never noticed any unusual rate of healing for whatever minor cuts and bruises I received. Could it be I've always healed quickly?

I feel Lorelei's eyes on me. "Are any of your wounds bothering you?" she asks.

"No, they feel much improved. How about yours?"

She rubs her torso where her dress is stained with blood. "Sore, but mostly healed, I believe. The Butcher of Stone Ninety-Four let my spear wound close before he put me in the iron chains. I think he liked his prey to put up a fight."

My throat feels tight as I recall his body, the root pierced through his chest. I blink the vision away. "What do we do now?"

She looks away, brow wrinkled as she ponders. Without meeting my eyes, she says, "We could go to Autumn. King Aspen will keep you safe."

I remember the version of him in my dream, the terror in his eyes when he implored me to wake up. My heart sinks to think of him, especially when I consider the truth. Aspen wasn't there. He's home safe in Bircharbor Palace with his new Chosen. Just like I said I wanted.

"No, I can't go there."

She doesn't question me or press further. Instead, she plays with a blade of grass, expression deep in thought.

"Is there anywhere safe to stay in Spring? We're already on the Spring axis. Perhaps there's somewhere I could lie low until my mother's trial."

She tilts her head as she contemplates. "Spring is a neutral seelie court, so you may be safe here. I don't dare bring you to the palace though. If word has spread about who you are and what the humans have planned for you, there could be many who would either take you to King Ustrin or return you to Eisleigh. The same goes for any seelie ruler, in fact."

"Maybe I should go back." I shudder. "I should have taken my imprisonment to begin with. None of this would have happened if I had."

"You don't belong in a prison."

"Neither does my mother."

She lets out a sigh. "If you feel you must go back, I can't forbid you. But I don't believe they will be kind if you do."

She's probably right. After what I did, locking me in the Spire would be a mercy. Mr. Duveau's bargain only stated no harm would come to my mother. He made no promise about me. There's a good chance he would force me to spend my days before Mother's trial in the care of another surgeon like Mr. Meeks, or perhaps he'd take me where he was planning on taking Lorelei.

"Do you know what the Briar House is?"

Lorelei's lips pull into a snarl. "A brothel, most likely." Her anger fades quickly, shoulders slumping. "Now that I know what the Butcher likes to do with his victims, I think Malan's fate may have been a kindness."

I remember the wings I saw on the shelves in Mr. Meeks' laboratory, the jars of hearts and blood.

"That's the only place I can think to bring you," she says. "To Malan's parents. I don't even know if they would agree to harbor you, but they're the only spring fae I know outside of the palace."

I can tell by her expression that's the last place she wants to go. "You feel the same way about Spring that I feel about Autumn."

She nods. "But I made Aspen a promise."

"You promised him you'd watch over me while I was in Eisleigh."

"*And* until the situation with your mother was settled. To me, that means until her trial. I won't leave your side."

"I can't ask you to take me to the home of your deceased mate."

She plays with another blade of grass, and we fall into

silence. After a while, she freezes, her stillness drawing my attention. "There's somewhere else I can take you."

"Where?"

She grimaces, and I already know this option doesn't make her any happier. "The Lunar Court."

14

"The Lunar Court?" I say with a gasp. "But they're unseelie."

Lorelei shrugs. "In this instance, that's not necessarily a bad thing."

"Why do you say that?"

"Like I said, there's a chance any seelie court will turn you in to either King Ustrin or Eisleigh's council. The radical seelie most certainly will, seeing you as a threat to the treaty. The radical unseelie will do...well, they will do far worse, if they think they can use you to purposefully break the treaty. The *neutral* unseelie courts, however, are probably the safest for you right now."

"I take it the Lunar Court is considered neutral unseelie?"

Lorelei nods. "They don't care about saving the treaty, which means they will have no qualms harboring you. However, they aren't determined to eradicate humans either."

"Are there any other neutral unseelie courts?" I try to

hide my trepidation with an air of nonchalance. The thought of seeking asylum with Queen Nyxia—a vampire fae—does not sound appealing. Then again, going to any unseelie court seems like a bad idea.

"Lunar and Wind are both neutral unseelie, while Winter and Sea are radical."

"You think Lunar is the best option?"

She meets my eyes and lowers her voice. "I heard what your mother said about Queen Nessina harboring your grandmother."

"You think Queen Nyxia has her mother's sensibilities?"

Lorelei rises to her feet, brushing grass from what remains of her tattered skirt. "I'm not certain, but she's our best chance right now. Besides, she owes me." She extends her hand and pulls me to my feet. "Come. The Lunar axis is the next one west of here. If we start walking now, we'll get there before morning."

I take a step, surprised to find that my muscles have stopped screaming. "Why does Queen Nyxia owe you?"

She nibbles her bottom lip. "Let's just say we have a history."

My curiosity is burning, but I force myself not to pry. If she feels like clarifying, I'm sure she will sooner or later. In the meantime, I can only hope she's right about her.

ALL RELIEF I FOUND FROM REST IS WASHED AWAY AFTER hours of walking. The only thing that keeps me going are my occasional bursts of anger. Each time I feel it rise, I allow it to grow, to burn away my exhaustion, to fuel my healing. That healing is all that keeps me on my feet, prevents me from succumbing to the torturous pain the earth causes my bare feet. I'm still not sure what to think of this newfound power with the element of fire and can't help wondering what else I might be able to do.

Of course, such thoughts take me down a dark path as blood and smoke and flames fill my mind.

We keep the fog of the faewall within our periphery at all times to help us navigate within the confines of the axis line. It feels like we'll never find anything but spring grass, sparkling dew, and delicate blossoms. Even in the dark of the night, it's clear we are traveling through Spring.

Luckily, due to our proximity to the wall, we cross no fellow travelers, save for several rabbits, a doe, and countless squirrels. Whether these creatures are regular animals or fae in their unseelie forms, I do not know. In Faerwyvae, is there even such a thing as a *regular animal*?

The sun is just beginning to rise, illuminating the early morning, when our scenery finally changes. At first, it's a shift in the light. The blush of the sunrise dims, throwing our surroundings under a hazy filter. It reminds me of the sky before a lightning storm or the eerie quality of light that falls over everything during a solar eclipse.

Lorelei lets out a sigh of relief. "We made it to Lunar."

The feeble hope that we can now rest sparks within me, but it's quickly dashed to bits when Lorelei quickens her pace and shifts direction. With a deep breath, I try to connect to my inner fire and follow her.

We move away from the wall and deeper into the Lunar forest. Even the trees look different here, with tall, slim trunks that disappear high overhead where dark branches in shades of deep indigo and violet mingle with the more familiar browns and greens. Clusters of elegant brambles blanket the forest floor while dark vines of ivy snake up the trees.

There's no obvious season, just a moderately cool temperature and the smell of night-blooming jasmine. As the sun rises higher, the forest grows somewhat brighter, but the eerie quality of light doesn't diminish.

We continue on, going deeper and deeper into the forest. It's quiet, as if most of the creatures here are asleep. In fact, I spot several animals in the midst of slumber. Tiny bats cling to branches, dozing upside-down, wings wrapped around their bodies like blankets. A feline purr rumbles behind a patch of flowers with glowing, bell-like blooms, revealing nothing but two black, pointed ears. Owls doze in the beams overhead, occasionally opening an eye to study us. Surprisingly, a few fully awaken when we pass, launching from their branches to take flight.

"Messengers," Lorelei says under her breath. "Nyxia will know we're here."

I suppress a shudder. "Are we nearing the Lunar palace?"

She nods, the movement revealing the tenseness in her posture. Her eyes are narrowed as she stares into the distance, attention fixated on the path ahead. "We've crossed the axis and have been transported about an hour's walk from the palace."

My pulse begins to race. While our arrival will mean relief from walking, I feel only trepidation about everything else regarding the visit. Meeting the Lunar Queen, in particular. My only experience with Queen Nyxia was her involvement with Aspen's challenge for his throne when she acted as mediator between Aspen and Cobalt. Even though she ultimately decided in Aspen's favor, before that, she'd supported Cobalt's claim. I'm not sure what to make of her. I swallow hard, preparing to keep my voice level. "Is there anything I should know about Queen Nyxia before we arrive?"

Lorelei seems uncertain of what to say. "She's very powerful." Her tone doesn't reveal whether that's a good or bad thing.

"Powerful in what way?"

"She's quite...dominating in both her seelie and unseelie forms."

I remember how she shifted into a towering shadow with red eyes and terrifying fangs when the fighting began after Cobalt lost. "What exactly is she in her unseelie form? I mean, I've surmised she's a vampire, but what does she become when she's a shadow?"

"In her unseelie form, she takes the shape of fear and can delve into others' minds, finding their darkest thoughts and bringing them to the surface. That's how she feeds. While she can terrify a victim any time of day, she specializes in feeding off nightmares."

I want to know if she feeds off more than fear—blood, specifically—but I can't bring myself to ask. What little I've heard about vampires always includes some tale of bloodlust and the sinking of fangs into an unwilling victim's flesh. I rub my neck reflexively.

Lorelei grimaces. "I'll warn you now that you might have odd dreams while we're there."

"That's comforting."

She halts, posture rigid as she holds an arm out for me to stop as well. "Someone's here," she whispers.

With my thoughts swarming with blood and vampires, I can't suppress the shiver that crawls up my spine. A sound rustles in the brambles up ahead before a dark shape launches into the trees. I let out a heavy sigh. "A raven."

Lorelei doesn't seem nearly as relieved. She turns her gaze to the branches overhead, lips pulling into a frown.

"Well, Lorelei, don't you look like the wrong end of a centaur." A low, drawling male voice trickles down from somewhere above us, but I can't locate its source. Is the raven talking? "And what is with that dress? I don't think I've ever seen you in pink. I do like how you've decorated it, though."

My eyes move to the blood staining Lorelei's torso, then to the layer of grime coating my corset and makeshift skirt.

Lorelei crosses her arms and bumps her hips to the side. "Did Nyxia send her dog?"

I hear a gasp. "Now that's plain rude."

"Rude? You just called me the wrong end of a centaur."

"But I don't even like dogs."

"And I like centaurs?"

A dark shape falls to the ground. As it lands, shadows unfurl, revealing a male figure. His frame is lean and tall, skin pale, eyes the most shocking shade of silver-blue above chiseled cheekbones flushed the palest rose. His hair is a silver blond that falls in silken wisps past his pointed ears. He wears a black silk waistcoat and trousers, both patterned with silver threaded designs, but he wears no jacket. His white shirt is unbuttoned at the neck, free of cravat or tie. There's something frighteningly seductive about his state of dress.

He leans against the trunk of the tree behind him, posture casual as he waves a hand toward Lorelei. "You have that...earthen magic. You're practically related to a centaur."

Lorelei scowls. "I'm a wood nymph, and you are clearly trying to get on my nerves."

He tilts his head, lips pulling into a sultry smile. "I didn't realize I had to try so hard."

She rolls her eyes. "Is your sister at the palace?"

"Why, is she back in your good graces? Come to rekindle that spark?"

"There's no spark, but I seek an audience with her. You'll take us to her."

His eyes fall on me for the first time, assessing me from head to toe. "Us? Is this your new plaything? I thought your heart was truer than that. Darling Malan has hardly been dead for—"

Lorelei lifts her hand, and a pointed root erupts from the earth at the fae male's feet. He can hardly flinch before it rises and hovers an inch from his throat, the sharp tip vibrating as if it begs to dart forward and sink into the fae's flesh. "Don't you dare speak of Malan or so much as utter a word about me being untrue to her memory. If anyone knows about being untrue, it's your sister."

His wide eyes are all that betray his composure. He holds up his hands in casual surrender. "My apologies."

With a violent sweep of her hand, the root burrows back into the ground.

He straightens his waistcoat and extends his arm. "To Selene Palace."

Lorelei brushes past him. Before I can take a step, he faces me and folds into a graceful bow. I can't tell if he's mocking me. "Prince Franco at your service. And you are?"

"Evelyn," I mutter through pursed lips.

"Evelyn. Is that your true—"

"Don't even start." With a scowl, I rush after Lorelei.

Prince Franco matches my pace, eyes burning into me. "I like you."

"Excuse me?"

He smiles, revealing the tips of elongated canines. A vampire. "You smell like violence. That's my preferred vintage." With a nod of approval, he streams to the head of our small retinue and leads the way.

With a shudder, I force my trembling legs to keep moving.

15

Queen Nyxia is a sight to behold, as is the lush palace that surrounds her. Upon an obsidian throne, she sits with such confident authority, you'd think she's the queen of the world. Walls of moonstone and opal make up the throne room while the ceiling ends in enormous domed glass, giving an open view of the sky above.

My eyes linger on this feature as Prince Franco leads us toward his sister. "You should see it at night," he whispers in my ear.

I avert my gaze without a reply, focusing on the Lunar Queen instead. Lorelei and I drop into curtsies. As we straighten, Nyxia rises from her obsidian throne and steps down from the dais to approach us while Franco sprawls on an elegant chair at the base of the throne.

My eyes are locked on Nyxia, stunned by her eclectic clothing. At the council meeting, she wore a slim black suit. Now she wears dark silk trousers with a top that is somewhere between a jacket and a dress. The material is a blue so dark it's almost black and shimmers indigo and violet when she moves. The collar is enormous, its stiff fabric lifting from the neck to frame her face at an angle. The front is cropped above her hips like a waistcoat, but the back is like an open-front skirt, trailing the ground behind her.

Like the first time I saw her, her short silvery hair is slicked back, and her smile reveals pointed canines. She assesses me from head to toe. "What an odd surprise. If it isn't Miss Evelyn Fairfield."

I force my words past my lips, hoping I can manage them without a stutter. "I come seeking your hospitality for a short period of time."

"Now, what would King Aspen's mate be doing seeking hospitality with me? Aren't you his beloved champion?" Her voice is laced with sarcasm. "Then again, he sure is collecting his share of mates these days, isn't he? I believe I'm supposed to witness yet another grand spectacle with a Chosen in a few days from now."

My breath hitches and I find my throat stripped of words.

Fortunately, she doesn't wait for a response, instead turning her attention to my companion. "And you, Lorelei. How wonderful to see you again. I didn't realize we were on speaking terms. You hardly said a word to me at Bircharbor." Her rosy lips pull into a pout.

Lorelei crosses her arms, throwing out all sense of formality. "Trust me, we wouldn't be on speaking terms if I didn't need to call in that favor you owe me."

She lets out a trill of laughter. "I can't believe you're still upset about what happened at Summer Solstice."

"Still upset? Solstice was less than four months ago."

"A silly accident."

Lorelei narrows her eyes at the queen. "You gave Malan traumatic nightmares. About *me*. She could hardly look at me for a week."

Nyxia shrugs. "I don't create the nightmares from nothing. They come from existing fears."

"And you fed off hers."

Another casual laugh. "I was jealous. You know how protective I am over you."

"If you wanted to be so protective, you would have tried harder to keep me around in the first place."

"If I recall, you were the one who ended things with me."

Lorelei grinds her teeth. "And if *I* recall, you cheated on me. With seventeen other fae. At once."

Nyxia waves her hands in a dismissive gesture. "It was Beltane."

My cheeks grow warm, and I wish I could shrink on the spot. This is not the kind of conversation I feel like I should be present for.

Franco watches me through slitted lids, then slides lazily from his seat. Nyxia and Lorelei are still arguing by the time he makes it to my side. "Come. They'll be at this for a while."

Lorelei whirls toward us, eyes furious as they lock on Franco. "Don't you dare take her anywhere."

"Don't worry about it," Nyxia says. "Until I make a formal decision about whatever you've come here for, she's under my protection. Franco can take her to the baths. Speaking of, you could use one yourself. Why don't we get you out of those filthy clothes."

Lorelei rounds on the queen. "Oh, that's just so like you. Turn every serious topic into a seduction—"

"Told you. Come on." Franco waves his hand forward. "I'll take you to the moon baths."

He starts toward the door, but I hesitate, eyes flashing from the prince to the arguing pair. With a sigh, I give in and follow Prince Franco.

The prince winks as I catch up to him. "Bet you didn't know you were in for that treat."

"Can't say that I did," I mutter.

"Don't worry, they'll cool off in an hour or so. Although, I doubt they'll be making up in the same fashion as they used to."

We continue down the moonstone halls in silence. My heart races with every step, both from the unfamiliar territory and my unsettling companion. I feel his eyes burning into me more often than not, and I wish he'd just keep his gaze to himself.

"So, you're the Evelyn Fairfield I've heard so much about."

I suppress an irritated grumble. "What exactly have you heard?"

"That you're King Aspen's mate."

"I am." The statement is a barbed defense against his unwelcome stare, but as soon as the words are out of my mouth, I realize their futility. I might be Aspen's mate, but it means nothing now. Not when I'll never see him again. Not when he's about to marry another. "I mean, no. Not really."

His lips quirk into a grin. "Not really. How interesting. Are you too proud to share him with his new Chosen? Or is it King Ustrin's venom against you that has you running to Selene Palace?"

"It's none of your business."

"It might be, if you are to stay here for a time. Selene Palace is not just my sister's home. It's mine too."

I keep my lips pressed tight as we continue through the palace. Finally, we come to an ornate sliding door. As the prince pushes it open, wafts of steam spiral into the hall. We enter, and I find three enormous pools inside the room. The ceiling is domed glass like the throne room, with that eerie light bathing everything in a dusky glow. The smell of jasmine and gardenia beckon from the calm waters.

Franco faces me. "Welcome to the moon baths. This is another place I recommend you come at night. I'll keep this room private and have a servant bring fresh clothes. In the meantime, make yourself at home." With that, he shudders and transforms into a black raven. I jump, hand to my pounding heart as I watch the raven prince fly into the hall.

Alone in the bathhouse, I stare at the pools. The size of the room and the vast sky above make me feel vulnerable. Even though I'm the only one here, I feel exposed, but the thought of cleanliness is too tempting to ignore.

Before I can change my mind, I hurry to peel off my filthy clothing. Luckily, my corset has been torn enough that I can remove it without aid. Then I slip beneath the soothing waters.

~

ONCE CLEAN, I FIND MY PILE OF CLOTHES HAVE BEEN replaced with a thick towel and a dress in a lightweight shimmery fabric the color of fire opals. I pull the dress over my head, relieved to return to the freedom of fae clothing after the confines of my corset.

Unsure where to go now, I take a few hesitant steps past the sliding door and into the hall. Lorelei leans against the far wall, arms crossed. She appears to have gotten cleaned and changed as well, all blood and grime wiped from her brown skin, a long, silky, black dress clinging to her form. Her expression looks relieved when she sees me. "Oh good, Franco didn't drown you."

"You should be surprised I didn't drown *him*."

"True." She gives me a halfhearted smile, then nods toward the other end of the hall. "Come. Nyxia has rooms for us so we can rest."

I follow her eagerly, the word *rest* like a tantalizing prize. The bath was merely a precursor to what my body truly needs after everything it's been through in the past twenty-four hours. But first, there are questions that need answers. "Did you explain my situation to the queen?"

Her expression darkens. "I did. She'll provide you hospitality so long as you need."

"You don't seem happy about that."

"I'm happy that we've found a safe place for you to stay."

"But you aren't happy that you have to see her because of it."

"Exactly."

"So...you and Nyxia?"

"Yeah," she grumbles. "We were a thing. Two years. She wasn't into settling down like I was. She was even less into seeing me move on to someone else. Hence her petty revenge on Malan."

It's hard for me to imagine my friend in a relationship with the domineering Nyxia. However, it's clear Lorelei can hold her own against the queen.

"That's why she owes me a favor," Lorelei says. "I nearly tore her head off, queen or no, after what she did to my lover. Like I said, prepare yourself for some uncomfortable dreams while we're here."

"Will do."

We come to a small room with walls of onyx and silver. The ceiling hosts not a dome but a glass window in the middle where faint light streams through. A bed with indigo velvet blankets beckons me from inside. Lorelei puts her hand on my arm. "You should get some rest. Do you...feel comfortable staying in this room alone? I can stay with you."

I try to offer a reassuring smile. "No, Lorelei, I'll be fine here by myself."

"Very well. I'll be in the room next door if you need anything."

She slips down the hall, and I enter my room, legs nearly puddling to liquid as I head straight for the bed. My head hardly hits the pillow before sleep overtakes me.

The nightmares begin without warning. I'm trapped in the underground laboratory again, and Mr. Meeks stands over me with a knife, the gaping wound at his neck trailing blood down the front of his apron. He cuts into my arms, my legs, my skull. I scream, but my lips are sealed shut. Fire roars around us, but instead of strengthening me, it burns the flesh from my bones. Mr. Meeks doesn't cease his operation, his knife digging into my very soul as flames char him from man to skeleton. The fire obscures my vision, but before it burns my eyes, I see the silhouette of a stag charging through the room.

Aspen.

I repeat the name like a soothing melody. The more I focus on it, the dimmer the terrifying visions become. Finally, the nightmare fades, blood and fire drifting to smoke as I follow the safety of the name. No longer is the dark lab surrounding me. Instead, a bridge spans before me, and I don't hesitate before crossing. At the other end, I find myself in the dining room at Bircharbor Palace, the sound of waves falling upon my ears.

Aspen stands at the rail near the open expanse, back facing me as he stares out at the night sky. My heart leaps at the sight of him, at his messy hair, his towering antlers, the wrinkled waistcoat that tells me he hasn't been sleeping well. Like before, a violet aura glows around him.

"Aspen." I say the word out loud this time.

He whirls, freezing when he catches sight of me. For endless moments we do nothing but lock eyes. Then his swift stride carries him across the room. His hands frame my face as his lips press into mine. My body responds to his, arms wrapping around his waist, moving up his back. Our kisses are hard and urgent, as if fighting against the strain, that discrepancy between what our touch feels like and what it *should* feel like if this were real.

It's the only thing that reminds me this is just a dream.

As if the realization comes to us both at once, our kisses slow. We separate our lips but our foreheads remain touching. "You're all right," Aspen whispers. "What happened to you?"

I swallow hard. "I don't want to talk about it."

"I wish you were really here."

"I wish I was too."

He pulls his head back, eyes swimming as they drink in mine. If only the evening light were brighter so I could better make out his beautiful eyes, the dark brown flecked with green, gold, and ruby. Eyes I should have done a better job at memorizing when I had the chance. His thumb trails over my bottom lip, then along my jaw. I take a hand from his back and place it over his chest, feeling the steady thrum of his heart beneath my palm. My breath hitches, eyes locked on his lips, ready to taste them again.

Before I can claim them, he speaks. "Where are you? I need to know you're safe."

"I'm safe. I'm—"

"Aspen." The voice that shatters the moment grates on my ears with nauseating familiarity. Maddie Coleman strides into the dining room draped in a robe—one of *my* old robes. "I thought you might show me the selkies like you promised."

Aspen stands at the rail again as if he never left it. Come to think of it, I can't recall him leaving my side. One moment he was in my arms, the next he was gone. He's no longer looking at me but at Maddie. His jaw is set, but I refuse to read more into his expression.

Because, of course, this is a dream. No. A nightmare. And if this nightmare is as visceral as my last, I can only imagine what I'll be forced to witness next.

I take one last look at Aspen. His expression falters as

his eyes meet mine before I close my eyes and try to remember where I am—where I *really* am.

The Lunar Court. The bed.

I jolt upright, blankets tangled in my limbs as I blink into moonlight. My head pounds. I look around the room, expecting a dark shadow to be hovering nearby, red eyes glowing as it drinks in my nightmare. But there's nothing. No one.

I let out a shaking breath and shove the blankets off me, forcing away the dream-images that linger in my mind. As much as I enjoyed the part about Aspen, it's Maddie's smug expression that prevails. The vision of her wearing *my* robe and speaking to *my* mate with such familiarity sends a wave of burning rage through me.

I nearly let it consume me before I remind myself that Aspen isn't my mate anymore. He's about to be *hers*, and there's nothing I can do about that. Not if I want Aspen to save the treaty.

With a grumble, I get out of the bed. There's no getting back to sleep now.

16

I find a small wardrobe in the room filled with an assortment of clothing. From within, I retrieve a midnight-blue velvet robe embroidered with stars and crescent moons. My dress is slightly wrinkled from sleeping in it, so the robe should hide that as well as warm me from the slight chill in the air.

I open my door, expecting to find darkness and quiet in the hall outside. What I don't anticipate is the bustle of activity that greets me. Dark has fallen over the hallway, but orbs of light that resemble moonlight hover along the walls. Fae float by in pairs and triplets, speaking animatedly. And I say *float* literally, as most of the fae appear to be sprites and specters, their bodies hovering above the ground like wisps of flame or smoke. Some are tiny, about as tall from the ground as my kneecap, while others are of average human height. A couple glance my way, but most are too distracted to pay me much heed. I can only guess they must be servants.

I scurry to the room next door and tap a light knock. "Lorelei."

A dark shape dives down from the opalescent beams of the ceiling, materializing as Prince Franco by my side. I lurch back. "Could you not do that?"

He leans lazily against the wall next to Lorelei's door. "I wouldn't wake her. She's sleeping deeply, and it wasn't easy for her to find restfulness."

"How do you know?"

He shrugs. "I can sense her dreams."

I bristle, wondering if he's to blame for my uncomfortable nightmares. "Are you like your sister then?"

"Not exactly," he says. "I'm not nearly as powerful."

I pull my robe tighter around me, then cross my arms over my chest. "What is it you do then?"

"I can sense dreams and feed off their energy in a similar way that Nyxia can. But she can do more. She can enter another's dream space, prompt fears and memories to the surface that she can use as nourishment. She can't control the dream, but she can give the dreamer a nudge in the direction she'd like them to go."

He flashes me a smile, revealing his pointed canines. It brings to mind a very specific concern I have yet to find clarity on, one I know I should handle with some delicacy. Which, of course, is not my specialty. "Is it always fear you and Nyxia feed off of?"

"Fear is one of the strongest emotions to use as nourishment as well as one of the easiest to elicit from another, but we feed off any emotion that offers an enticing taste."

Perhaps I was too delicate. "Is there...anything else you feed on?"

He looks at me through slitted lids, the corners of his lips revealing his amusement. "I take it you're hinting at something. Perhaps you should ask me directly."

Heat flushes my cheeks. "Do you drink...blood?"

He smirks. "Depends whose blood and how tempting it is to taste it."

Great. This is just great. It's a struggle not to bring my hands up to cover my neck.

Franco lets out an amused chuckle. "No, I don't drink blood. I'm a psy vampire, not a sanguine."

I can't tell whether I'm more relieved at the truth or annoyed at his teasing. My eyes flash to his teeth again. "Then why do you have elongated canines?"

"Can you think of no other reason to have such a feature aside from drinking blood? What do other creatures use them for?"

I refuse to answer.

"To spear their prey, of course. I may not drink blood, but I'm not above a good hunt."

This time, I can't help but cover my neck, resting my hand over my collarbone. "And what exactly do you hunt, Prince Franco?"

He leans closer and winks. "Beautiful human-fae hybrids like you, of course. But only if I want them badly enough." He straightens and offers me his arm. "Now that that's settled between us, will you allow me to show you the beauty of the palace at night?"

I take a step away from his leering stare, arms crossing tighter over my chest. "You just named me your prey. Whether it was in jest or truth, I have no desire to be alone with you."

"I only named you my prey if I were to want you badly enough."

I burn him with a scowl. "And just how badly do you want to eat me, Your Highness?"

His lids grow heavy, eyes falling to my lips. "How badly do I want to eat you? Now that is a loaded question."

My heart hammers in my chest. I whirl toward my door. "I'm going back to sleep. I prefer my nightmares to this."

He intercepts me before I can reach my door, expression jovial. "I'm joking, Miss Fairfield. I'm not going to eat you. Unless you ask me nicely and we aren't talking about dinner at all. In that case..."

"Can you be serious for once?"

He gives me a mock bow. "My apologies. I admit, I enjoy getting a rise out of you, testing your response to fear and flirtation. I like the taste of the energy you emit. Most of it tastes like fire."

"What is it with aggressive males testing my resolve?" I mutter.

"It's the Old Ways in us. Our instincts make us want to determine who's alpha, who's omega. It's in our nature."

"Well, it's getting old."

"Spoken like a woman who has clearly had much experience with the follies of aggressive males seeking her attention."

My mind goes to Aspen, to the nightmare. To the kiss we shared. To Maddie Coleman taking my place. My heart clenches.

He offers me his arm again. "Let me give you an intermission from your worries. I promise I'll be less of an ass. I'll even show you Selene Palace's finest feature."

I roll my eyes. "Don't you dare say it's your ass."

His eyes widen as he gives me an approving grin. "I can't believe I didn't think of that myself. We're going to get along just fine."

I let out a grumble before placing a hand at his elbow. My other hand seeks to pat my thigh until I remind myself my dagger is long gone. If only I'd been of sound-enough mind to steal one of the knives from Mr. Meeks' laboratory.

As we move through the halls, we encounter more and more fae. Many are like the ones I first saw, sprites, wraiths, and specters in various shades and forms. Others appear more like Franco or Nyxia, and there are several nocturnal animals that scurry about the halls. Each fae bows to the prince as we pass.

I've been determined to say as little to the prince as possible, but my curiosity gets the better of me. "Why is the palace so busy right now? There was hardly a soul out and about earlier."

"Selene Palace is the liveliest at night," he explains. "This is the Lunar Court, you know. Most of our residents, servants, and guests are nocturnal."

"And you?"

"I prefer a nocturnal lifestyle as well. In fact, I was sleeping soundly until a rather rude owl came hooting about two foreigners covered in blood traipsing through the woods. That's when Nyxia sent me out to find you."

We reach a staircase and continue up several flights in what seems to be a wide spiral. When the summit is in sight, cool night air greets us. The staircase ends at a circular balcony that rings an enormous glass dome. The night sky opens overhead, speckled with countless stars in such unfathomable quantity I've never witnessed from any other viewpoint.

Franco points at the bubble of glass before us. "That's the roof of the throne room. And this," he pulls me forward until we reach a platform that juts out from the balcony, "is the observatory."

My mouth falls open, hand slipping from Prince Franco's elbow. Upon the platform stand several telescopes in varying sizes and designs. "Are these for viewing the moon?"

He approaches the largest telescope, a hulking device constructed of gold and crystal. "This one is for viewing the moon. And other planets, of course. You'll find only one telescope to rival it in Faerwyvae, and it belongs to the Star Court. Come see what it has to offer."

My intellectual hunger is too ravenous to do anything but obey. Prince Franco adjusts the dials on the telescope, then extends his hand for me to take a look. I place my eye to the viewing glass, which reveals the waxing moon in such detail that I've never seen. The sight makes my throat feel tight, awed over the beauty and terror of seeing such a fixture of the night sky as if I were floating before it. "It's beautiful."

"You'll have to see it again in a few days when it's full."

It's almost painful to force myself away from the sight. "What do the others show?"

"Whatever its previous user was looking for. Go ahead and see."

I move from telescope to telescope, greeting different planets, stars, and nebulae. I haven't felt this happy and alive since...since...well, probably since the night in the cave with Aspen.

The thought dampens my joy, and I pull away from the final telescope. With a sigh, I walk to the edge of the platform and look out at the landscape around the palace. I wasn't in the best state to care about my surroundings when we first arrived, so I can hardly recall what it looked like during the day. But the moon illuminates plenty for me to see, revealing lush meadows, towering trees, glittering lakes and streams. To my right, I see a marsh upon which tiny blue lights glow.

Franco comes up beside me, shoulder brushing mine as he follows my line of vision. "Wisps," he says. "They used to live more often in the Fire Court, but they've taken a liking to Lunar. However, don't rely on them to guide you if ever you are lost at night. They like to cause more mischief than good, although they aren't harmful."

The heat of his body next to mine is an unexpected distraction, sending my pulse racing just the slightest bit faster, but I do my best to ignore it. Instead, I squint deeper at the blue lights. "Wisps? But I've seen this phenomenon back in Eisleigh. Are the lights not a result of combustible marsh gases?"

"Perhaps where you're from. I assure you the wisps are more than a trick of light and gas."

I leave Franco's side to reach for one of the smaller telescopes and swivel it until I have the marsh in sight. I adjust the dials until the blue lights come into focus. To my surprise, the light has some semblance of form—swaying arms and legs, a hint of eyes and mouth. I know I shouldn't be surprised, but I can't help it. Now I wonder if the strange blue lights I saw in Eisleigh had been fae after all. "You say they used to live in the Fire Court?"

"Wisps are related to fire sprites, making the Fire Court a decent home. However, they are nocturnal. In Lunar, all night-dwelling fae are welcome, as well as lovers of the moon. We are also home to many fae who are shunned by other courts, especially the unsightly or ghoulish varieties. They feel safer here beneath the cover of night."

I shudder. "You mean like banshees and harpies?"

"Banshees, harpies, lycanthropes," he flashes me a toothy grin, "and vampires."

"Aren't they dangerous?"

"About as dangerous as I am. Or you."

"I'm not..." I can't bring myself to finish the sentence, knowing it would be a lie. I may not be as dangerous as the fae male before me or the monstrous creatures that lurk in the dark, but I killed a man and burnt his laboratory to a crisp.

"Look!" Franco points over my shoulder, a welcome diversion from my thoughts. "The kitsune are gathering at the Wishing Tree."

I turn around and seek where he's pointing. All I find is an enormous willow tree with flickering orange lights beneath it. Again, I reach for the telescope and bring the tree into focus. My heart leaps at the sight. Dozens of lithe, white foxes gather around the trunk of the tree, balls of flame hovering at their mouths or tails. They appear to be speaking with one another, but I can't hear a word from here.

"Another type of fae that once held their allegiance to the Fire Court," Franco says. "Most kitsune choose Lunar as their home these days. Actually, thousands of unseelie fae have migrated from Fire to other courts as King Ustrin grows less and less patient with them. Not when his radical seelie ways keep him in such good standing with the council."

"King Ustrin is radical seelie?" I remember his orange, scaly skin, his slitted nostrils, and forked tongue. "I would have thought King Ustrin was unseelie based on his appearance. He seemed more lizard than anything."

"The fire lizard has always been a powerful type of fae in the Fire Court. Retaining similar features when in seelie form is another way to show his power. It doesn't impact his political affiliation, however."

A shadow falls over us, and I find my attention drawn to the sky where a black silhouette passes over the glittering stars.

"A moon dragon," Prince Franco says. "Yet another type of fae that fled Fire to live in Lunar. Many of the fire lizard's draconian cousins have moved to other courts." He lowers his voice. "Rest assured, you are far from being the only one who isn't a fan of King Ustrin."

I tense. "The more accurate statement is that he isn't a fan of me. I couldn't care less about him."

"Even though he's responsible for orchestrating the charges against your mother?"

My head whips toward him. "You know about that?"

He nods. "My sister filled me in on the details Lorelei shared."

A question rises to my mind, another that requires much decorum. "Is your mother the same as Nyxia's?"

"Yes. Why do you ask?"

"Do you know much about Queen Nessina's involvement with the war? Were you alive back then?"

He shakes his head. "Nyxia and I were born centuries after the war ended and Mother didn't tell us much."

That might mean he knows nothing about his mother harboring my grandmother. Did Lorelei share that part with Nyxia? With Franco? I don't want to ask directly, in case the secret isn't safe with him. "Where is your mother now?"

"She is no longer with us."

"She died?"

"Not in the way you're imagining," he says. "Fae rulers tend to remain at court until they pass the throne to the next in line. For most unseelie, that means when an heir proves their worth as alpha. It didn't take long for my sister to demonstrate her alpha status after she reached maturity, and I didn't dare challenge her. She's the strongest alpha the Lunar Court has seen in generations. Anyhow, after my sister became the new queen, Mother left court and sort of...reverted to the Old Ways entirely."

"You mean she took her unseelie form indefinitely?"

He nods. "It is our way."

My eyes meet Franco's, and I find myself fascinated by his words. Everything he's said about the lunar fae, the unseelie, the Old Ways—it's intriguing. *He's* intriguing, when he isn't being annoying. That alone is worth my awe. Even a day ago, I would have thought befriending an unseelie fae was out of the question. Now, here I am genuinely enjoying my time with an unseelie prince.

A flash of guilt seizes my chest, and I avert my gaze.

A pair of light footsteps approach from the balcony, and Nyxia comes into view. "I thought I might find you here, Miss Fairfield." She offers me a grin before her gaze moves to her brother. "Thank you for showing our lovely guest such kind hospitality."

"It was my pleasure," he says, adding a wink for me.

"I have no doubt about that. May I ask for my turn to speak with her?"

Prince Franco nods, then takes my hand in his. Before I can react, he pulls the back of my hand to his lips, brushing a light kiss over my skin. "I do hope we can speak again soon." With that, he shudders and shifts into a raven, taking off into the night sky. I follow his silhouette until it's out of sight. Only then do I force my gaze to return to Nyxia.

Alone with the most powerful lunar alpha in generations, I suppress a shudder.

17

Nyxia approaches me with slow, confident steps. She's changed out of the elaborate outfit she wore earlier and now has on a pair of black silk slacks and a matching tunic. "Let's take a stroll," she says.

Falling into step beside her, we walk the circular balcony ringing the perimeter of the dome. I force my breathing to remain even, natural.

"My brother seems quite taken with you," the Lunar Queen says.

I let out a bark of laughter before I can stop myself. "We've hardly spoken."

"I think you've learned by now that the fae know what they want quite quickly."

I press my lips tight, refusing to follow the train of thought that I know will lead me to Aspen. To the gaping wound left in his absence.

"Regardless," Nyxia says, "he wouldn't be a terrible mate to make an alliance with."

My head swivels toward her. "What are you implying?"

"I'm implying that I understand the precarious position you are in. You're considered a criminal by the humans and would be used as a bargaining chip by many of the fae, if given the chance. Unless you can secure your position in Faerwyvae, you'll be exiled to a slow death on the mainland."

I stop in my tracks. "I'm not staying in Faerwyvae. That would be treason. It would break the treaty."

Nyxia halts, then slowly spins on her heel to meet my gaze with a delighted grin. "Then let's break it."

"That will bring war."

She shrugs a delicate shoulder. "I guess we should try to win it then."

I shake my head and continue walking, quickening my steps as if I can outpace her treasonous suggestion. "That's not why I came here. I came to seek refuge while I await my mother's trial."

She matches my hurried stride with little effort. "Yes, but there's another option open to you. If you were my brother's mate, you'd be Lunar royalty. You'd have a shot at earning enough respect to take the throne that is rightfully yours."

I round on her. "The Fire Court isn't rightfully mine. My ancestor was exiled. The treaty states his descendants cannot live in Faerwyvae ever again."

This time, she's the one who walks ahead, and I'm forced to race after her. "The treaty was made with human rules. King Ustrin likely never would have become king according to the Old Ways. As cousin to the exiled King Caleos, Ustrin claimed the throne based on human traditions of male bloodline succession, but he never proved himself the alpha blessed by the All of All."

I have no idea what she's talking about, so she must be referring to some unseelie custom. "It doesn't matter what King Ustrin did or didn't do. A fae Legacy Bond keeps the treaty in place and forbids me from claiming the throne. A man named Henry Duveau will put a bounty on my head if I try to stay in Faerwyvae."

She waves her hand dismissively. "Don't you understand? If the treaty is broken, so is the Legacy Bond. Besides, if this human wants to place a bounty on you, I'd like to see what great fool would try to claim it. A human bounty hunter will get himself killed before he so much as crosses the axis line. And no fae would turn on you if you were a respected leader."

"Oh, you mean like when Cobalt stole King Aspen's throne?"

She shrugs. "King Aspen was challenged and came out the victor. With your help, of course. Your success in the Twelfth Court is exactly what makes me think you have what it takes to claim the Fire Court throne according to the Old Ways."

Her words send my heart racing, both from the fear and excitement they generate within me. There's a part of me that rises to meet her words with a spark of hope, igniting a fire of indignation against those who would stand against me. I hate it. I hate the part of me that wants her to say more.

She continues. "I'll be honest with you. I don't like King Ustrin or any of the radical seelie. I don't like the Council of Eleven Courts or how much they seek control over the unseelie. The very name of the council is blasphemy against the Old Ways. You cannot be fae and disregard the Twelfth Court. I'll support any effort that puts an unseelie queen on the Fire Court throne."

My mouth falls open. "Unseelie," I say with a gasp. "What makes you think I'd be *unseelie*?"

She seems unperturbed by the bite in my tone. "You'd have to be unseelie to go against the treaty. I suppose you could call yourself seelie, but it comes down to this: you don't want to be controlled. You don't want your true nature suppressed or for your freedoms to be taken away. That's what being unseelie means."

Again, that secret part of me stirs and rises. It wants to shout in agreement, to wail a battle cry and fight for what is mine. *No. Not mine. Nothing in Faerwyvae is mine.* "You know nothing about what I want," I say through my teeth.

Her voice takes on a soothing, ethereal quality. "I know your dreams. Your fears. I can see them even when you're awake. They float around you like specters."

I shake my head, crossing my arms over my chest. "This conversation is pointless. I will not break the treaty nor will I stay in Faerwyvae. I'm going to my mother's trial, and there I will face my fate."

"You will choose death."

"I will choose my mother. I will not abandon her. If I do, she will be executed."

"But you would live. I'm sure she'd want that, wouldn't she?"

I open my mouth to argue but snap it shut. There's no way I'll admit Nyxia is right, but I can't deny the truth in her words either. Finally, I say, "Just because I'm here, and just because I'm part-fae, doesn't mean I've turned my back on the humans."

We've reached the other end of the loop where the staircase opens beneath the balcony. Nyxia faces me, looking down her nose. "When you're ready to take a side, let me know. A crown awaits."

"I don't want a crown forged from blood."

"All crowns are forged from blood."

"Then I never want one."

She lets out a trilling laugh. "What about the one the All of All gave you?"

The gold crown of swaying leaves. If it's where I left it, it remains on the table in my parlor. "It was never mine. Aspen's new wife can have it for all I care."

"She'd look awfully silly wearing a crown of flame, don't you think?"

A crown of...flame? My breath hitches as the swaying leaves emerge in my mind's eye. What if they weren't leaves after all? What if they were flames?

I shake the questions from my mind. What does it matter now?

Nyxia takes a step closer. "I think Aspen knew exactly what he was doing when he placed that crown on your head."

THE FOLLOWING DAYS PASS WITH FAR LESS EXCITEMENT, BUT my circadian rhythm is totally thrown off. Nightmares plague my sleep, and I find myself most often awake at night. When this happens, I visit the observatory, watch the moon, the stars, and the unseelie fae that play about the landscape. Few fae pay me much heed, aside from the occasional attentions from Franco, which I must admit

I'm beginning to grow more and more comfortable with. His lighthearted persona has its charm, and even his irritating moments tend to rouse a secret smile from me. Nyxia, however, seems preoccupied most of the time, which I'm grateful for. I have no desire to continue our conversation from before.

During the day, I spend idle time with Lorelei. She, however, seems perfectly capable of sleeping at night, so there are times when I'm left without her company. Whether alone or with my friend, I try my best to keep busy, forcing myself not to consider the upcoming event...

Aspen's wedding.

Every time I think about it, nausea churns inside me. I wish I could burn the thought of him and his soon-to-be wife from my mind. I wish I could feel anger at him instead, fury that he's really going through with this. But I can't even drum up the ghost of my rage. Not when I was the one who made him promise to marry her. Not when I know it's for the best. Not when it's the only way to stop a war.

It's the eve before the dreaded occasion when I wake from a string of unpleasant nightmares involving none other than Aspen and Maddie. My only relief is that tonight's dreams were not the visceral kind like the one in Bircharbor's dining room; those are far more difficult to decipher between dream and reality.

Sweat soaks the sheets as I finally give up on sleep and force myself out of bed. I dress in a cream gown and pace my room. There's only one matter I can count on to distract me. A matter of life and death...and a certain unseelie prince.

I retrieve the prepared sealed envelope from my

dressing table and stuff it beneath the sash around my waist. I've been working on the letter for two days now and only settled on my final draft earlier this evening.

When I enter the hall, I'm greeted by the bustle of nocturnal activity. With slow steps, I make my way down the corridor, eyes flashing to the ceiling, seeking black feathers hidden in the shadows of the beams overhead. However, all I find are wraiths and owls. If only I knew where the prince's bedroom was.

The thought stops me in my tracks, a barrage of unanticipated images flooding my mind as I picture myself showing up at his private quarters unannounced. He would only be too pleased. And I...how would I feel about that? I shake my head to clear it.

As I continue down the corridor, a black shape catches my eye from a beam just ahead. With careful steps, I approach it, craning my neck to see if it might be—

"What are you looking at?"

I startle, finding Franco at my side, matching my posture as he stares up at the ceiling. A blush heats my cheeks as I'm forced to recall the discomforting visions I had of him just moments ago. I square my shoulders and steel my expression. "Do you take pleasure in scaring me each time?"

"I take any pleasure you'll give me. But why were you so fascinated with the soot sprite?"

"A soot sprite?" I return my attention to the black shape, part from curiosity, part to obscure the fire that I'm sure still shows in my cheeks.

Franco lets out a whistle. In response, the sprite moves, opening a pair of glowing red eyes that lock on mine. Now I can clearly see it is not a raven at all but an orb of soot, motes of black swirling as it hisses in irritation before scurrying across the beam and out of sight.

Franco turns to me, brow lifted, mouth open in mock surprise. "Wait, did you...were you looking for *me*?"

I roll my eyes. "Don't flatter yourself. I have a favor to ask of you."

"A favor? I can only imagine—"

"Can you get a message to another court without drawing attention?"

The grin slides from his lips. "I think you have me confused with a messenger fae."

"Not you personally, but someone in your employ."

"I suppose," he says. "What court are you trying to infiltrate? If you're intending to reach your beloved mate, I'm sure Nyxia could deliver the message herself. She'll be leaving for Bircharbor at dawn."

I ignore the pressure in my chest, the wave of sorrow that threatens to drown me on the spot. Crossing my arms over my chest, I dig my nails into my arm, the sharp sensation a welcome point of focus. "It's not King Aspen I'm trying to reach. It's an unseelie court I need to get a message to, and I need it to reach someone specific."

He looks surprised by this. "Which court would that be?"

"Sea."

His expression darkens. "Queen Melusine is a keen-eyed ruler. Not much gets past her."

"Yes, well, she won't be at court during the wedding, will she?"

"Ah, so you would like this message delivered while Queen Melusine is distracted."

I nod. "And if the recipient isn't at the Sea Court, I need her found as soon as possible. This message must get to her at once."

"It sounds like you need a spy more than a messenger."

I uncross my arms to put my hands on my hips. "Do you have someone in mind or not?"

He leans lazily against the wall, a smirk playing over his lips. "I may have someone who will perform this duty, but it won't come free."

"How much will it cost?"

He eyes me from under his lashes. "Your company. Tomorrow night. At the full moon revel."

"My company?" My pulse quickens, but I manage to keep a straight face. "I'm not going on a date with you."

"You can call me a chaperone if that makes you feel better. The Lunar Court can get quite...rambunctious on the full moon. With my sister away at Bircharbor Palace for the wedding, you'd do well to keep close to me."

"Or perhaps I should stay in my room and avoid such rambunctiousness altogether."

He shrugs. "Suit yourself. However, that is my price."

"Fine," I growl. I pull the letter out from under my sash. "But this isn't a date."

"I dare not dream of it." He accepts the letter, then turns away and stalks down the hall, but not before whirling back around and shouting, "Wear something scandalous."

I purse my lips and shoot him a glare, but as soon as I face ahead, it turns into a half-hearted smile. I'm left with the smallest comfort—that if I must endure the night of Aspen's wedding, at least I won't have to do it alone.

18

Lorelei isn't too pleased when she learns of the promise I made to Prince Franco. "You agreed to do what? To go to the full moon revel? Do you have any idea how these celebrations tend to end?"

Her raised brow tells me it isn't fear I should feel, but a heated blush. "Well, no," I confess.

"Every moon revel in Lunar might as well be Beltane."

I lift my chin to hide my trepidation and make my way to my wardrobe. "Then you better come with me and make sure the prince keeps his hands to himself."

"Or we could skip it altogether," she says.

"I sort of...owe him," I say as I begin rifling through the dozen or so dresses in the wardrobe. The first is black, which I immediately deem too dour before flipping to the next. Pink? No, reminds me too much of Amelie. Blue chiffon? No. Reminds me too much of Aspen. My heart plummets, and I'm forced to consider what's happening at this very moment. Queen Nyxia departed for

Bircharbor at dawn, and now it's nearly evening. Surely the treaty has been sealed with a wedding at this point. I swallow the lump in my throat and blink the tears from my eyes as I bite the inside of my cheek until I taste blood. Only then can I breathe again and return to examining the dresses.

Lorelei puts her hands on her waist, oblivious to my moment of pain, and bumps her hip to the side. "Are you telling me you made a bargain with Prince Franco?"

I pause my search to meet Lorelei's eyes. When Franco offered me his terms to deliver my letter, I knew it was a bargain of sorts. But the weight of that fact didn't strike me until now. I'm suddenly aware of how careless I've become ever since Mother told me I'm part-fae. Somehow, the knowledge has made me grow less wary around the fae, less guarded.

Having fae blood doesn't make me invulnerable, though. In fact, I still have nearly all the human weaknesses and very little fae power. I can still be glamoured or tricked into a bargain. The incident long ago with Amelie and the goblin is proof that a part-fae can be glamoured. Although, whether her relationship with Cobalt is additional proof is impossible to know. Is the Bond the only reason he controls her, or did he glamour her into the Bond to begin with?

I return to sorting through the dresses. Gold? No, it's too scandalous. Prince Franco would be all too happy about it. Purple silk? Another heart-sinking reaction. *Definitely not.*

"Perhaps it wasn't the best idea," I admit, keeping my voice level, "but I needed him to do something for me. I needed him to find Amelie. He agreed to send a spy to deliver my message to her discreetly while Queen Melusine is at Bircharbor. I must know if she's coming to Mother's trial."

"Why would you ask Franco? I could have handled it for you. I could have gone and done it myself."

"I needed it to be done in secret. Your presence at the Sea Court would certainly arouse suspicion. Besides, can you even visit the Sea Court? Is it not underwater?"

She rolls her eyes. "I would have sent someone. I have my own contacts, you know."

I sigh. "I know. I'm sure you would have done it, but I didn't want to wake you. Also, I don't think Franco is so bad. His flirtations irritate me to no end, but I can't say I despise his company." My eyes flash to Lorelei. "You know him better than I do, though. *Should* I despise his company?"

Her posture relaxes. "No, he's not despicable. I hate him, of course, but it's more like the disdain for a little brother. He was basically that to me when Nyxia and I were together. We were at each other's throats with teasing more often than not. Still, I wish you would have let me help you instead." She places a hand on my arm. "I feel just as useless as you do, you know. I want all of this to work out, and I hate that nothing is going the way I wish it would."

I bite the inside of my cheek again as my lungs constrict. I hardly trust myself to speak. "How do you wish it would go?"

She gives me a sad smile. "I wish you would decide to stay. I wish you would storm over to Bircharbor right now and stop Aspen from sealing the treaty with his new Chosen."

A wave of shock runs through me. "That would mean—"

"I know what it would mean. Sometimes I agree with King Aspen about the treaty. Sometimes I question whether it's worth saving."

I clench my jaw. "It is, Lorelei. That's one thing I know. If it saves lives, it's worth it."

"Is it truly saving lives? Or controlling them?"

Heat floods my veins with the effort it takes not to argue. My anger is a welcome alternative to the sorrow that threatens to crush me, but I'm in no mood to affirm my stance yet again. Instead, I let my rage burn away my pain and change the subject. "Come with us tonight. The prince may not be the worst fae in the world, but I don't want to be alone with him."

"I suppose I could go. If it's a moon revel, there will be wine. But there better be Midnight Blush or I'm out."

"What's Midnight Blush?"

"It's a wine made from night blooming jasmine and obsidian pyrus—a cousin of honey pyrus. Don't worry, there are no dreadful hallucinations to go with it. And it's the only thing that's going to allow me to endure hours of Franco's company."

I force an emotionless laugh and return my efforts to sorting through the dresses. My fingers fall on the one I first dismissed as being too dour—a black dress with silver moons stitched at the hem of the skirt. The sleeves are a sheer spider silk draped with strands of pearls. The neckline is lowcut and lined with white feathers. Best of all, it doesn't remind me of autumn, Bircharbor, Amelie, or Aspen.

I hold the dress against my figure. "Does this look scandalous to you?"

She quirks a brow. "No. Definitely stunning, but not scandalous."

"Perfect," I say. "Scandalous was not the bargain I agreed to."

AT MIDNIGHT, PRINCE FRANCO ARRIVES AT MY ROOM TO claim his bargain.

He stands in my doorway, looking like a storybook vampire indeed, with his black leather trousers and a white linen shirt unbuttoned to the middle of his chest. His silver hair is slicked away from his face, revealing the hard planes and angles of his jaw and cheekbones. A long strand of hematite beads hangs around his neck, drawing my eyes to his chest. For the first time, I notice dark ink tattooed on his skin, crescent moons and other geometric symbols peeking from beneath the open collar.

"Lovely females." He extends both arms, not seeming at all surprised by the presence of my companion. I place my hand in the crook of his elbow, while Lorelei takes his arm with a grimace.

Franco's eyes drink me in. "Nice dress."

I ignore his compliment even though it sends a flutter of pleasure through me. "Where is this revel taking place? The observatory?"

"Not a chance. Moon revels are far too crowded for the observatory to accommodate."

He guides us through the dark halls lit by the warm glow of the moonlight orbs to the lawn outside the palace. The moon is full and bright overhead, enormous and near-blinding with its glow. In the distance, the sound of laughter and voices and animal noises mingle with the beat of a drum. The latter reverberates in the ground beneath my feet. As we near the source, an enormous tree comes into view with hundreds of glowing lights surrounding it. The lights are from wisps, wraiths, sprites, and dozens of other kinds of fae I have no name for.

Franco points at the tree. "Do you recognize it?"

It takes me a moment to realize it's the same tree we saw from the observatory, the Wishing Tree. At its base stands a fae with pearlescent skin, silver hair, and a flowing gown of white gossamer. She speaks a language I don't recognize, lifting her arms to the moon, then lowering them over a silver cauldron of water. The water reflects the moon as if the fae holds the celestial entity before her.

"Priestess Dionna," Franco says. "She performs the moon rituals at every revel."

I'm entranced by the flowing motions of the priestess' arms as she lifts and lowers, bends and sways. Her movements seem sacred and ancient. I'm surprised to find not everyone is watching her. A crowd of reverent onlookers surrounds the priestess, but most of the fae are elsewhere, dancing, drinking, running, flying. The freedom I see is both terrifying and exhilarating.

"Where's the wine?" Lorelei asks in a bored tone.

Franco guides us away from the ritual to a long table made of white quartz edged with gold. I certainly never noticed this enormous piece of furniture in all my views through the telescopes over the last few days, so it must have been transported for the revel. I don't bother wondering how. Surely some impossible feat of magic is responsible.

Upon the table are trays of fruit and flowers and hundreds of bottles of different colored liquids. Lorelei paces the length, eyeing the bottles with heavy scrutiny before she finds the one she's after. It's a pale blue that shimmers in the moonlight. Franco finds three glasses and Lorelei fills each nearly to the rim. Once we each have a glass in hand, she raises hers. "Midnight Blush. Drink up."

"In honor of the full moon." Franco gives me a wink and knocks back his glass, swallowing the liquid in a single gulp.

I stare at the contents of my glass, knowing I shouldn't risk even a sip of the fae wine. But there's a void inside me, one that wants nothing more than to forget, even for a time. I raise my glass in a silent toast. *To forgetting what I'm missing and enjoying what I have while it lasts.* I take a deep breath and down a hearty sip.

Franco takes my hand in his and pulls me away from the table. "Let's dance."

19

The night wears on and the wine continues to flow. I find my sorrows are swept away, leaving me with the most luxurious ecstasy. Lorelei was right; the effects of Midnight Blush are far less troublesome than honey pyrus. There are no psychoactive properties, only intoxicating relaxation and a calm euphoria.

My two companions and I sway to the beat of the drums while the priestess continues to chant. All kinds of fae surround us; wisps bounce and undulate with every pound of the drum, bats swoop overhead, humanoid fae dance with graceful motions, cats pounce and claw their way up the Wishing Tree, dark shadows writhe as they expand and contract with the tempo. Even banshees, harpies, and dragons soar through the night sky, joining in the revel, but I can't find it in me to be bothered by their presence. Instead, I let my body loosen, let my arms swing as if they're made of air. This dance is unlike any I've ever witnessed.

Only one other dance compares. One with ribbons, masks, and vows, and a fae male with a sensuous smirk...

No. None of that tonight. This dance is everything I need.

I close my eyes, feel deeper into the drums. A new kind of fire floods me—a mixture of my life force and unfurling passion. I follow it, become it, let it rise. When I open my eyes, a purple haze falls over my vision, blanketing everyone beneath an ethereal glow. It reminds me of my journey to the Twelfth Court, and—more recently—my dreams. Again, unwelcome thoughts threaten to shatter my peace, so I push them away, focusing instead on the joy and passion, on the beauty of the purple haze.

"You're glowing." Franco's voice sharpens my mind, and the violet begins to dim. After a few moments, the scenery returns to what it was. Still beautiful, of course, but no longer filtered through the strange vision. My eyes meet the prince's, finding them alight with wonder. He repeats his words. "Evelyn, you're glowing. It's like flames."

I slow my dancing and examine my hands. He's right. My body has taken on a golden, shimmery aura. It's enough to surprise me and snap me even further from my daze. In a blink, the glow is gone.

Perhaps Lorelei hadn't been entirely correct about Midnight Blush after all. It obviously elicits some psychoactive effects.

Still, it isn't enough to worry me, and before long, I return to my dance. Lorelei takes my hands and we begin to spin. When we stop, we fall into fits of laughter and tumble onto the grass. It reminds me of being with Amelie.

Another thought I quickly smother. I'm not thinking of Amelie tonight. Not Amelie. Not Aspen. Not—*Oh look!*

I let out an unrestrained squeal of delight as a pair of sleek white kitsune dart by, the first with a glass of wine over its muzzle, the second chasing the orb of flame on the other's tail.

Franco chuckles as he offers me a hand to help me rise to my feet. "I knew you'd have fun." Once I stand, he turns the same hand to Lorelei, but she bats it away, shoulders slumping as her expression crumbles.

"I miss Foxglove," she says with a pout. "He's supposed to be my drinking partner."

Franco and I exchange an amused glance. "This is what happens when you drink too much Midnight Blush," Franco says, then lowers his voice so only I can hear. "We should take her back to her room."

My heart sinks at his suggestion. All I want to do is dance and drink and drink some more. All I want is drums and rhythm and the feel of my body moving without care. But a rational part of me remains intact, and it can understand the reason for his concern. Lorelei looks like she's on the verge of falling asleep, and it can't be safe for her to doze in the middle of a dance floor.

Franco bends to lift her, which is a struggle as she fights him. Once she's righted, he pulls her arm over his shoulders and helps her walk. It's slow progress as we make our way from the revel to the palace, but I don't mind. Every step I take carries the rhythm with me, and I continue to feel the drum, even once indoors. My hips bounce to it as Franco lays Lorelei on her bed. My arms sway to it as he walks me to my room, his hand on my lower back. I can feel the heat of his touch even through my dress.

Too soon, we reach my door. I face him and our eyes lock, trapping us in a bubble of silence. The wine still spins inside me, burning my blood with euphoria. I don't want to move from this moment. I don't want any of this to end. All I want is to stare at the beautiful fae male, to avoid sleep for as long as possible. To avoid the reality that awaits me with the coming dawn.

He grins, his sharp canines glinting in the glowing light of the hall. This time, they don't make me flinch. Like Foxglove's pointed teeth, the prince's now seem charming somehow, safe, even as he steps closer. "Did you enjoy yourself tonight?"

"I did. Thank you."

Again, silence falls between us, making the distance separating our bodies feel too vast. I crave to return to the revel, to throw my arms around his neck and resume the dance right here in the hall. With the beat of the drums still pounding inside me, my body proceeds to move and sway. It's only natural when that beat brings me toward the prince, draws our lips together to continue the song. His lips are tantalizingly soft, our kisses slow and lingering. The brush of his tongue against mine is like fuel for the Midnight Blush, renewing its ecstasy as heat ignites in my core, tingling between my thighs.

A word comes to mind, one that encompasses the desire that has taken over. Only it isn't a word, exactly, but a name. *Aspen.*

I pull away, my pleasure drowned in a shocking sense of sobriety. My eyes fill with the prince's face, with the hunger in his eyes. It isn't the face I wanted to see.

Franco is beautiful and seductively alluring, but one problem remains. He isn't Aspen.

A string of expletives runs through my mind ending with *bloody iron*. No matter how much I try to deny it, my feelings for Aspen run deeper than I can contain. Yet, at this very moment, he's likely in bed with his new mate, his new Bonded, his new *wife*. And here I am with a gorgeous male who stirs my passion, yet all I can think of is *him*.

Rage courses through me at the unfairness of it all. Aspen is certainly enjoying the pleasures of the flesh with someone new. Why shouldn't I?

Franco's brow furrows. "Is everything all right?"

If I close my eyes, I could pretend it's him.

No, that's disturbing.

"Yes." I force my lips into a smile.

"Do you want me to stop?"

Yes, yes, yes. A million times yes. Stop this at once. "No."

He leans in to kiss me again, but not before something catches my eye at the end of the hall. Blue-black hair. Narrowed eyes. Antlers.

As Franco's lips meet mine, I turn my head, and his lips graze my cheek. "Aspen?" This time I say the name out loud. But the hall is empty. There's no sign of the Autumn King, or of anyone, for that matter. Most fae are likely still at the revel. My chest heaves as I blink at the place I thought I saw him. Of course, I *hadn't* truly seen him at all. I'm thoroughly drunk on Midnight Blush. My dreams are beginning to weave into reality.

Without me realizing it, Franco has taken a step away from me, his expression wounded when I meet his eyes.

An embarrassed flush heats my cheeks. I put a hand to my forehead as I lean against my door. "I'm sorry," I say breathlessly. "I'm clearly not in the right state of mind."

Franco's face shifts into a smile, but his eyes retain the hurt I caused with my outburst. "I should let you get some sleep." He offers me a low bow, which gives me a chance to better compose myself. When he rises, he studies my face for a moment before reaching a hand to my cheek. He gives my skin a soft brush of his fingers, then leaves.

I hurry into my room and strip off my dress, not even bothering to toss on a nightgown. All I want to do is disappear beneath my covers, and I do just that. My mind reels from the events of the night, from the beauty of the dance, to the ecstasy of the wine. To the unfathomable fact that I danced alongside unseelie fae and never once feared for my life. Perhaps my chaperone was to thank for that, or maybe it was the Midnight Blush. Whatever the case, I truly enjoyed myself. That is, until that strange kiss. I mean, the kiss itself was delightful. But how it ended...

Thoughts of Aspen threaten to sober me further, but I refuse to let it happen. In the morning I know my sorrow will return, but until then I seek the beat of the drum, still heavy in my veins. I let it rock me, soothe me, and pull me into the deepest, dreamless sleep.

20

In the morning, the drums continue to pound, but it isn't the beat of the revel that carries the thrum. It's a pulsing headache that has me wincing against the morning light. Even with the muted quality of the Lunar Court's daylight filtered through the single glass window in the ceiling, it's too much. I groan, realizing I can't have slept longer than four hours.

I should have known better. Of course drinking that much fae wine—or any wine—would leave me with a hangover. At least it isn't nearly as bad as I felt after eating honey pyrus. And at least it was the very distraction I needed to get through the night.

Even if it ended in such an odd manner.

I pull myself out of bed, surprised to find I'm naked before I recall the haste in which I'd gone to bed last night. My black dress is a crumpled heap by the wardrobe. I obviously couldn't be bothered to hang it up last night. With a shake of my head at my former intoxicated self, I hang the dress in the wardrobe and slip into my velvet robe. Every movement sends a shard of glass through my skull, but I manage to make my way to the dressing table where a pitcher of water sits. I down one glass, then another, until my throat no longer feels like sand. Only then does the pounding in my head begin to lessen.

My thoughts then turn to Lorelei; if I feel this awful, she can't be faring much better. Then again, being full-fae could be in her favor. Still, she was quite indisposed.

I straighten my robe, pulling the sash tight around my waist to hopefully conceal all traces of my nudity underneath, and leave my room. When I reach Lorelei's door, I'm surprised to find it open. Animated voices come from within. One of the voices sounds like...

I rush inside. "Foxglove?"

He grins when he faces me, then pulls me into an embrace. When we separate, he studies me, his smile shifting to a grimace. "Evelyn, dear, what in the name of oak and ivy have you been doing with your hair? It looks terrible."

I run my hand over it, finding tangles. If I'd been expecting to find anyone but Lorelei next door, I would have brushed it. However, that is the least of my concerns. "Foxglove, what are you doing here?" I look from him to Lorelei.

Lorelei seems to be in full health, seated on the arm of her couch with bright eyes and a glowing smile. She's obviously thrilled to see her friend, but when her eyes meet mine, there's trepidation in them. She bites her lower lip. "We were just talking about that."

"We arrived before dawn," Foxglove says. "It's been a whirlwind, I tell you. I haven't slept a wink."

"We," I echo. "Who's *we*?"

"Aspen and I, of course. And a few of his soldiers."

"Aspen's here?"

"Yes," Foxglove says.

"Right now? He's been here since before dawn?"

He nods, a sympathetic frown pulling his lips. "I'm sure he would have come to you at once if there wasn't so much to attend to. I only just left the throne room myself."

My legs turn to water beneath me, my hand flying to my chest as my breaths grow shallow. Foxglove is wrong. Aspen did come to me at once. He came to me and saw me...

"You said you just left the throne room? Is he there?"

"He is, but—"

I don't wait to hear another word. On flying feet, I tear down the hall. The palace layout isn't entirely familiar to me, but I know I can find the throne room without guidance. I've visited the observatory plenty of times on my own, and the throne room is just beneath it.

After a few wrong turns, I finally find a set of enormous double doors. Two shadowy wraiths stand before them. Guards. I'm taken aback, realizing this is the first time I've seen guards at Selene Palace. This can't be good.

I address the two wraiths. "May I have permission to enter?"

They say nothing.

"I am Evelyn Fairfield, guest of Queen Nyxia. Might I speak with her?"

Again nothing.

A lump rises in my throat, desperation mingling with frustration as my palms grow hot. I'm about to do something reckless, although I'm not sure what, when one of the doors opens.

Queen Nyxia squints at me. "I thought I tasted violence."

I'm surprised by her appearance. Her black suit is wrinkled and torn in places, her silver hair no longer smooth and sleek but sticking out at odd angles. I blink a few times and open my mouth to speak. Although, now that the queen is before me, I'm not sure what to say. I should bow, offer a formal greeting, ask an intelligent question. But I can only say one thing, and it comes out like a croak. "Aspen."

She rolls her eyes and opens the door wider. Inside the throne room, a group of fae are huddled around a table. I recognize them as fae royals—the white wolf from Winter, the fae with curling horns from Earthen, and the blue fae with flowing hair from Wind. All are in similar states of disarray as Nyxia—wrinkled clothing, messy hair, skin covered in grime or blood. But my eyes seek the figure standing at the end of the table.

Aspen's eyes meet mine. His hair falls in disorderly waves around his face, and his russet waistcoat is unbuttoned, gold cravat hanging loose around his neck. I want to run to him, to fold myself in his arms like I did in my dream. His eyes, however, keep me at bay. There's no warmth in them. It confirms my fears—Aspen really was there last night. He saw me kissing Prince Franco.

My voice comes out with a tremor. "May I speak with King Aspen in private?"

The wolf lets out a low growl. Aspen silences him with a shake of his head. "It wasn't her," he says, although

I'm not sure what he's referring to. He says nothing to me, though.

Queen Nyxia speaks, her tone casual and exasperated at once. "We are in the middle of a very important discussion."

"I need to speak with him."

She crosses her arms and stares daggers at Aspen. With a grumble, he turns away from the table and stalks toward me. I expect him to stop when he approaches, but he brushes past me and out the door. I give Nyxia a belated bow before following Aspen into the hall.

I find him leaning against a wall, expression bored. He watches me through narrowed eyes, taking in my appearance from head to toe. "You look like you had a fun night." There's no mirth in his tone as his gaze lingers over my chest.

My hands fly to the neck of my robe, where I find it has slipped in my haste to get to the throne room, exposing a little too much skin. That's when I realize what this looks like. I'm dressed in a robe and naked underneath. I take a step toward him. "Aspen, nothing happened last night. It's not what you think."

He averts his gaze, and his voice comes out with a lazy drawl. "It's none of my business. You are free to choose any mate you desire."

"It's not like that." A thousand arguments, justifications, and questions soar through my mind. *I was drunk. I was upset you were marrying someone else. Wait, did you marry someone else? It was just a kiss. I wanted it to be you.* But nothing makes it past my lips.

"Nyxia told me about her offer," Aspen says, punctuating each word with clear disgust.

I shake the cacophony from my head. "What offer?"

"That she'll support your claim to the Fire Court throne if you take Prince Franco as your mate." His jaw shifts back and forth, but vulnerability tugs at his carefully curated facade. "I wouldn't blame you for accepting."

My mouth hangs open. "I'm not taking Prince Franco as my mate. And I'm certainly not bidding for the Fire Court throne."

He furrows his brow, posture stiffening. "Then why are you here?"

"To await my mother's trial. I needed a safe place to stay until then, and I..." I can't finish what I was going to say. *I couldn't come back to Autumn and watch you with your new Chosen. The new Chosen I told you to accept.*

Aspen pushes away from the wall, anger twisting at his features. "You're going back to the humans? After everything they've done to you?"

I take a step back, surprised at his sudden rage. "I'm not going to let my mother die for me."

His hands curl into fists. "They had you strapped to a table, Evie. You cannot go back to Eisleigh."

I blink at him a few times. "How do you know about that?"

"For the love of oak and ivy, I was there. Do you not recall?"

I shake my head. "That's impossible. It was a dream." Even as I say it, I know my words are folly. If he remembers, then it had to have been more than that. Memories flash through my mind, awakening every instance I've dreamed of him, the more visceral experiences blending with the horrible nightmares I've had of him and Maddie.

That brings up a vital question. "Wait, why are *you* here? What happened last night?"

"I left Bircharbor."

"Why?"

"There was a fight."

"Obviously." I wave a hand at his unkempt appearance, at the blood staining the collar of his tattered linen shirt. "For the love of iron, Aspen. Tell me what happened. Did you break the treaty?"

"I did not fulfill it."

I swallow hard. "Did you refuse to marry Maddie Coleman?"

"Yes."

Relief and anger wash over me at once, followed by terror for my mother. If Aspen broke the treaty, will Mr. Duveau maintain his bargain not to kill her before the trial? Will there even be a trial? Rage prevails, and my words come through my teeth. "You promised me."

"I promised you I'd make a choice neither of us would like. I was never going to marry the new Chosen."

"By breaking the treaty, you put my mother's life at risk. She could be dead right now for all I know!" I realize I'm yelling, but I don't care. Let the entire palace wake from my fury.

Aspen's lips pull into a snarl. "I may not have fulfilled your precious treaty, but as far as the humans are concerned, it isn't broken."

"How is that possible?"

"My brother fulfilled it."

My mind goes blank as I process his words. "Cobalt...fulfilled the treaty? You mean..."

"He is now King of Autumn, according to the council."

"You gave up your throne after everything we did to save it?"

He shrugs. "It is but a partial loss. I have every intention of remaining King of Autumn."

"How? If the council has determined Cobalt has the throne—"

"I am claiming Unseelie King of Autumn according to the Old Ways. The rulers of Earthen, Wind, Winter, and Lunar support me. When Cobalt is defeated, I will once again be the only King of Autumn."

What he's saying shouldn't be possible. Since when is there both a seelie and unseelie ruler in one court? The question is quickly overshadowed by what it suggests about Aspen's allegiance. *Unseelie King of Autumn.* My blood goes cold, even as flames lash my palms, begging to be unleashed. "You're turning unseelie? What about the balance of the council?"

"All hope of maintaining balance on the council has been lost. I've had enough. The only thing to do now is to break the council completely."

My rage grows to a fiery inferno at his matter-of-fact tone. "If you destroy the council, what is left to secure the treaty?"

He throws his hands in the air. "Why not ask a better question? If we destroy the treaty, what is left to enforce your exile? Evie, if the treaty breaks, you can't be forced to leave. The Legacy Bond breaks with it."

My voice comes out barely above a whisper, shoulders trembling as I fight to suppress my fire. "They have my mother, Aspen. Without the Legacy Bond, the promise to keep her alive until her trial will be nullified. The humans will execute her on the spot."

His expression alternates between stoic and wounded as silence falls between us. Finally, it settles on steely. "If you are so determined to return to your vile human world, we won't make our stance known until you and your mother are safely on the mainland."

"Your actions will still condemn all the people of the Fair Isle to war. All the people I'm trying to protect with my exile."

"Once you leave the isle, it won't be your problem anymore." His words hold a bitter edge.

"It *is* my problem. This ruins everything. Everything I care about!" Hot tears spring to my eyes, a sob building in my chest.

Aspen's face falls, eyes turning down at the corners. He lifts a hand as if to bring his fingers to my face but stops himself halfway. He lowers his arm, tensing as he pins it stiff at his side. "Maybe it's time to reevaluate what you think you care about and make a different choice."

"What's that supposed to mean?" I say through my tears. "Are you insinuating I don't care about the right things? Are human lives not worth saving?"

He lets out a low grumble. "*Human* lives. Even with proof of your heritage, you still care more about them than the fae."

My breath hitches when I realize what I said. I didn't mean to say *human* lives. I meant to say lives in general, but the word came so naturally. In all honesty, I've been growing more and more enamored with the fae, even the unseelie, as of late. I still don't trust them, especially outside a controlled environment, but I've seen for myself how amiable they can be. How wild, beautiful, and unrestrained.

Before I can say any of this, Aspen takes a step away, shoulders rigid. "I must return to the meeting." His eyes lock on something behind me, narrowing as his lips raise into a snarl. "Perhaps Prince Franco can see you back to your room. He's quite adept at that."

He stalks back behind the double doors, leaving me feeling empty in his wake.

21

When I turn around, Prince Franco stands in the middle of the hall. He smirks at the closed doors of the throne room until his eyes meet mine. His expression softens, cheeks flushing to a pale rosy hue.

With hesitant steps, he approaches me, lips flickering between a frown and a wary smile. "I should apologize."

"It's not your fault." *It's everyone's fault. Everyone's including mine. Everything is ruined.* White hot rage continues to burn after my argument with Aspen. I let it sear away my sorrow and pain, let it char the remnants of my hangover-induced headache to nothing. The result is a sharpening of clarity. Strength.

"I said I *should* apologize, but that doesn't mean I'm sorry. Causing you pain was never my intention, but I don't regret kissing you."

I'm at a loss for words, surprised by his candor. I, however, don't have any honest words to meet his. Do I regret kissing him? Do I regret the fun and freedom I had last night? I regret that Aspen is under a false impression about my involvement with the prince, but it's hard to be sorry when my anger at the king is stronger.

The *unseelie* king. The king who is plotting war at this very moment.

"Anyhow, I came to give you this." Franco holds out an envelope.

My heart leaps into my throat as I take it. The envelope holds no seal, no address, and I tear the letter from inside with trembling fingers.

Franco doesn't say a word as he leaves me to read the letter alone.

I'm grateful for the privacy because I'm quickly undone by the words I read.

> *Dear sister, I thank you for your concern. I assure you, I have received word of the allegations against our mother and the summons for my presence at her trial. However, as Faerwyvae is my home, I will not leave it to attend.*

The letter ends there, unsigned. However, the script is familiar and written without haste, Amelie's elegant loops and swirls intact. Could she have written so neatly under duress? Were these words forced from her by Cobalt's demand through the Bond? Or are they entirely her own?

Anger and sorrow clash as I fall to my knees. My sob is accompanied by a shout as I slam my fist into the opalescent floor. The ground rocks beneath me, and I feel a wave of heat burst from my palm. I'm so startled, my emotions drain in an instant. When I turn my attention to the floor, I find several fissures darting from where my hand made contact. The damage isn't deep, but it's obvious. With a gasp, I leap to my feet and run from the scene of my destruction.

I DON'T REALIZE WHERE I'M GOING UNTIL I FIND MYSELF outside Lorelei's open door. She and Foxglove rush toward me, taking in my blank expression. My tears have already dried with my violent outburst in the hall. I'm not sure what to say, so I hand Foxglove the letter.

He and Lorelei read it in tandem, then their wide eyes meet mine.

"I'm so sorry," Lorelei whispers. She puts a hand on my shoulder and guides me into her room until we reach her couch. "Here, sit."

I do as I'm told, finding a glass in my hands a moment later. As I bring it to my lips, a familiar aroma sends my head spinning. "Midnight Blush?"

Lorelei grimaces. "I might have smuggled a bottle under my gown from the revel last night."

I don't hesitate a moment longer before I take a drink, letting the wine slide down my throat and warm my stomach. With eyes closed, I savor the way it eases my breathing and slows my racing heart. It helps me find a sense of calm amidst the chaos in my mind. Once I've managed to regain some semblance of composure, I say, "Tell me everything. What happened last night?"

Foxglove takes a seat on the couch next to me while Lorelei perches on the armrest. "It was madness," Foxglove says, adjusting his spectacles. "We knew it would be messy, of course, but things went far worse than the king expected."

"What did Aspen expect?" I say, forcing my words to come out evenly. "How long had he been planning on refusing to marry his Chosen?"

"I doubt he ever planned to marry her at all, so long as he could guarantee his actions didn't put you or your mother in danger. When Queen Nyxia informed him in private that you were safe in Lunar, he was confident in his decision to refuse the marriage alliance. However, I do believe he was under the impression that if you were in Lunar, you were resigned to stay in Faerwyvae."

That explains why he seemed surprised when I told him I still planned to attend my mother's trial. "Did Nyxia not tell him the truth? That my stay here is a temporary one?"

Foxglove frowns. "Omission is a great form of deception when one can't lie. Especially when the result suits one's needs quite well."

Of course Nyxia wanted Aspen to compromise the treaty. Her omission helped hurry his resolve.

Foxglove continues. "Once the king made his stance clear to the council, the majority reacted as he anticipated. The unseelie supported him, but most of the seelie were in an uproar. The king even expected what happened next, although it was a surprise how it came to pass."

I sit forward in my seat. "What?"

"Queen Dahlia suggested the council allow Prince Cobalt to secure the treaty and strip Aspen from his throne."

"Queen Dahlia made that suggestion? Why am I not

surprised?" I knew there was something about her I didn't like. Well, aside from the grudge I've carried against her for not taking better care of Faerwyvae's only other living Chosen—the aging Doris Mason, a lonely woman spending her miserable final days at Queen Dahlia's Summer Court. After my most recent unsettling conversation with the queen, I thought perhaps it was Aspen's affection she wanted. I wouldn't have guessed she was after his demise.

"I always thought she was fake," Lorelei says with a sneer.

"Aspen had his suspicions about her as well," Foxglove says. "It's unclear whether she was in contact with Cobalt during her entire stay, but it can be assumed the betrayal was set up from the start."

"What happened when she petitioned for Cobalt to take the throne?" I ask.

"Well, it certainly put the council further at odds. Arguments were made that Cobalt had lost his right to rule Autumn when the All of All chose Aspen. But other council fae insisted the ruling of the All of All encompassed that incident alone, and that Cobalt could still be considered an eligible heir now that Aspen was compromising the treaty yet again. The debate went on and on without resolution as the council was split half-and-half. You see, one ruler was missing from the festivities up to that point."

His grim expression sets me on edge. "Who?"

"Queen Melusine. Queen Dahlia got the council to agree that the Sea Court would have final say over the ruling. And that, my dear, is when Cobalt came waltzing into the palace like he owned it."

Lorelei mutters a string of curses.

A rush of indignation heats my core. "How did Cobalt have the nerve to show his face before the ruling was made for or against him?"

"He was protected," Foxglove says, "by his claim that he was now King of the Sea Court."

"Wait, did Melusine...give her throne to Cobalt?"

His voice lowers, tone grave. "Not willingly. He made his apologies, stating he was late because he'd spent all day dealing with the murder of his mother."

My throat goes dry. "Murder?"

"He went on to claim she was found dead in one of the collapsed underwater caves near the shore with an iron blade buried inside her. *Your* iron blade, to be exact."

"Mine?" The room begins to spin around me, the blood leaving my face. I remember what Aspen muttered to the wolf king in the throne room. *It wasn't her.* "The council actually believed it was I who killed her?"

Foxglove wrings his hands. "It was a devious accusation, one that served several purposes. Not only would your guilt weaken Aspen's position, but your innocence would reveal your whereabouts to King Ustrin. You see, neither Aspen nor Nyxia could provide you an alibi without giving away your location."

I shake my head, wondering how long this plan has been in motion. All this time, Cobalt had my missing blade, the one I lost when he captured me in the coral caves. He's likely been waiting for the perfect opportunity to use it as revenge, and what better way than to condemn me and his brother while earning himself a new crown? Then again, the iron blade should have made my dagger impossible for him to wield...

A chill runs up my spine. *But not impossible for Amelie.*

My heart races as another chilling thought creeps upon my awareness.

Melusine knew this would happen.

I put my hand to my heart as I sink into the back of the couch. "It's my fault," I whisper.

Foxglove and Lorelei exchange a glance. "Why would you think that?" Lorelei says.

"The day the letter came, after the explosion and the attack on the coral caves, she came to me while Aspen was still fighting Cobalt's fae. She told me she feared for her life, begged me to petition Aspen on her behalf. With everything that happened after, I never gave her request a second thought. I...never said a word to Aspen."

Foxglove's eyes turn down at the corners. "That doesn't make it your fault."

"I may not have killed her like the council thinks, but her death is on my hands."

Without a word, Lorelei refills my glass with more Midnight Blush.

I down it as quickly as I can. "Let me guess what happened next," I say, voice hoarse. "Cobalt ruled in favor of himself on behalf of the Sea Court and became King of Sea and Autumn in a single day."

Foxglove nods. "It created a violent divide between the council. The unseelie held their stance that making Cobalt King of Autumn was the worst kind of blasphemy against the All of All and deemed the council disbanded. The meeting ended, as you might imagine, with bloodshed."

"Was anyone fatally wounded?"

He returns to wringing his hands. "Guards, mostly,

but none of the royals. Aspen made the call for his allies to retreat, although it pained him greatly to leave his household staff behind. But with Cobalt ruling the Sea Court, Bircharbor had become too vulnerable for him to try and stay. We fled in the night and came here to Lunar."

"Are those in the throne room Aspen's only allies?" I ask.

"For now," Foxglove says. "They were the royals firmly against Cobalt. However, some of the neutral seelie might be persuaded, like the Earthen King was. It will be a challenge to convince all the neutral seelie to join the rebellion, though, when it would mean fighting for the Old Ways to return, for with that comes the end of the treaty and the dissolution of the Council of Eleven Courts. And war."

The final word chills me, but my attention snags on something else. "I've heard the term the *Old Ways* before. What does it even mean?"

"The Old Ways were how Faerwyvae operated before the war began. The Council of Eleven Courts was only established to mirror the humans' efforts at the start of the war. When the treaty was forged at the end of it, the fae council was solidified in turn, and the Old Ways fell out of favor."

"And the Old Ways state Aspen can rule as Unseelie King of Autumn even though Cobalt has claimed power?"

"Yes," Foxglove says. "Long before there was ever a fae council, the All of All chose its rulers by blessing an alpha during a show of dominance. When humans came to the isle and fae started taking on seelie forms, there were often two rulers in each court, a seelie and an unseelie. Of course, that was when seelie and unseelie lived in balance and both agreed to follow the Old Ways. But simply declaring a return to the Old Ways isn't enough to bring that balance back. Not with the remaining council fae determined to maintain their authority at all costs. The rebels must overthrow the council. Aspen will have to take down Cobalt."

"It sounds like the fae are at civil war."

His expression turns bleak. "They are. Not everyone knows it yet, but there's no turning back now."

Anxiety tickles my chest. "What does this mean for the treaty? Do we know for sure that Cobalt secured it? Are the rebels considered a threat to it?"

"As far as the humans are concerned," Foxglove says, "the treaty is secure. Nyxia's spies have confirmed that Cobalt performed all three steps to secure the pact. The spies say the humans are aware of the unrest amongst the fae royals but have been assured the threat will be dealt with."

"So, my mother might be safe," I say under my breath. *For now,* I add, the contents of Amelie's letter hitting me like a blow to the heart. "This is a mess," I whisper. "Not only are the fae at civil war, I have my own personal matters of life and death to deal with. If Amelie doesn't come to the trial, my mother will be executed. I doubt my willingness to attend will count for much, as Mr. Duveau assured me my sister's presence is vital. Even if I show up, they...they'll kill me alongside my mother."

Lorelei puts a soothing hand on my shoulder while Foxglove leans in close. "You have one option," he says. "I know about the offer Nyxia gave you."

My eyes go wide. "You think I should make a bid for the Fire throne? Nyxia will have me paired with her brother for it." I say this last part with disdain, although that doesn't reflect my true feelings about the matter. In all honesty, I like Franco. As a friend, at least. But do I like him enough to make him my mate? I can't imagine the term *mate* belonging to anyone but Aspen. Then again...

My chest squeezes as my argument with Aspen echoes through my head.

"Evelyn," Foxglove says, tone gentle, "you don't have to do anything you don't want to do. Nyxia is a clever fae. She will support her own cause in any way she can. In this, she is simply trying to secure an alliance between her court and yours. I have no doubt she would support the Unseelie Queen of Fire regardless of mate, and if so, those allies you saw in the throne room would be your allies too. I wouldn't underestimate that kind of backing."

Unseelie Queen of Fire. I shudder. "How would that help my situation?"

A spark of excitement lights his eyes. "If you were queen of your own court, you would have a say alongside the other royals. You could use your influence to temper the most violent whims of the unseelie. Your position would give you the means to protect those you love and shape the future of the Fair Isle. If you wanted, you could strive to maintain the treaty after the rebels win the war against the council fae."

My pulse races at the last part. If what he's saying is true, there's a chance I could prevent a second war with the humans. Still, there's something missing. "I don't see how that saves my mother."

His expression falters. "It doesn't, honestly. I hate to

say so, but saving her might be a lost cause. At least this way, you can save your own life and secure your place in Faerwyvae. You said so yourself; if you attend your mother's trial without Amelie, they will kill you."

"There must be another way. Please, Foxglove, you must have some idea how I can fix this."

He lets out a heavy sigh. "There's only one last hope."

I sit straighter, heart pounding.

"Make the humans a bargain they can't refuse."

22

"How do I make a bargain with the humans?" I ask. "One so tempting they can't say no?"

Foxglove squints, then rises to his feet and begins to pace. "Give me a moment," he says, shaking out his hands and stretching his neck right then left. "Creating bargains to appease the humans is what I excel at, but this is a complicated matter."

I watch him eagerly, and Lorelei leans forward with keen interest.

Finally, he stops and faces us. "There is a loophole in the treaty. You know how the council has been able to adjust the timelines required by it? And how the humans were able to offer Aspen a final set of Chosen before deeming the treaty broken?"

I nod.

"That's because the treaty allows for changes to be made. The exact wording is lengthy and complex, but it basically states that mutually beneficial concessions that support the treaty can be created. These amendments are rare, however, and never so drastic as what I'm about to propose."

My heart leaps into my throat. "And what is it you're suggesting?"

"That they amend the treaty and remove the clause that forbids King Caleos' descendants from living in Faerwyvae."

I'm stunned into a moment of silence. "Can the humans even do that without permission from the fae council?"

"Technically," Foxglove says with a wary grimace. "Considering the humans were the ones who requested King Caleos be punished for the human village he burned, they have the right to revoke the agreed-upon term concerning his exile."

Hope flutters in my heart for a moment before it's crushed by reason. "If this were possible, wouldn't you have suggested this option to begin with?"

He adjusts his spectacles, a frown tugging his lips. "If I thought it had a chance of working, yes. Considering this proposal is highly unlikely to pan out, I'm only voicing it as a last resort."

I deflate and lean back into the couch. "Well, that's comforting."

"At least highly unlikely isn't impossible. Would you like me to go on?"

With a sigh, I nod.

"So, I know King Ustrin has the council wrapped around his finger." He nods at the fae next to me. "Lorelei filled me in on the situation earlier. Here's the thing; if you want to get the humans to amend the treaty in your favor, you first need to compel them to abandon their allegiance to King Ustrin and convince them to place it in you."

I shake my head. "This is sounding more impossible by the minute."

Foxglove ignores me. "To do this, you'll need to promise them something better than anything he can provide. What exactly is he offering them?"

I shrug. "Threats, as far as I know. If the humans don't exile my family, they will be blamed for breaking the treaty."

He shakes a forefinger. "Then it will need to be something bigger than a threat, something only you can provide as a queen. It must be tempting enough to encourage them to look past their fear and see opportunity instead. This will be a challenge because their fear will be strong regarding you. The terms about King Caleos' descendants are woven tightly into the treaty. The humans know that if you claim the throne, the act alone will break the pact."

"I can't break the treaty, Foxglove."

"I know. Which is why you need to convince them to amend the treaty *before* you claim rule as Unseelie Queen of Fire."

I ponder for a moment, collecting my thoughts. "All right," I say, nodding to myself. "I attend the trial, plead my case, and present some tantalizing bargain to win their allegiance. In exchange, they will remove the clause in the treaty that requires exile of King Caleos' descendants. Then Mother and I go free."

Foxglove nods, but his expression isn't optimistic.

With a furrowed brow, I ask, "What am I missing?"

"Nothing dear. It's just...you must follow up with claiming your place as queen."

I take a deep breath. "With Nyxia's support, I think I can do that."

"And you must defeat King Ustrin according to the Old Ways."

"Defeat...King Ustrin," I echo slowly, hating the taste the words leave in my mouth.

"Well, yes," Foxglove says. "Even if the treaty were amended to allow you to stay, he'd never acknowledge your right to rule. He'll put up a fight."

What he's saying is obvious, but hearing it stated aloud highlights the ridiculousness of this entire plan. "This really is crazy, isn't it?"

Lorelei leans in closer to me. "It's not impossible to defeat him, Evelyn. I know it sounds that way, but all you need according to the Old Ways is the All of All's blessing. The fact that you already petitioned the Twelfth Court and were blessed with a crown shows you have an advantage over King Ustrin. He never faced the All of All for his throne. It was given to him by the two councils."

"What makes you think he won't gain the All of All's blessing just because I unwittingly managed to?"

Foxglove and Lorelei exchange a glance. "There's no way to know for sure," Foxglove says, "and I can't say it won't be a huge risk."

I shake my head and rise to my feet. Now I'm the one who's pacing. "I can't do this."

"You could at least try," Foxglove says.

"Or give up this whole idea," I say under my breath.

Lorelei approaches me, taking me by the shoulders to halt my steps. Her expression is fierce, though not unkind. "What's the alternative? Are you going to beg Mr. Duveau for your life? Plead with him to exile you?"

My skin crawls at the thought of begging Mr. Duveau for anything. I force my words past my teeth. "If I must."

"And where will that get you?" She gives my shoulders a light shake as if she's trying to stir my anger. I almost wish it would ignite. Anything is better than this overwhelming despair. "I know you'd never forgive yourself for leaving the Fair Isle on the brink of chaos without at least trying first. You're better than that. Fiercer. You're above begging scum like Henry Duveau for your life."

Finally, her words meet their mark, like flint striking steel. The fire of indignation burns inside me, forcing my posture to straighten. However, the intangible odds continue to batter my resolve.

"I don't know what to do," I say, surprised at the heat in my tone. "I need to save my mother, the treaty, and the fates of two races. Oh, and if there's time, I'd like to save my life too. To do so, I'll have to bargain with a council that hates me, defeat a fae king who hates me more, and once that's all taken care of, I'll have to help the rebellion win a civil war. For the love of iron, how the hell am I to accomplish all this?"

Foxglove's lips pull into a frown. "I agree with what you said. This is too much. If you don't take a side, you spread yourself too thin. But if you're determined to try and do everything at once, then this scheme is the only way."

Tears spring to my eyes, the sheer impossibility of the task at hand threatening to crush me back into despair. This time, I refuse to buckle beneath its weight. Lorelei's right. I'm fiercer than this. Things may have swung far out of my control, but there's still a way for me to gain an upper hand. There's an option that might make everything right...or as right as it can be.

If I do this, I could save the treaty.

I could save my mother.

I could prevent bloodshed.

I could protect fae and humans alike.

There's another benefit to this scheme, one that takes me by surprise.

I could be with Aspen.

It's the first time I've considered our relationship since this conversation began. Of course, after the words we exchanged in the hall, I'm not sure we even have a relationship. Still, I can't deny the way my pulse races at the idea that, if we wanted to, we *could* have one.

Maybe. If this works.

"I'll do it," I finally say. "With all things considered, the worst that can happen is I die trying. At best...well, at this point, I'm not sure if there is an at best. But at least this way, I'm part of the fight *and* the solution."

Lorelei lifts her chin, giving me an approving smile, while Foxglove claps his hands.

"We don't have much time," I say. "The trial is in less than a week. I know I must come up with an offer compelling enough to convince the humans to bargain with me, but what can I do in the meantime?"

"First step is," Foxglove says, "you need to gather supporters."

23

After night falls, I meet Queen Nyxia outside the palace. Lorelei insisted on coming along, but Nyxia arrives alone. The queen spots us hidden in the shadows of a moonstone column on the southern end of the palace, and when her eyes find mine in the dark, a smug smile spreads across her face.

"I almost didn't believe Foxglove when he arranged this meeting," she says in her smooth voice. "Please tell me this isn't an ill-constructed assassination attempt." Her eyes flash toward Lorelei, her smile turning a hint seductive.

Lorelei tosses her a seething glare but says nothing.

I pull my cloak close to my body and take a step toward the queen. "Have you told anyone else about this meeting?"

"Like your mate?"

"Like anyone." While Aspen certainly is on the top of my mind in this regard, I'm not ready for word of my plans to spread just yet. Not until I'm far more certain of its possible success. At this point, anything could go wrong. For now, I don't want the pressure of others' hopes riding on my shoulders.

Nyxia rolls her eyes with an irritated sigh. "No, I didn't tell anyone."

"Promise me you won't say anything. Not until I'm ready."

Her fingers flutter dismissively in the air. "Sure. Silence on this matter benefits my cause as well, you know. I don't want to present you to the rebel leaders until your footing is more secure."

"That wasn't exactly a promise."

Her tone sharpens. "If you want a solid promise, you're going to need to be a little more direct in your wording. If I must tell no one that you plan on taking the Fire Court throne, how am I to introduce you to the fire fae? Perhaps you should trust that, in this matter, our interests are aligned."

Despite her often-indifferent air, I'm reminded of her terrifying power. This is not a fae to anger. I square my shoulders. "Very well."

Nyxia's smile returns. "Come along then."

Lorelei and I follow the queen away from the palace. At first, I think we might head where the full moon revel took place, but instead, she leads us into the forests beyond. My pulse quickens as we move deep into dark trees, bleak shadows punctuated by clusters of glowing mushrooms and towering, bell-shaped flowers that emit near-blinding luminescence. It's breathtaking and terrifying all at once.

We continue in silence until Queen Nyxia speaks. "Now that you have accepted my offer to support your claim to the Fire throne, I do wonder if that means you've also accepted the terms I'd presented alongside it?"

I clench my jaw. I was wondering how long it would be before she brought up a mate alliance with Franco again. However, broaching the subject in the dark of the woods is not ideal. Not with so many convenient places to bury my body.

"Honest but tactful," Lorelei whispers in my ear. "And strong," she adds.

With a deep breath and careful consideration over my choice of words, I construct my reply. "Queen Nyxia, I appreciate your support of my claim to the throne and am honored—"

"Don't pander to me," the queen says. "It's unbecoming."

Lorelei emits a low growl, but I place a hand on her arm to still her.

"Fine," I say. "I understand you want our alliance made formal by pairing me with your brother, but I cannot accept. If you believe in my right to rule the Fire throne, then I claim that right alone. My choice of mate will be mine to make and shall have no bearing on my rule."

Nyxia watches me out of the corner of her eye, then lifts her chin. "Spoken like a true unseelie queen. I will continue to support your claim."

I exchange a look of relief with Lorelei.

Nyxia continues. "It would be hypocritical of me to condemn your desire to claim your throne by yourself when I too have yet to take a mate." She glances at

Lorelei, her seductive smile tugging her lips. "Although it isn't from lack of trying."

Lorelei scowls. "Oh, I'd say those seventeen fae at Beltane would disagree."

She shrugs. "It was a mere slip in judgment. You know I was never good at being monogamous before. It was a difficult adjustment..."

And the bickering begins.

BY THE TIME WE REACH THE MOUTH OF A CAVE, LORELEI and the queen have already cycled through several rounds of verbal assaults and steely silence. I tuned them out long ago for my own sanity.

The queen stops outside the cave's opening, her mood unflustered, while Lorelei's irritation wafts like a tangible essence as she stands at my side with her arms crossed. "Here we are," Nyxia says in a sing-song voice. She enters the cave, and Lorelei and I follow.

"The fire fae are gathered inside?" I ask, trying to hide the tremble in my voice as the damp cave walls seem to close in on me.

"Yes. Those who received my summons in time, that is."

"How did you gather them so quickly?" Foxglove couldn't have requested this meeting more than a few hours ago. I was surprised when he told me it would happen tonight.

"Owls." She says it like it should be obvious. "They are the most astute messengers and spies my court has."

As we venture deeper into the cave, a faint light

begins to glow up ahead. It soon proves to be from more glowing mushrooms protruding from the walls of the cave, joined by the luminescence of enormous crystals.

"Where are we?" I say with a gasp.

"Oh this? It's Venitia's house."

"Venitia?"

"A moon dragon. You'll meet him."

I swallow hard. The light grows brighter as we continue on, and soon comes the sound of voices, growls, and yips. We come to a wide chamber, its walls lined with more glowing fungi and crystals. Throughout it, various fae are gathered including several kitsune with their orbs of fires hovering over their mouths or tails, blue wisps, a black dragon, and something I at first took for an overgrown fungus but now see is some kind of crustacean-mushroom hybrid with curious eyes peeking beneath its shell.

The fae grow quiet as we enter the chamber, eyes falling on Queen Nyxia. She addresses them with a smile. "Thank you for gathering to meet me on such short notice and being so willing to greet my guest." She flicks a finger at me, and I come up beside her.

My mouth dries up as all eyes lock on me, some with boredom, others with keen interest, and a few with open hostility. "I am pleased to meet you," I manage to say.

Nyxia frowns at me for a moment before returning her attention to the fire fae. "It is my great honor to introduce to you King Caleos' granddaughter, Evelyn."

Gasps and yips emit from my audience. Some of the expressions have now turned reverent while others seem a bit more fearful.

Nyxia continues. "With King Ustrin growing more and more militant in his rule as the centuries pass, your kind have sought shelter in other courts. You've always been welcome here in Lunar and will continue to be. However, I ask you to consider what it might be like if an unseelie ruler were on the Fire throne. Not just any ruler, but the blood of the great King Caleos."

Whispers, grunts, and other animal noises rumble throughout the cave. When they subside, a kitsune steps forward on graceful paws, a ball of flame hovering in the air above its muzzle. Its eyes move from me to Nyxia. When it speaks, the words come through like Aspen's had in stag form—not from its lips but from somewhere inside it. Or inside my mind. "I see the blood of King Caleos, but I see no unseelie ruler but you."

Nyxia extends her hand toward me. "Evelyn plans to stake her claim as Unseelie Queen of Fire according to the Old Ways. Once she defeats King Ustrin, she will be the only ruler of Fire and the unseelie will be safe to return to the Fire Court if they wish."

The kitsune doesn't look convinced, nor do the majority of the fae in the crowd. "What is her unseelie form, then?"

Several voices echo their support of the question. A blue wisp bounces forward, her ethereal voice slow and smooth as she says, "Yes, I too want to see her unseelie form. I want to see she's truly one of us."

The blood leaves my face. Do they honestly expect me to be able to *shift forms*? Surely, they must know I'm not full-fae.

Queen Nyxia gives the crowd a placating smile. "She

will show you her unseelie form when the time is right." I shoot her a look of surprise, but she ignores it. "This is but an introduction so you can spread the word that hope is coming to Fire. That an unseelie rule is soon to return."

Voices rise, calling out demands to see me shift. I feel like I might be sick.

"Why doesn't she speak for herself?" the crustacean-mushroom says in a low, gravelly voice. A rumble of agreement moves through the crowd.

Nyxia gives me a pointed look before nodding.

My palms grow hot as, once again, all eyes fall on me. I want to run, to forfeit this entire plan and forget I ever thought I have what it takes to do this. This is what it would mean to be queen. I'd be required to give speeches, to represent a people I hardly understand.

I take a step back to catch my bearings, but my heart leaps into my throat as my lungs constrict.

"Breathe," Lorelei whispers. "You can do this."

I close my eyes, the cave spinning around me.

Lorelei's whisper takes on a harsh quality. "Would you rather beg Henry Duveau for your life?"

Her words ignite a ripple of fire, and with it comes a sense of clarity. I connect to the fire, let it burn away my fears. *All I can do is try,* I remind myself.

With a deep breath, I step forward and meet the eyes of my audience—*my people*. They don't truly feel like my people, not only because they are fae but because they are unseelie. However, that must change. If I am to become Queen of Fire, I will have to consider the term *unseelie* without fear or disgust. I will have to fight for them as strongly as I fight for the humans.

"Your kind are suppressed by the radical seelie like King Ustrin," I say. The hesitation in my tone is obvious, but I call forth more fire to burn it away. Thoughts of King Ustrin allow my anger to rise. I think about what he did to my mother, to the apothecary. Until I can fight for the unseelie without forcing it, I can at least fight against *him*.

"King Ustrin maintains his power by turning his back on the Old Ways." I'm not even sure what I'm saying, but my voice is stronger now. "He betrays his own kind to keep a throne he never earned. The council he supports grows more and more seelie every day. If allowed to fall too far into the hands of the radical seelie, the Old Ways will be eliminated entirely. The unseelie will be eliminated. You'll be forced into clothes, forced to obey laws that strip you from the traditions you've held onto for countless centuries."

Even though my words only echo what I learned from Aspen, I find myself feeling the truth in them. My audience seems intrigued, their gazes intent upon me. I continue. "The Council of Eleven Courts has been broken and a war between the fae is coming. The radical seelie seek control while the rebels seek freedom." I put my hand on my heart. "I am part of that rebellion. As Unseelie Queen of Fire, I will fight the forces that threaten your way of life. I will fight against King Ustrin and win us back the Fire Court. I will win back our home."

A kitsune lets out a bark that sounds like approval, while other encouraging sounds emit from several other fae.

Nyxia looks almost impressed.

Movement at the back of the crowd snags my attention and the masses return to quiet. The black dragon uncoils, extending its lithe neck toward me. "You are of human blood." The voice is part hiss, part whisper. "You may promise to fight for us, but how do we know you won't fight for them more? How can we trust you won't be worse than King Ustrin?"

My confidence falters. To say I won't fight for the humans would be a lie. Am I ready to promise I'll at least fight for them equally?

Nyxia seems to sense my loss of momentum and takes a step forward. "Like I said, dear ones, this is but an introduction. We know it will take time for you to trust what Evelyn has to offer. In the meantime, I ask you to trust *me*. Trust me when I say that I believe Evelyn is the answer to tipping the balance in our favor. Spread word of what you learned tonight, but do it discreetly. Rally the unseelie fire fae and anyone who seeks an end to King Ustrin's reign. We will gather again when Evelyn is ready to make her move against him."

"Will she show us her unseelie form then?" asks an orange sprite.

Queen Nyxia plasters an exaggerated smile over her lips. "Yes. Until then, do as I've requested."

The cave erupts with commotion, and the three of us turn to leave. All I hear is the pounding of my heart in my ears as we exit the cave, my feet flying beneath me. Once we return beneath the forest trees, I halt and round on Queen Nyxia. "You lied."

"I cannot lie."

"You told them I would show them my unseelie form next time I meet with them."

"And you will."

My eyes bulge as I stare at her. "You don't understand. I don't have that kind of power. I can't shift like the full-fae can."

"Sure you can." She walks on ahead, leaving me gaping behind her.

I turn to Lorelei, silently begging her to argue some sense into the queen.

Instead, she says, "She's right."

"How do you figure?"

"You've already proven yourself capable of using fae magic," Lorelei says. "That's all you need to shift. It's simply a matter of knowing how, which you have yet to learn."

"How can you be so sure? I'm only one-quarter fae."

She shrugs, and we hurry to catch up with the queen. "The half-fae children of the Chosen have always been able to shift, and none of them seem any more adept with magic than you."

This takes me by surprise. "They can?"

Nyxia turns to look over her shoulder at me. "Yes, and so will you. It is your only hope of winning over the unseelie fire fae completely."

I rub my temples. "Great. Let me just add that to my list of unrealistic things I'm supposed to do to save the isle."

"Evelyn, you've been to the Twelfth Court," Lorelei says. "That's all it takes. That, magic, and intent. All magic stems from intent. You'll learn."

I open my mouth to argue, but Nyxia comes to a

sudden halt, forcing me and Lorelei and to stop as well. An enormous owl swoops down from the sky and lands at the queen's feet. "Urgent," the owl says. "Unwelcome guests have traveled through the axis. They're heading for Selene Palace."

24

"Who do you think it is?" I ask Lorelei as we hurry back through the woods toward the palace. Nyxia already took off in her shadow form as soon as the owl delivered its message.

"I don't know," Lorelei says, "but it can't be good."

We continue on as swiftly as we can. The forest remains eerily silent, as if the message has every creature in the woods on high alert. I'm hyper aware of every snapping twig, every rustling leaf.

"Evie." The sound of my name has me nearly leaping out of my skin. I draw back as a figure materializes seemingly from nowhere. A scream builds in my throat and I nearly release it until the moonlight illuminates a pair of antlers.

"Aspen! What are you doing here?"

He takes me by the shoulders. "For the love of oak and ivy, where have you been? Are you safe?"

All I can do is nod, startled by the concern written over his expression.

His eyes leave me to scan my surroundings. "Why are you in the woods?"

I blink a few times, confused by the question. Then I recognize that familiar purple aura around him and realize he isn't really here. I take a deep breath to steady my nerves as I consider how to answer his question. I'm not ready to tell him the truth about what I've been doing. Besides, the longer he stands in my presence, the more I recall I'm still mad at him over our argument in the hall. I don't owe him an explanation. Not yet. "I'm with Lorelei," I say curtly.

He purses his lips, hands sliding from my shoulders as if he's suddenly uncomfortable with the physical contact. In the absence of his touch comes a sting of regret. "Stay there," he says without warmth. "Do not come back to the palace."

"Why? What's happening?"

"King Ustrin is coming."

My throat goes dry. "What does he want?"

"Just stay where you are." With that, he's gone.

When my vision adjusts to Aspen's sudden disappearance, I find Lorelei in his place. Her hands are on her hips, head cocked to the side as she watches me with a raised brow. "What the bloody oak and ivy just happened?"

"You didn't see him?"

"See who?"

I almost don't want to explain, but her expression tells me she won't let me off that easy. "Aspen was here."

She lifts a brow. "Aspen? He was here just now?" Her tone is flat, full of skepticism.

I let out a sigh. "It's something that's been happening

since I left Bircharbor. At first, I thought they were dreams, but they're...something else."

Her posture relaxes. "Wait, you're serious?"

I nod. "I don't understand it, but there are times when we're able to see each other. It...might be linked to the Bond." Since finding out my dreams were true occurrences, I haven't given the phenomenon much thought. But now, it's beginning to make sense. "I think we've been using the Bond to visit each other somehow. When I use his name and think of him in a certain way, I can see where he is. And when he uses mine...likewise. That's why he knew I was in trouble in Eisleigh. Lorelei, he was there in the underground laboratory."

"That's a lot to take in," she says. "But all right, I think I understand what you're saying. Although, I don't believe that's a common feature of the Bond."

"Well, whatever the case, there's something far more pressing. He told me King Ustrin is coming and urged me to remain hidden."

She gapes. "He's coming? Where, to the palace? That's who Nyxia went to confront?"

"That's what it sounded like."

Lorelei darts forward, then hesitates. "No, he's right. You need to remain in hiding."

"Like hell," I say. "I need to know what's going on."

"A lot of good that will do if he kills you."

I feel the blood leave my face, but I refuse to back down. "Even so, what if he already knows I'm here? What if he's coming to threaten Lunar for harboring me? I can't let anyone get hurt for me."

"What are you going to do? Sacrifice yourself?"

"If I must."

She rolls her eyes. "What is with you and the constant need to put others before you? Is your life not worth more?"

The question catches me off guard. I've always wanted to help others and save lives. That's why I wanted to become a surgeon. But her words bring to mind an unsettling question; what is my own life worth? I shake my head. "If there's anything I can do to keep others from getting hurt, I have a right to do it."

"Fine. But I'm making you invisible."

"Invisible? How?"

She lifts her hands. "I'm putting a glamour over you."

I step away, blinking furiously as a flash of betrayal ignites within. "You're going to glamour me?"

She clenches her jaw. "No, Evelyn. You can stop blinking now."

I take a deep breath and force my eyelids to stop fluttering.

Her hands remain raised. "I'm putting a *physical* glamour over you. It's different from a mental one. A physical glamour doesn't interfere with a person's mind."

"All right," I say slowly. "You think you can really make me invisible?"

"I'll try," she says. She remains still for a few moments before lowering her hands with a shrug. "Well, let's hope it works."

"What do you mean, let's hope? You can't tell if it worked?"

"It's my glamour. Since I know it's there, I can see through it. You look as clear as day to me."

I sigh and start back down our path. "Good enough."

Lorelei shakes her head. "King Aspen better not have my neck for this."

My feet ache by the time we reach the edge of the forest outside the palace lawn. Despite my glamour, we remain hidden behind the trunk of a tree while Lorelei scans the landscape. She tenses, and I follow her line of vision. Outside the southern end of the palace, where Lorelei and I had met Nyxia mere hours ago, stand dozens of armed fae, mostly wraiths and ghouls with weapons as ethereal as their forms. Their bodies are angled away from us as they face the distant tree line.

We creep forward, crossing the lawn toward the palace. Once we reach a row of towering hedges near the building, we make our way forward until the retinue comes further into view. We slip beneath shadows until we reach the nearest column. There we peek around it for a better vantage.

Before the soldiers stand Nyxia, Franco, and Aspen, as well as the rulers of Wind, Winter, and Earthen. Their postures are tense as they stare ahead at what appears to be nothing. Endless moments of chilling silence pass until movement flickers in the distant shadows. Three figures approach, and as they near, I recognize the middle as King Ustrin. He wears a red suit, its color dim against the radiance of his orange scales glinting in the moonlight. The fae on each side of him look like guards. They have scaled bodies like the king, but their coloring is pale yellow. The one to Ustrin's right seems to be trembling, his steps slower than his companion's.

The three figures stop several yards away from the gathering before them.

I hardly breathe as I strain to hear over my pounding heart.

"Queen Nyxia," Ustrin says, his voice quiet but loud enough to carry to us. "How good of you to greet me with such a charming welcoming party. Although, when I requested my right to a peaceful exchange of words, I didn't expect so many soldiers to take part. Did your owl not make my intentions clear? I did not come for a fight."

Nyxia gives him a toothy smile, her canines conveying the hidden threat in the gesture. "Why are you here? You were not invited."

"That's no way to speak to a fellow council fae."

"You and I both know I am no longer considered a council fae. The same goes for the rulers who stand beside me."

"Ah, well I did want to hear it from your lips before I assumed too much," King Ustrin says, a false smile on his lipless mouth. "Then my next order of business can commence. By order of the Council of Eleven Courts, I hereby deem you, Nyxia of Lunar, stripped of your right to rule. The same goes for you, Aspen of Autumn, Aelfon of Earthen, Minuette of Wind, and Flauvis of Winter." He nods at each of the rulers in turn. The tension in the air is palpable, and even I bristle at this blatant omission of their royal titles.

The wolf fae—King Flauvis, that is—lets out a deep growl. King Aelfon, the stout fae with curling horns and deep, brown skin, pounds his hooves into the grass beneath him. The ethereal Queen Minuette lets out a windy hiss with her blue lips.

"You don't have that kind of power," Nyxia says, unperturbed by the threat. "We have deemed the council disbanded. Nothing you say has any weight over our actions, decisions, or rights to rule."

King Ustrin narrows his beady eyes. "We'll see what tune you're singing once you're outnumbered on a battlefield. You see, the council is electing seelie rulers in each court." His eyes flash toward King Aelfon. "A *new* seelie ruler, in some cases."

A snarl rips from the Earthen King's lips. I'm surprised he can manage not to launch for the Fire King's throat. With only two guards, King Ustrin could easily be overpowered.

"Go ahead and play at being in power while you still can," Nyxia says. "You won't be much longer."

I feel a chill at her words, sensing the double meaning. Not only does she mean the council, but him personally. King Ustrin seems to sense it too, the smile slipping from his face. "Now onto my next order of business. I'd like to offer one of your subjects an alliance with the council. Prince Franco, the council offers you the position of Seelie King of Lunar."

Nyxia visibly tenses, shadows curling from her fingertips. "Excuse me?"

Franco's eyes bulge, but he says nothing.

"Now, now," Ustrin says, "there's no need to get your shadows involved, Nyxia. This is a peaceful exchange of words, remember? If Prince Franco would like to accept the offer, he should be free to do so. Or is all that talk about freedom of choice simply...talk?"

Nyxia snarls, but it's cut off as Prince Franco takes a step forward, then another. She watches in horror as her brother closes the distance between himself and King Ustrin.

The Fire King greets the prince with a triumphant grin.

"That slimy, son-of-a-harpy," I say under my breath. Rage burns inside me, turning every fond memory of the Lunar Prince to ash.

Ustrin extends a hand, which Franco accepts. In a blink of an eye, the prince pulls Ustrin toward him, and his free hand collides with the Fire King's flat nose. "That's what I think of your offer," he says, arms wide as he sweeps into a mocking bow.

All right. I take it all back. Prince Franco is—

One of the guards, the one who was trembling earlier, unsheathes his sword and buries it in Franco's stomach. I let out a shout echoed by Nyxia as the prince falls to his knees. Nyxia's shadows unfurl and her soldiers begin to surge forward. The guard convulses before releasing the hilt and falling to the ground motionless. The second guard takes his place, gritting his teeth as his fingers stop inches from the hilt.

"It's iron." King Ustrin's voice halts the oncoming melee. "One more step and I'll have the prince beheaded with it."

Nyxia's shadows disappear, and she motions for her soldiers to take a step back.

"Think about the rules, Nyxia," Ustrin says. "In a peaceful exchange of words, violence is forbidden. It can only be met blow for blow. As of now, equal blows have been exchanged and it can stop here. But if you attack me, it will be my right to end his life."

"Let him go," Nyxia says through her teeth.

Franco moans in pain, head lolling to the side.

"I'll let the prince go if you let me speak with Evelyn Fairfield."

A hush falls over the crowd, punctuated only by Franco's whimpers.

"Oh, let's not play dumb," Ustrin says. "I know she's here. As my final order of business, I ask only that I speak with her. The rules made by the peaceful exchange of words will be extended to her, and she will not be harmed tonight. I give my promise."

Aspen burns Nyxia with a glare, but Nyxia keeps her lips pursed tight.

I look from King Ustrin to Prince Franco. "Release the glamour," I whisper to Lorelei.

"No," she argues. "He may have promised not to harm you today, but once he knows you're here, there's no stopping him from returning tomorrow."

"I'll give you a count of five," King Ustrin shouts. "If you don't reveal Miss Fairfield in that time, I'll be the next to deliver a blow, and it will cost your prince his life." His guard's fingers flinch toward the sword. "Five."

"Release the glamour," I hiss at Lorelei.

"Four."

"I'm not letting Franco die."

"Three."

"Damn it, Lorelei—"

She lets out a frustrated grumble and lifts her hands toward me. "Fine."

"Two."

I dart from my hiding place.

"One."

"I'm here. Let the prince go."

Aspen whirls toward me, expression unreadable. He takes a step forward as if to stop me from approaching. I meet his gaze with a subtle shake of my head, hoping I can convey my meaning through the gesture. *Do nothing, Aspen.* His chest heaves with suppressed rage, but I can't tell if it's for me or Ustrin.

King Ustrin faces me with a feral grin. "The rumors are true after all."

"Let. Him. Go."

He waves his hands dismissively. "Once we're done speaking, he's all yours." He nods at his guard, who takes a step away from the prince.

I cross my arms over my chest to keep them from shaking. "What do you want?"

His forked tongue flicks toward me. "I simply wanted to know what your intentions are. After I learned of your escape from imprisonment, I wanted to be sure you weren't doing anything...unwise."

"I didn't escape from imprisonment," I say, my words walking the blade's edge between truth and lie. "The human council gave me permission to await my mother's trial wherever I pleased."

"So you chose Lunar? How quaint."

I shrug.

"And you still plan on attending your mother's trial?"

My mind races as I weigh the impact of my words. "I'm considering it."

He hisses. "What is there to consider?"

"I want a bargain from you."

He erupts with a violent laugh. "A bargain? From me?"

"It will serve us equally."

"What terms do you offer?"

"I want my last days in Faerwyvae to be peaceful ones. That's all I ask. I want you to promise that neither you nor any ally of the Council of Eleven Courts will engage the rebel alliance in violence so long as I remain on the Fair Isle."

His slitted nostrils flare. "What do I get out of this promise?"

"In return, I promise to attend my mother's trial and accept my exile without argument if the human council allows us to leave unharmed."

"And that you will never return," King Ustrin adds.

I swallow hard, preparing the words that could seal my fate. "In addition, I promise that once I leave the Fair Isle, I will never return."

The Fire King's expression shifts with a pleasant smile. "That's all I ever wanted. For your grandfather's ilk to be gone for good. You see, I am not a violent man. I could have you, your mother, and your sister executed, yet I am giving you this mercy."

"Mercy indeed," I say through my teeth.

He lifts his chin. "I agree to this bargain." With a flick of his fingers, the standing guard pulls the sword from Franco and shoves it into the sheath at the incapacitated guard's hip, then hefts him off the ground. The three retreat behind a line of fire that springs from the earth, stretching out in a wide arc behind them.

I run to Franco as does Nyxia. Some of her soldiers pursue Ustrin, breaking through the wall of fire, while the rest set up a perimeter around us. I kneel at the Lunar Prince's side and call for wine and clean cloth. His shirt is soaked with his bright red blood, his face even paler than usual, a gray tinge beginning to creep up his neck. I know what happens to fae who sustain iron injuries. I can only hope the sword wasn't embedded in his abdomen long enough to do severe damage.

I grasp the collar of his linen shirt and tear it open. Black patterns cover his chest and stomach, mingling with the blood. With a shock of relief, I realize the black is not from veins of poison but from his intricate tattoos. I let out a sigh, the tension smoothing from my shoulders. His wound is deep, but with his abdominal cavity free from poison, he will heal much faster than Aspen did.

With the thought of his name, comes the awareness of his proximity. Aspen stands near Franco's head, his presence heavy in the space he occupies. I meet his eyes for a moment, finding a flicker of confusion in them. Then they go steely, and he turns away. Before I can consider him a moment longer, a wraith's gray hand comes into view, bearing a bottle of wine. I quickly pour the liquid over the wound and my hands, then get to work.

25

With every move, I call upon my fire, let it tingle my fingertips as I pour all my intent into Franco's healing. In a matter of minutes, the wound is cleaned and the bleeding is staunched by the remnants of Franco's shirt. Only then do the guards lift him and transport him to his bedroom. That's when I'm finally able to seek out a splinter of bone and spider silk thread to stitch his wound.

In the prince's room, I'm joined by three petite fae with enormous black eyes and pale moth-like wings. I quickly learn they are Lunar Court's healers. They flutter around me, helping where they can. Like Gildmar, they aren't adept at handling injuries from iron or any kind of human weapon. Luckily, Franco's affliction proves to be minimal. I assess internal damage and find that a lesion in his small intestine is already knitting back together before my very eyes. With no further surgery needed, I finish cleaning his wound and begin stitching him back together.

One of the healers hands me a cluster of silky green moss. "Moon moss," she says. "Use it beneath his bandage once you finish his stitches."

I take it from her. "Thank you, but what does it do?"

"It will speed his healing. It only grows near the Wishing Tree when the moon is full."

I finish my ministrations with the help of the fae. Prince Franco begins to rouse by the time I finish tying off his bandage with the moss packed beneath it. His eyelids flutter open, accompanied with a groan of pain. He tries to sit, but I place a hand on his shoulder to steady him.

The moth fae flutter about, and one darts toward the door. "I'll tell Queen Nyxia he's awake." Another pours a cup of Midnight Blush and hands it to me.

"Drink this." He takes the wine from me, and immediate relief crosses his face. Midnight Blush might not be as effective as honey pyrus extract, but considering the mildness of his injury, it should suffice.

He takes the cup and drinks the liquid down, then meets my eyes with a furrowed brow. "You...saved me. With a bargain."

"So you were conscious during that."

He shakes his head, silvery hair sticking out at odd angles. "Sort of. I hope you didn't bargain away anything too vital."

I purse my lips. "So do I."

He studies my face. "Why did you do it? Nyxia would have taken him down before he managed to kill me. Her shadows would have wrecked his mind and each of his guards before they made another move. That's if he had any intention to follow through with his threat to begin with. You know he was baiting you, right?"

At the time, it didn't occur to me that Nyxia would have saved her brother or that Ustrin might be bluffing. In retrospect, of course the powerful alpha would have saved the prince. King Ustrin's threat was a trick for me alone. And it worked.

I try for a nonchalant shrug. "Maybe I wanted to make the bargain."

A corner of his mouth quirks. "For me? Or for some devious plan of yours?"

I blush. Even with the presence of the moth fae, I'm still painfully aware of my proximity to a shirtless Franco in his bedroom. It hadn't seemed improper when he was unconscious. Now all I can see is his heated expression, his bare, inked chest. I clench my jaw and take a step away from his bed where I can more easily maintain my composure. "If I had a devious plan, I wouldn't tell you about it."

"Then I'll pretend you did it for me."

"Pretend all you like, but don't leave this bed for the rest of the night."

His lips pull into a mock pout. "That will be so boring. Unless you plan to stay in it with me."

The sound of buzzing wings and stifled giggles deepens my blush. The prince certainly has no shame. I cross my arms and give him a pointed look, although I can't hide my amusement. "I'm a medical professional, and you are my patient. You are going to stay in this bed *alone* and try to get some sleep. Iron injuries are no joke."

He rolls his eyes. "Fine. You sure know how to take all the fun out of a near-death experience."

I shake my head and pour him another glass of wine. "Drink this, then go to sleep."

He accepts it, and I watch him down it in a single gulp. He winces as he returns the glass to me, then settles back on his pillows. His lids grow heavy and his expression turns serious. "Thank you," he says, "for what you did for me."

"You're welcome." I place a hand on his shoulder to give him a comforting squeeze. Just as I'm about to pull away, he lifts his hand to rest it over mine. Our eyes lock the way they did outside my bedroom after the revel. I can't help but think of the kiss we shared that night. But, of course, that kiss is impossible to consider without thinking of Aspen. About the hurt it caused. About our fight, about the passion and fury I still carry for the king.

My heart sinks, and I gently pull my hand from under his.

Maybe in another life, Franco and I could have been something. Or even in another time. If Aspen and I are unable to mend the rift between us...

I can't finish that train of thought. Instead, I smile at the prince. "Goodnight, Franco."

He returns the grin, blinking slowly as the Midnight Blush begins to take hold. "Goodnight, Evelyn."

I move away from the bed, and one of the moth fae flutters over to me. "We'll watch over him tonight," she whispers.

I give her my thanks and continue to the door, only to come to a halt. In the doorway stands Foxglove, expression forlorn as his eyes rest on the sleeping prince.

"Oh, were you coming inside?" I ask, nodding toward my patient.

He shakes his head as if to clear it. "No, I came to find you."

I join him in the hall, but as we turn away from the door, his attention snags once again on the room.

"Are you sure you didn't want to—"

"No." A blush creeps up his neck as he pushes the bridge of his spectacles.

I can't stop the grin from stretching over my face. "You fancy Prince Franco, don't you?"

His expression turns wistful. "He's just adorable, Evelyn, how could I not?"

"Are you...well acquainted?"

"We've hardly spoken a word. I doubt he knows I exist. Besides, I can admire him from afar, can't I?"

I chuckle. "Yes, I suppose you can."

"Now, enough about that beautiful prince. I came here to talk about you and what happened with King Ustrin."

"Did you witness it?"

"I watched everything from the observatory and nearly died when I saw what that guard did to the prince. It is a crime most foul for a fae to use iron against another."

"I was shocked to find a fae could use iron at all."

"As was I. It's nearly debilitating to so much as touch iron. I'm certain even sheathed, it leeched strength from that guard. I hope he was gravely afflicted." His words carry venom, and I can't help but feel the same. The guard went immobile after he stabbed Franco, making me wonder if he survived the act at all.

"How did King Ustrin come to own an iron blade anyway?" I ask.

"It's likely a relic from the war. We stumble across such weapons, often buried in some forgotten area. You can usually tell by the dying earth surrounding it. However, with all the deserts in Fire, it may have been easier to go undetected for much longer."

I nod, but my mind lingers on Foxglove's mention of the desert. I've never seen desert lands and always imagined them with equal parts fascination and terror. If I take the Fire Court as my home, that desert will belong to me.

"More pressingly," Foxglove says, interrupting my thoughts, "we should talk about the bargain you made. I couldn't hear the words spoken from the observatory, but Lorelei told me what was exchanged. How you sacrificed our great plan to save the prince. I can't say I blame you. I'd have been tempted to bargain for the fair prince's life, but...we came so far." His shoulders sink, expression crumbling.

"I'm not sure I did sacrifice our plan, Foxglove."

He furrows his brow. "How do you figure?"

"Well, I'm not clear on how this all works, so you must correct me if I'm wrong. When I made the bargain, I told him I'd attend my mother's trial. I have every intention of fulfilling that promise as stated."

"But you told him you'd accept exile too, did you not?"

"I told him I'd accept exile without argument if the human council allowed us to leave unharmed. Well, I can't accept my exile if it isn't offered, and if the council agrees to my bargain, then they won't offer exile."

Foxglove's eyes widen. "Well, now, aren't you clever!"

"There's more. I don't know if I did this correctly, but I tried to use the power of intent. When I said I'd accept my exile if the council allowed us to leave unharmed, my intent for the word *us* was myself and my mother. That way, if it comes to begging Mr. Duveau to allow her and I to leave the isle, Amelie's absence from the trial will have no bearing on the bargain."

Foxglove's lips pull into a wide grin.

"Did I do it right? The power of intent?"

"Yes, I believe you did. Very well done. However, you also promised you wouldn't return if exiled."

"And I'm willing to keep that promise," I say. The thought alone makes my heart sink. "But, most importantly, was his side of the bargain. I agreed to all this in exchange for his promise that he and the council fae wouldn't engage the rebels in violence so long as I remained on the isle. If all goes according to plan, and I'm able to stay in Faerwyvae forever, we'll have an upper hand. The council won't be able to attack us...ever."

His mouth falls open. "Brilliant, Evelyn. Simply brilliant."

"You think it will work? Did I leave too much room for interpretation?"

He tilts his head one way and another, as if weighing the various scenarios in his mind. "Depending on the exact words used, I don't think that will stop the civil war from breaking out between the rebels and the council, but it will prevent them from engaging us first. They will only be able to attack on the defensive."

"Then that's enough for us to have an advantage, right?"

We arrive at my bedroom door and stop outside it. Foxglove grins. "My dear, I think you're right. I could hug you if you weren't covered in blood. Instead, I will have to settle for a goodnight. Will you be ready to leave in four days' time?"

The blood drains from my face. It's both too soon and not soon enough. I'm far from ready to face the council at the trial, and yet I'm eager to get this over with. To free my mother. To face my fate.

He continues, "You should arrive the day before her trial so you can get settled in. Well, I should say so *we* can get settled in. I'm most certainly going with you."

The statement surprises me from my frazzled thoughts. "But you represent Autumn, Foxglove. Why would you attend Mother's trial with me?"

He squares his shoulders. "You will be Queen of Fire, my dear. It's time you start acting like a royal. No fae queen would face the humans without an ambassador, and until you have one of your own, I am more than happy to play the part."

"But...will Aspen even let you?"

He lets out a tittering laugh. "I assure you, I won't have a choice in the matter. He'll think it was his idea."

I furrow my brow. "I'm not so sure. Things have been...strained between me and the king."

His expression softens. "I know things aren't exactly comfortable at the moment, but King Aspen cares for you unlike he's ever cared for anyone. Trust me. You'll work out whatever is amiss between you."

My heart yearns to feel the optimism of his words as if it were my own, but I don't allow myself to dwell on it. Instead, I shift the subject to more practical matters. "You're certain you can manage not to tell him about our plan?"

"So long as he doesn't ask, I don't have to tell the

truth, although," he twists his fingers together in a nervous gesture, "I implore you to tell him the truth. If he had hope—"

"I don't want his hope." My tone comes out sharper than I intend. "I don't want anyone's hope right now. Not until I think this might actually work. If I can get the council to agree to my terms, then I'll make our plan known. Until then, it's folly."

"Hope is never folly, Evelyn."

I swallow hard, steeling my expression. "It is when it could break your heart."

26

The next four days pass in a blur of anxious preparations. I hardly see a soul as I spend most of my time in my room going over every word I've prepared to say at Mother's trial. Only Lorelei and Foxglove come to visit, and I try not to read too much into Aspen's absence. Even the few times I've left my room to seek him out, he's nowhere to be found. The doors to the throne room remain firmly closed throughout most of the day, and Foxglove tells me Aspen and the rebel allies are busy plotting their first move against the council fae.

Perhaps it's for the best I haven't spoken to Aspen. I'm still not sure what I intend to say when I finally do. Should I apologize? Yell? Force his lips onto mine until that spark returns between us?

Only one thing is clear: we're running out of time. If I don't see him soon, there's a chance I might never see him again.

On the day we are to depart on our journey to Grenneith, I'm an anxious mess. With pacing steps, I cross my room, rehearsing the terms of the bargain I'll be presenting. I try to anticipate every argument the council could counter my proposal with, and plan out answers to those as well. It's maddening and hopeless, and I just want this to be over already.

As a hazy sunset throws my room beneath a dusky glow, I discard my mental preparations in favor of physical ones. We'll be leaving by nightfall to arrive in Grenneith by tomorrow morning.

My hands tremble as I pack my bag, wishing I had more to bring, if only to keep my hands busy. Yet, all I'll need is a nightdress, undergarments, and extra shoes. I don't bother trying to dress in human clothing this time, considering not even my corset was salvageable after my arrival at Selene Palace. However, Nyxia did loan me some cream silk trousers and a blue linen blouse, which I'm wearing now beneath my velvet cloak.

A knock sounds on my door, almost too quiet to hear, as if the visitor is unsure of their intent. When I open the door, I'm speechless to find Aspen on the other side. My breath catches in my throat as our eyes lock. Silence envelops us, leaving nothing but a tense hum of energy I can sense down to my bones. The energy feels wrong, the air too thick. Does he feel it too?

He clears his throat, the sound so loud it startles me. "Can I come in for a moment?" His tone is cold, formal, catching me off guard.

I blink a few times, realizing we're still standing under

my threshold. "Of course," I say, hating how my formality matches his.

He enters, striding to the center of my room, back facing me. He wears russet trousers, a white shirt, and a bronze waistcoat—wrinkled again. It's an effort not to reach for him, to place a hand in the middle of his back and soothe whatever has him so rattled. But I can't touch him, not when everything about this is wrong—his posture, his formality, the way he's been avoiding me. I get that we've yet to reconcile our grievances toward each other, but the way he's acting has my stomach in knots.

This can't be just about my stolen kiss with Franco. Surely anger would suffice his feelings over the matter. Rage, I can handle. Rage, I can counter with my own. But this distance, this strain...I know neither how to confront it nor how it's come to lie between us. There must be something else I've done to deserve his coldness.

I run through our last few interactions and consider everything that's happened between leaving Bircharbor and now. So much has changed but—

Then it dawns on me. His mother died and it was my fault. Does he know? Did Foxglove or Lorelei tell him what I admitted to? Does he realize I could have prevented her death if I'd mentioned her plea before I left? The blood leaves my face, sweat beading over my forehead.

Finally, he speaks, attention fixated on the empty wall in front of him. "I want to come with you to the Spire."

My mouth feels dry as I search for words. The way he refuses to look my way tells me the offer to accompany me pains him greatly. But why? "All right," I say, my voice tenuous.

He remains facing away from me, each heartbeat tugging on the air between us. When he speaks again, it's drowned out by my own words. "I'm sorry about your mother."

He whirls toward me. "What?"

I swallow hard. "I said, I'm sorry about your mother. I heard about her...murder." My unspoken question echoes in my head. *Does he know the truth? Does he know it's my fault?*

He nods but says nothing in reply.

Another stretch of silence. Aspen opens and closes his fists, a nervous gesture I've never seen him do, one that makes the air in the room feel suffocating. I can't help but feel that this marks the end. That nothing will ever feel right between us again.

I wish he'd yell. I wish *I'd* yell. I wish anything were happening but this painful quiet.

Tears spring to my eyes as the room begins to spin. There's only one thing left to say. "It's my fault."

His expression softens. "Excuse me?"

"Her death. It's my fault."

"I don't understand. You were here when she was murdered. Nyxia vouched for you. I know Cobalt had your dagger, he—"

I shake my head. "I could have prevented it." I inhale a trembling breath, preparing my confession. "She spoke with me the day I left Bircharbor, telling me she feared Cobalt. Feared for her safety. She begged me to speak to you on her behalf, to form an alliance. She wanted your protection. And I...I never said a word."

He closes the distance between us, stopping a few feet away. His hand lifts toward my face, and my heart races in anticipation of the touch. A flicker of hope rises inside, as if everything will be set to rights with this one caress. But it doesn't come. Like he did in the hall, he pulls his hand away before he can touch me, curling his fingers into fists as he purses his lips. "It isn't your fault." His words come out with a tremor, as if filtered through suppressed rage.

My throat feels tight, seeing his repulsion in the set of his jaw, in the fists balled at his sides. I call upon my fire to steady me as I fix him with a glare. "Obviously you don't believe your own words," I say through my teeth.

"How can you say that? You had nothing to do with her death. If anyone is to blame, it's me. She came to me with the same request, the same fears. I didn't trust her." A flash of pain crosses his face. "But you, Evie. You're innocent of blame."

My mind reels to comprehend him. His words sound so genuine, but his body betrays the truth. If he isn't upset about that, then why does he find it so hard to be in the same room with me? Why does he look like he'd rather be anywhere but at my side? I'm about to give voice to the questions when footsteps sound outside my room. My eyes flash to the open door where Foxglove emerges from the hall.

Aspen takes a step away from me, and the hum of that unsettling energy shatters. "What is it?" he asks, voice gruff.

Foxglove's expression flashes with surprise, as if he hadn't expected to find Aspen here. "Queen Nyxia has prepared her carriage for our journey. It's time."

My hands tremble at his words. "I should finish readying my things."

"I'll meet you at the carriage," Aspen mutters without looking at me. With that, he leaves my room.

Foxglove gives me a knowing grin. "See, I told you things would be better between you soon enough."

I open my mouth to argue but can't find the words to express the truth of what just occurred. Because honestly, I have no idea what any of it meant.

A ROUND, WHITE, OPALESCENT CARRIAGE AWAITS US outside the palace. At the front are two skeletal equine creatures, thin and white with lipless mouths and red eyes. Instead of a mane, each creature has a set of sharp ridges that run from their heads to the middles of their backs.

Nyxia stands before one of the creatures, hands framed on each side of its face as it nuzzles her. The queen's expression is delighted, as if she's playing not with a terrifying beast but a puppy. Lorelei leans against the side of the carriage, arms crossed, but straightens when she sees us.

When we meet, she pulls me into a hug. I'm surprised by the gesture—I never knew Lorelei was the hugging type—but I wrap my arms around her petite frame without hesitation. "Stay safe," she whispers.

We pull away, and her arms wrap around Foxglove next. Seeing their worried expressions as they embrace reminds me just how dangerous this journey is. Not only are we traveling to the human lands, we're going to Gren-neith, the capital city of Eisleigh. The most densely populated human location on the isle. There won't be familiar faces or childhood friends—neither of which I have reason to trust anyway.

My beloved mentor betrayed me.

What could strangers do?

When Foxglove and Lorelei separate, she eyes us each in turn. "Good luck with everything. I *will* see you again." She says the last part for me alone, then leaves toward the palace.

We turn to Nyxia, who is still showering affection on her creatures. Her gaze meets mine as we approach. She gives a final pat to the horse and kisses its bony nose. "Sylvia and Mernog are well-fed and ready for the journey. They'll make it to the Spire without needing to rest and they won't need to eat again until they return."

I'm about to ask what they eat, but I don't think I want to know the answer.

She continues. "If you need to stop for any reason, Franco will communicate with them. They listen to him almost as well as they listen to me."

Foxglove and I say the same thing in unison. "Prince Franco's coming?"

"But he's wounded." As soon as I say it, I know my argument is feeble. Four days is plenty of time for a fae to heal from such a wound.

"He's fine," Nyxia says. "He's fully healed as if nothing even happened. Besides, if you want to get to the Spire quickly, you'll have to take the moon mares. We don't employ any other carriage-drawing creatures in Lunar but them."

"And that has to do with the prince...how?"

Nyxia glares, making me immediately regret my tone.

However, the thought of Aspen and Franco together in one carriage...it gives me no small amount of trepidation.

Foxglove elbows me. "What she means is, for what reason do you give us the great honor of his presence? Surely such a task is beneath the sweet prince."

She gives a casual shrug. "Like I said, the moon mares listen to him."

I squint at her, wondering if there's more to this plot than she's letting on. Is she still hoping she can get me to take Franco as my mate?

Nyxia ignores my scrutiny. "Go on. My brother's already inside the carriage."

"What about Aspen? Has he come yet?" I ask, scanning the grounds.

"Why am I not surprised he's going too?" she says with a roll of her eyes. "I'll have someone fetch him."

Foxglove and I move toward the carriage, and I step inside first. Franco greets me with a warm smile. "Evelyn, I'm so pleased I get to be your chaperone once again. We had such a nice time before, did we not?" His grin is suggestive, making my pulse race. I look from the empty seat next to him to the unoccupied bench on the other side of the carriage.

"I'm grateful for your generous offer to accompany us," I say and take the bench across from him.

Foxglove's cheeks flush pink as he enters with an audible sigh. His expression is dreamy as he takes the seat next to me.

"Are you sure you're recovered enough for the journey?" I ask, giving the prince a pointed look.

Without warning, he lifts the hem of his shirt,

exposing far more flesh than necessary. "Not a scratch. You have a real healing gift."

I blush and look away from his lean stomach, while Foxglove emits an awkward giggle.

The carriage sways as a new figure enters. I meet Aspen's eyes before they shoot toward Prince Franco and the only empty seat at his side. "Why are you here?"

The prince gives Aspen a charming grin. "King Aspen, what a pleasurable journey this will be. Cramped, but pleasurable."

With a grumble, Aspen lowers himself into the seat, his antlers snagging the white silk roof above him. I look from one male to the other, noticing for the first time how much taller Aspen towers over the prince, and that's not including the extra height his antlers provide. Franco doesn't seem intimidated in the least, his eyes resting on me.

I feel Aspen's burning into me as well and avert my gaze to the window.

The carriage lurches and rolls into motion.

"King Aspen," Franco says, "I was just telling Miss Fairfield how grateful I am for her healing gifts. She has the gentlest yet most powerful hands."

Aspen lets out an irritated grunt while Foxglove erupts with another giggle.

I shake my head at the window and grit my teeth. This is going to be a very long ride.

27

The capital city of Grenneith is unlike any place I've been before. I watch out the carriage window as we roll over the cobblestone streets. Even though it's barely past daybreak, the streets are already busy with commotion. Towering factories clutter the skyline behind endless rows of merchant shops, townhouses, and elegant city manors. I gasp as I watch an automotive vehicle roar across the cobblestones like some mechanical beast. Such contraptions are far more common on the mainland, but even there they are considered a rare luxury.

Once the vehicle is out of sight, I study the people, their fine dresses and stylish suits, the way they carry themselves almost like royalty. My stomach takes a dive as I realize how out of place I feel. And it's more than just the fae carriage drawn by skeletal moon mares that makes me feel that way.

Luckily, no one seems to notice our passing as we make our way down the bustling streets.

"Are we beneath a glamour?" My voice cuts through the silence that's fallen since we entered the city. The mood has gone from tense to frightened.

"We are," Franco says, brow furrowed as he stares out the window. After a while he meets my gaze, his face pale and tinged with green. "I've never been in a human city before. There's a lot of iron."

"Not even I have been in such a place as this," Foxglove says, covering his nose with his hand. "I think I might faint."

"We're only here until tomorrow," Aspen says, stoic as ever. He doesn't so much as glance out the window, as if our surroundings are far beneath his care. "We'll manage."

Our eyes lock, and his expression softens, but we don't exchange a word. We've hardly spoken to each other at all during the entire journey. With so much left unsaid after our last conversation, it's hard to believe any words could suffice.

I move away from the window and settle back into my seat. The deeper we move into the city, the faster and faster my heart races. "What's the plan now that we're here?"

"We'll need to find somewhere to stay the night," Foxglove says. "Beneath a glamour, of course. Then I'll act as your ambassador and go to the Spire to sort out all the details for your mother's trial. All communication I've exchanged so far has assured me trials at the Spire begin at noon. However, if there are any others scheduled for tomorrow, your mother's may not be the first."

I inhale deeply to steady my nerves. "Will I be able to

see my mother beforehand? I want to speak with her before the trial."

"It isn't safe to go anywhere near the Spire before the trial," Aspen says. "If anyone sees you, there's a good chance they'll lock you up."

"I'll take you," Franco says. "A raven can infiltrate many places. I should be able to orchestrate a visit with your mother without a hitch."

"You don't know that," Aspen says with a growl. "It could be more danger than it's worth."

"I think it's worth anything if it's the last time she sees her mother before the trial," Franco argues.

I look from Aspen to Franco, wishing they'd stop opposing each other at every opportunity. "I'll do what it takes," I say. "Even if I get caught and thrown into prison with her, I don't care. I want to see her tonight."

Franco leans forward and places a hand on my knee. "I'll make it happen."

Aspen clenches his jaw, eyes burning into Franco's hand until the prince pulls it back to his lap. "We'll all make it happen," Aspen says through his teeth, "if you're so keen to squander your last night of freedom."

My last night of freedom. Considering the chances of my plan's success are slim to none, he very well might be right.

~

WE FIND A DECENT HOTEL ON THE OUTSKIRTS OF THE CITY, far enough away from the bulk of the crowds yet not too far from the Spire. Foxglove covers me with a mild glamour to help me blend in better with the other humans—I'm assuming that means he's made my clothing look a little less fae—and my three male companions don their own. I, of course, can't see the effects of their glamours, but the looks we receive as we enter the hotel are ones of curiosity, not terror.

We each get a room of our own, which I'm grateful for. Part of me expected I'd be forced to share a room and be put in a position to choose my sleeping companion. At this point, I most likely would have chosen Foxglove over the two other males. I still can't get over Aspen's odd behavior in my room before we left. It infuriates me each time I recall how he nearly reached for me before snatching his hand back, as if he couldn't bear to touch me.

If it isn't blame over his mother's death that has him acting in such a way, then is it truly my kiss with Franco? Surely such a misunderstanding isn't worth this level of disgust on his part. It's not like I thought I'd ever see my mate again. In fact, I thought he was married when I kissed Franco. *Married*, for the love of iron.

I pace inside my tiny room at the hotel, teeth clenched. Now that I'm alone, I can let out my irritation, although it doesn't really get me anywhere. It provides no answers. All I know is before Mother's trial, I will force Aspen to speak to me, even if it ends with a fight. Maybe a fight would do me good. A fight. A fiery kiss. A final night of reckless passion before I meet my fate.

My fate.

The thought sobers me quickly, and I sit on the narrow yet well-made bed, shoulders slumped with sudden fatigue. The daunting task ahead sets my head spinning. My eyes dart to the single window in the room, one which showcases a view of the sprawling city and smokestacks reaching high into the sky, puffing black smoke.

To the right of my view stands a tall, stone building, its central tower reaching dozens of floors high. The Spire. I remember learning it's one of the oldest architectural structures in Eisleigh, built as a castle when humans first settled here. Considering its ability to withstand not only the war with the fae but the tests of time, it's no surprise the building has been converted into a prison. From what I know, the top of the tower hosts the prison cells, while the bottom floor houses the courtrooms. My eyes lock on the highest point of the tower, wishing I knew how my mother fared.

Foxglove has already left for the Spire. Soon he will gather all the information we need. Her courtroom location, her trial time. Meanwhile, Franco will fly to the tallest portion of the building and find my mother.

Then tonight, we infiltrate the prison.

28

Night covers the city streets in a blanket of shadows as we reach the Spire. The bustle of Grenneith has been laid to rest for the evening, save for the occasional shouts of merriment floating on the air from the nearby taverns.

Aspen stalks close to my side while Prince Franco flies overhead in raven form. When we reach the side of the building, Foxglove steps out of the shadows and greets us.

"Everything has been settled," he says, although the wringing of his hands doesn't make me feel too confident in his words.

I raise a brow. "Is there anything I should be worried about?"

He sighs. "What's not to worry about? The iron in this building is making me feel like I'll melt into a puddle at any moment."

I'm reminded of how difficult it must be for my companions to be here. Although, Franco seems to have recovered at least partially from his initial response to our arrival. You'd never guess by the smooth motions of his wings that he or his magic was suffering from the city's ill effects. Aspen too seems to be managing well. It makes me wonder about the power of the two royals compared to fae like Foxglove or Lorelei. Perhaps the stronger fae are less impacted by being so far from the faewall.

"What are the details?" Aspen asks.

"Maven Fairfield's trial is set for noon tomorrow, the first trial of the day. I was given the location of the courtroom as well. We'll be able to arrive promptly before it begins."

"And my mother?" I ask. "Where is she now?"

The black raven begins his descent in slow circles until Prince Franco materializes next to me. He rocks unsteadily on his feet before he catches his bearings. "This place is the worst. I never get dizzy from flying."

"Where's Evie's mother?" Aspen asks, a hint of irritation in his tone.

"Cell block four, room seven," the prince says. "She's the only prisoner on that floor and the guards make their rounds on the hour. Once the clock strikes eleven, we'll wait ten minutes before I fly Evelyn up to the cell block. We'll be out again before midnight."

Aspen tenses next to me, while I remain struck by something he said. "What do you mean by *fly me up*?" I ask.

"I'll shift into my winged form, but only partially so I maintain my size. Then I'll carry you up and fly you through the window in the hall outside the cell block. The windows are old and glassless in the tower hall."

"You're going to fly. With me. In your...arms."

"That's reckless," Aspen says, taking a forbidding step toward Franco.

Franco meets his glare with a nonchalant grin. "I've never dropped anyone yet."

"There must be another way inside."

Franco points to the top of the Spire. "You mean, up through the central tower of the building, past several cell blocks, and nothing but a hope that we bypass the guards without notice?"

"What about an invisibility glamour?" I ask.

His eyes widen. "Invisibility glamours are hard enough in Faerwyvae. I can't maintain one over the both of us in a building filled with iron."

Aspen throws his hands in the air. "Oh, but you can maintain your winged form no problem."

Franco takes a challenging step toward Aspen. "Shifting is in my blood. I don't have to use much magic to do it. Even you know that, Stag King."

Aspen looks like he's on the verge of showing the prince exactly what he knows about shifting, but instead, he clenches his jaw and faces me. "It's your choice, Evie. I know you want to see your mother, but I'd rather you didn't risk your life with *him*," he tosses the prince a scowl, "as your only lifeline."

When his eyes return to mine, I see the concern in them, rendering me speechless. Just then, chimes sound from the city center, and I don't need to count to know there are eleven. Once the echo recedes, I square my shoulders with resolve. "I'm willing to take the risk."

At that, Franco shudders and spouts a pair of enormous black wings from his back. A few stray feathers protrude from his neck and shoulders, but the rest of him remains unchanged. He winks and extends his arm. "Let's do this."

"You said you'd wait ten minutes," Aspen growls.

"Yes, but I'm not going to wait *here*. We need to get deeper into the shadows before someone spots us."

Aspen's jaw shifts side to side. "Fine. I'll keep watch here and make sure no one heads your way."

Foxglove wrings his hands. "I suppose I should stand guard around the front of the building."

Aspen nods, then leans against the building's wall, arms crossed over his chest, but his gaze remains on me. My eyes are glued to his for several breaths until I force myself to take Franco's arm.

We round the back of the building and wait beneath the boughs of a well-manicured tree, my pulse racing with every minute that passes. Finally, Franco leans in and whispers, "It's time."

I let out a shaking breath and Franco pulls me close, wrapping his arms around my waist. I don't look at him as I put my arms around his neck.

"Ready?"

I nod.

We launch into the sky, Franco's enormous wings beating at the cool night air. I suppress a shout as we rise higher and higher, shutting my eyes against the ground falling farther beneath me. My stomach dips in a way that makes me fear I might be sick.

It only takes a few seconds for us to gain enough height before I feel our weight tip to the side. Franco tucks his wings around us, and I open my eyes to see us dart through a window and into a long, narrow hall. With a lurch, he brings us to a skidding halt, just in time to avoid smashing us into the wall at the other side.

"I'm glad that worked," he whispers while I put a hand to my spinning forehead.

Franco nods toward an unmarked door. We enter it into a dim room lined with cells. Musty aromas of dirt and unwashed bodies flood my nostrils, but like Franco said, there's only one prisoner on this cell block.

Franco gives my hand a squeeze. "I'll stand guard outside the door."

Once alone, I make my way to the occupied cell to find my mother sleeping on a cot. Like Mr. Duveau promised, she seems to have been given decent amenities. Trays of half-eaten food and a cup of tea rest on a simple table, while Mother's sleeping form is draped in thick wool blankets.

A sudden presence at my side makes me jump. Aspen stands next to me, and it takes me a moment to understand how that could be. He's only here through the Bond, his violet aura rippling around him. "I'm not going to leave you alone," he says, his voice a casual drawl. However, his expression betrays the true concern that his tone tries to mask.

"I thought you wanted to stand guard?" I whisper.

"I'm getting better at doing...whatever this is. I can sort of see both places at once now. This way, I can actually warn you if I notice anything concerning from my vantage on the ground."

I nod, his nearness a steadying comfort. It's almost enough to help me forget the strain of the last few days.

His eyes flash from me to Mother. "I'll give you your

privacy." He hesitates as if he wants to say more but makes his way to stand by the door.

I return my attention to my mother and press myself close to the bars. "Ma."

She stirs, blinking at me with a furrowed brow before she springs to her feet. "Evelyn! You're all right."

I can't stop the tears that flow as she approaches the bars. It breaks my heart to have bars between us, twice now, but knowing she'll soon be free serves as a minor comfort. In a matter of hours, she'll be out of here.

Then one of three options will prevail: we'll either be allowed to return to Faerwyvae, exiled, or...dead.

"You really came back," she says. There's a note of disappointment in her tone. "Part of me hoped you wouldn't. That you'd return to Faerwyvae and never look back."

"You know I couldn't abandon you to be executed."

She sighs. "I know." Her eyes leave my face to look around me. "Where is your sister?"

My lower lip trembles at the hope in her eyes. A hope I'll have to crush either with truth or a lie. I think it's time she knows the truth. She'll find out tomorrow regardless.

"Amelie isn't coming."

Her eyes widen for a moment. "Why? Did she choose freedom...or is it something else?"

I grip the bars of the cell to stop my hands from shaking. "Shortly after we arrived in Autumn, Amelie bargained her name to a fae male in exchange for his love. I don't know if she refused to attend because he forced her to do so, or if..."

"Or if it was her choice." Tears glaze Mother's eyes. "Either way, it doesn't matter, I suppose."

"No, I suppose not. The fact remains that she's not coming, and Mr. Duveau will use that as means to execute us both."

She puts a hand to her heart, but I reach through the bars to grab the other.

"I'm not going to let that happen."

Her eyes widen with surprise. "What are you going to do?"

I glance at Aspen from the corner of my eye, wondering if he can hear us from where he stands. "Whatever it takes."

She lifts her chin. "That's the fire I wanted to see in you."

Her look of pride fills me with a greater sense of accomplishment than I've ever felt—greater than Mr. Meeks' praise or any compliment I've ever received regarding my intellect. In this moment, my mother sees me for who I am, and I finally understand that she's seen it all along. I was the one who never saw it. I was the one who refused to acknowledge the truth.

In what may be one of the final hours of our lives, we understand each other. It makes my heart ache, wishing she'd been honest with me and Amelie from the start. Would that have changed anything?

It's too late to wonder.

"Do you think she's happy?" Mother asks. "Was the love she bargained for worth it?"

Again, I debate truth or lie. "I'm not sure, Ma. I wouldn't say the cost was worth the kind of love she got in return, but only she knows for sure. And she won't speak to me. I don't think...I don't think she's the same

Amelie she used to be. I think the bargain and the Bond changed her."

Mother nods, face drooping with sorrow as her gaze falls to the floor. Then her eyes snap back to mine. "What about you? Were you happy in Faerwyvae? Or did you despise it as much as you thought you would?"

I'm taken aback by her question. This, at least, I can be truly honest about. "I hated it at first, but after a while, I came to find...something very unexpected."

Her expression brightens, lips pulling into the ghost of a smile. "And the fae you were forced to be with? Did he treat you well?"

I can feel Aspen's eyes burning into me from across the room, perhaps more so due to his presence through our Bond. Part of me wants to keep my lips pressed tight on this matter just to spite him, but there's a truth I can't keep hidden. Mother deserves to know. Maybe Aspen does too. "He was that unexpected thing."

Tears glaze her eyes, and her voice comes out with a croak. "Did you find happiness with him?"

A lump rises in my throat, and for several moments I'm paralyzed, still wondering if Aspen is paying as close attention as I imagine he is. My words don't seem to come, so all I give her is a subtle nod.

"Love?"

The word destroys me, crumbling my walls, dousing the anger that I've kept burning between me and my mate, the only thing that has prevented me from falling apart over the strain between us. My expression plummets, which seems to be answer enough for Mother. She reaches her arms around me and pulls me close. Even with the bars between us, we find a way to embrace, and I let myself cry. I cry for the words I never got to tell Aspen, words I still might not get to say. I cry for my uncertain future, for my mother's precarious fate.

Mother's hands smooth my hair, her soft voice hushing my tears. After a while, I manage to regain my composure, although I can't bring myself to let go of my mother.

"What's it like?" she asks in a whisper.

I pull away enough to see her face. "What do you mean?"

Her tone takes on an air of wistful wonder. "Faerwyvae."

It suddenly dawns on me that after all this time she's been alive, coming and going from the isle to the mainland and back again, she's never been beyond the wall. She has no idea what the different courts are like, what it feels like to travel through different seasons and climates. She's never seen the vibrant orange leaves of Autumn or the moon and stars the way they look in Lunar.

So I tell her.

29

Mother's lips curl into a smile of contentment as I express the delights and terrors of Faerwyvae. I tell her about the puca, the kelpie, and the Twelfth Court. I relay my experiences with honey pyrus and fae wine, describe the fae food and dresses. I'm so immersed in my stories that I lose track of time.

It isn't until I hear a noise in the hall that I begin to wonder how near we are to the next hour, the next round the guards will make. I look toward the door, surprised when I find no sign of Aspen. When did he leave? I could have sworn I felt his presence during most of my conversation with my mother. Perhaps some of what I said made him uncomfortable. Maybe he didn't like the feelings I implied I still have for him.

I frown at the door before I turn back toward my mother. With a jump, I find Aspen materializing next to her, my name on his lips.

"What—"

"Someone's coming," he says. "Foxglove saw several

figures enter the front of the building. He says one is a man named Henry Duveau."

Aspen disappears as suddenly as he came, leaving me reeling over what the councilman's presence means. He's here? This late? It's almost midnight!

The door swings open to reveal Franco charging forward. "We have to go. Now."

Mother's eyes widen as they take in the fae prince. I cling to Mother's hands, words pouring from my lips. I don't know why I feel compelled to say them now, but I do. "I hope you know how much I love you. I'm sorry for every grief I caused. I'm sorry I never listened to you. I'm sorry I didn't respect you and your craft. I'm sorry I rebelled."

"Evelyn, we must hurry." Franco circles his arms around my waist, but I cling tighter to Mother's hands.

"I'm not sorry," she says, smiling through a sheen of tears. "Your rebellion taught you independence. It taught you about fire before you even realized it."

She swims inside my vision as tears flood my eyes. Franco gives me another tug, and this time, I let him pull me away. "I love you," I shout. "I'll see you tomorrow."

I hardly hear her echo the sentiment before we speed out of the room and into the hall. We race to the far side, and Franco grips me tighter. He takes off, sprinting us toward the window. I see guards racing up a set of stairs before he jumps out the window with me pressed close. We fall for endless seconds and I'm sure it will be to our doom. Then I hear Franco's wings beating the air, and our momentum shifts.

My heart hammers in my chest as I cling to Franco, the Spire shrinking as he flies us away from it. The city clock strikes midnight, and we stop in the shadows of an alley several blocks from the Spire. If it's the same place we agreed to meet earlier in the case that anything went wrong, then we're between a milliner and a baker. I can almost smell the remnants of stale bread in the dumpster nearby.

Franco sets me on my feet, and I lean against the alley wall, head spinning as I gather my bearings. I'm not even worried about rats or the overflowing canisters of garbage further down. All I can think about is filling my lungs with air. Slowing my pulse.

When I can finally form a coherent word, I ask, "What happened? Why did the guards make their rounds so early?"

He shakes his head. "I don't know. I watched them for most of the afternoon today. Not a single round was made before the hour, and no guards came outside these scheduled rounds aside from delivering meals or to escort prisoners to their trials. Neither of those occurrences should be happening this late."

I can't help wondering if it had anything to do with the presence of Henry Duveau. "Did anything else happen?"

"Nothing that I saw."

A dark silhouette enters the mouth of the alley, but I know at once that it's Aspen. He rushes to me, hands framing my face. I'm surprised by his touch, and he seems to think twice about it as well. He straightens, pinning his arms to his sides, but remains close. "You're all right."

"Do you know what happened?"

"No, but Foxglove had me worried. He seemed to

think the presence of the man he saw was something to be concerned about."

"It might be worth some distress," I say. "The guards made their rounds too early. They may have seen us escaping before we fled."

"At least you're safe."

My eyes lock on Aspen's, the words I said to my mother about him ringing in my mind. Did he understand what I hinted at? What my tears meant to convey to her? Who knows what he actually heard. How long he was there.

Franco clears his throat. "I'm going to fly back and see if I can figure out what triggered the guards. Wait here. I'll let you know if there's anything we should be concerned with."

"Good idea," Aspen says.

The prince shifts into his full raven form and flies off, leaving me alone with Aspen. I avert my gaze away from his face. "Is Foxglove all right?" I ask.

He nods. "He took a different way back to the hotel. I told him I wanted to find you first."

"I'm worried," I say. "Mr. Duveau is the councilman who holds the Legacy Bond with my family's names. He's not a good man."

"Do you think he'll hurt her?"

I shrug. "He made me a bargain that I could do whatever I wished before her trial, so long as I vowed to attend. He promised he wouldn't hurt her in the meantime."

Silence falls between us, and with it, the energy between me and Aspen hums like it did in my room. His posture stiffens, fingers twitching and closing into fists.

When he speaks, his voice is quiet. Strained. "Did you mean what you said to her?"

My eyes flash to his, breath hitching. "About what?"

"Finding happiness with me."

I swallow the lump in my throat and give him a hesitant nod. "Does that bother you?"

His brow furrows, a pained expression. "Why would it bother me?"

A blush of anger rises inside me, heating my cheeks. I'm so tired of this discomfort, this divide between us. "I don't know, Aspen, why would it? Why do you seek to protect me, take comfort in my safety, then act revolted whenever you're alone with me?"

"I'm not revolted."

"Then what is it? Why do you keep doing that?" I point to his trembling fists.

His words come through his teeth. "I can't stand to be around you because it feels impossible to do so without having you in my arms."

I study his face, reconciling his words with his posture, his tense shoulders. "And that's a bad thing?"

"Yes, it's a bad thing when the effort to keep away from you feels like a blade in my chest."

A thousand questions pound through my mind. *Why do you want to keep away from me? Why am I causing you so much pain? Why do you sound like you want me, yet act as if you despise me?* But no words make it to my lips. Nothing comes but tears and tremors as I try to gather my thoughts into something coherent.

Aspen closes his eyes and lets out a sigh. With it goes some of his rigidity. "It's a bad thing when this is your last night here."

I almost argue, almost reveal my plan. My fear over its improbability keeps my lips pressed tight.

Aspen continues, voice breaking. "It's a bad thing when I'm not sure if there's someone else you'd rather be with."

A tear rolls down my cheek, and I hardly know why I'm crying. My words come out a breathless whisper. "There's no one else."

His jaw shifts. "No one? No one you'd rather spend your final moments on the isle with?"

My flash of anger ignites again, and I take a step toward him. "No, Aspen, there's no one else. There's never been anyone else and there will never be anyone else."

His expression flickers with a hint of vulnerability. "Not even the Lunar Prince?"

Irritation sends another wash of ferocity through me. "No. How can you ask me that?"

"You kissed him," he says through his teeth. "I saw the two of you together. Then I saw how you bargained for his life, trading every last chance of your freedom for him. I watched you run to him when he was injured like he was the only person left in the world. Then you brought him here."

"I didn't choose for him to come here," I say. "Nyxia did. But he has every right to be here because he's my friend. When I bargained for his life, I did it because it was the right thing to do. I treated his injuries with care because he was my patient."

"And the kiss?"

Guilt seizes me, and I have the overwhelming urge to defend myself, to tell him all the misconceptions and mistakes that led to that moment. I want to beg for his forgiveness, to convince him how badly I wanted that kiss to have been with him. But there's a calm warmth beneath my guilt, something that feels far truer. "Yes, Aspen, I kissed Prince Franco. I kissed him because in that moment and in that situation, I wanted to."

His eyes narrow, but I refuse to shrink beneath that look.

I continue, fighting the quaver in my voice. "I thought you were married. Even though I made you promise me you'd do it, it crushed me. Killed me inside. The fact that I found the will to smile or dance or kiss anyone that night is a miracle. I can't regret that I managed to find joy on your wedding night, even if it hurt us both in the end. Regret doesn't change what happened, and the truth is, I don't owe you an explanation. The same way you wouldn't owe me an explanation if you'd gone through with marrying Maddie Coleman. We aren't each other's property."

"Is that how you see me?" he growls. "As someone who wants to own you?"

"No, and that's exactly why I'm not going to debase myself before you. I've never wanted to be another male's property, nor have I wanted someone else to be mine. You and I have made our choices in the past, but our relationship—if we have one—is in the present. I'm sorry things haven't felt right between us since I used your name against you, but I can't apologize for the snippets of peace I've found between then and now, even the ones I found with another male when I thought we were over."

My truth sizzles between us, and the hard look on his

face makes me wonder if I should have gone with my first instinct to beg. *No,* I tell myself. *I do not beg for love.*

Finally, he takes a step closer to me, his chest a mere inch from mine. Even beneath the pale moonlight, I can see the full color of his eyes, the browns, rubies, emeralds, and golds. "You're terrible at apologies," he says.

"I know. That I'm very sorry for."

His lips pull into a tentative grin and the sight of it fills me with more comfort than I think I've ever felt. He lifts a hand to the side of my face, and this time he doesn't snatch it back. With trembling fingers, he brushes a strand of hair away from my forehead as he stares deep into my eyes. The gesture is gentler and more heartwarming than any kiss could be in this moment. But a kiss is what I yearn for. My lips tingle with their craving as my gaze falls to his full mouth.

"The day you left Bircharbor, you wouldn't let me hold you," he says. "You pulled away from me when I asked for more time together. Do you still feel the same? Or will you allow me this before the end?"

Another truth is on my lips. One I've been fighting not to tell him for days. Do I dare give him hope? Give *us* hope? "This might not be the end."

His eyes widen. "What do you mean?"

I open my mouth, but I don't want to talk. I just want to feel his lips on mine already. My fingers reach for the collar of his shirt, and I pull him down to me. He pushes me against the alley wall as a furious passion unleashes between us. We gasp for air as our lips lock together. His tongue brushes mine with tangible need, each stroke a plea for more. My hands twine in his hair while his move to my lower back, my hips. I arch against him, needing more of his warmth, his strength.

"I don't mean to interrupt," a voice calls overhead. Aspen and I pull away, breathless, to find Prince Franco perched on the roof of the bakery.

"What?" Aspen growls.

"I have bad news. The trial is happening now."

30

I furrow my brow, staring up at the prince. "What do you mean the trial is happening now? How is that possible?"

"I don't know," Franco says, "but I watched the guards escort your mother down from the prison to a courtroom."

"But it's midnight. Her trial isn't supposed to be until noon."

He shrugs. "You'll have to tell them that. The trial has already begun."

My heart pounds in my chest as my mouth goes dry. All the pleasant feelings conjured by my kiss with Aspen have evaporated.

"Take her," Aspen says. "Take Evelyn and fly her back to the Spire at once."

The prince leaps from the roof of the bakery and lands in a crouch with surprising ease. His wings spout from his back as he rights himself and extends his hand.

I reach to accept but hesitate for a moment. There's

still so much left unsaid between me and Aspen. So much I wanted to tell him before the trial. "Aspen—"

"I'll be there," he whispers. "I'll be with you the entire time. Now go. Hurry."

With a nod, I allow Franco to pull me close. In a matter of seconds, we're high above the alley and flying toward the Spire.

When we land, we dart toward the front doors of the building. "I know where the courtroom is," Franco says. I pull open the doors. The lobby of the Spire is quiet and empty, with not a soul in sight. Franco shifts fully into a raven and darts down one of the halls. My feet fly beneath me as I follow, pulse pounding with every step.

He stops outside a closed door, then circles in the air in front of it, cawing wildly. I push it open and find a courtroom in full session. On one side of the room sits a gathering of men in black robes. Jurors, I can only assume. On the other side are men in black suits. I recognize one as Mayor Coleman. These must be the men of Eisleigh's council.

At the center of the room stands Henry Duveau, outfitted in a black robe like the jurors wear, but upon his head rests a black cap. A judge's cap.

He's the judge? Fury sparks within me, but only for a moment. My attention is quickly diverted to what's behind him—my mother.

Flanked by several guards, her arms are extended to each side of her, wrists strapped in iron cuffs which are secured to two marble columns. The lower half of her is submerged in an iron tub of water. By the way she shivers and the blue tinge of her skin, I can only assume the water is ice-cold.

A black shape swoops past me—Franco—then disappears high in the rafters overhead. The confused jury and councilmen stare from the raven then back to me.

Mr. Duveau greets me with a cold smile. "Miss Fairfield, how good of you to attend."

I stride into the courtroom, each step echoing on the marble floor beneath my feet, pounding in a fraction of my heart's racing tempo. "What is the meaning of this? My mother's trial was scheduled for noon."

Mr. Duveau seems unaffected by my rage. "We have every right to change times of trials."

"And when were you going to inform me?"

"You were given the proper notice as required by law. We sent a message to the hotel the Autumn ambassador said you'd be staying at when he came to inquire earlier on your behalf. If you weren't there to get the message, then perhaps you should have stayed put." His last words are punctuated with venom.

I grit my teeth. It's impossible not to suspect this was part of the ultimate plan all along. No wonder the guards came when they did. They weren't alerted of our infiltration; they were coming to take Mother to her trial. All to make it difficult for me to meet the terms of the bargain and serve King Ustrin's whims.

"It comes down to the fact that you're late," Mr. Duveau says. "You were supposed to attend Maven Fairfield's trial, otherwise her sentence—and yours, mind you—would be execution."

I lift my chin. "The bargain never stated I had to attend from the start of the trial. I'm here now. Her trial is still in session, is it not?"

The councilman narrows his eyes, a tick at the corner

of his jaw. "Very well. We will allow you to be present for the remainder of her trial. Have a seat." He extends his arm to an empty chair next to my mother. One with iron cuffs on the arms and legs.

With trembling steps, I make my way to the chair, bristling as I sense Mr. Duveau following in my wake. Once seated, the councilman closes the cuffs around my wrists and ankles, then returns to the middle of the floor. I try not to recall the last time I was locked up this way, ending in fire and smoke and blood. My eyes find Mother's, and I force a smile. She forces one in turn, but it's nothing more than a flick of her lips as she continues to convulse from the chilled water.

"To catch you up to speed, Miss Fairfield," Mr. Duveau says, "the council has presented their evidence of your mother's treason and the jury has determined her guilt."

I toss him a glare, although the ruling doesn't come as a surprise.

"I'm going to tear out his throat." A gravelly voice comes from beside me, and I turn my head to find Aspen has materialized, violet aura shimmering as his eyes burn into Mr. Duveau. I say nothing, not wanting to look like I'm talking to an invisible specter before the council and jury.

Mr. Duveau's attention turns to the men. "Let us continue, shall we?"

A round of "Aye," is uttered from the jurors and councilmen.

"The punishment for Maven Fairfield's crime is exile," Mr. Duveau says. "However, that merciful punishment was only to be extended if Amelie and Evelyn Fairfield attended this trial and accepted their exile with her. Considering only one daughter is present today," he waves a hand toward me, "that mercy has been made void. Agreed?"

Another round of ayes.

"Then it can only be surmised that Maven Fairfield and her two daughters are sentenced to death. The two present will be executed immediately following the conclusion of this trial, and a bounty will be placed on Amelie Fairfield for her life to be claimed as soon as possible."

Mother and I exchange a glance, while Aspen lets out a roar only I can hear. A furious caw echoes from the rafters, eliciting gasps and mutters from the jury.

"All in favor—"

"Wait!" I shout. "You haven't given me permission to defend myself."

Mr. Duveau turns slowly on his heel, expression both haughty and amused. It's as if he'd been waiting for me to speak up. "I don't believe allowing you the chance to speak on this trial was part of our bargain."

"But it is my right," I say. "As a citizen, I have a right to defend myself."

He turns toward the jurors. They hesitate, exchanging whispers before the majority utters their agreement that I may speak.

"Very well," Mr. Duveau says, taking a few steps toward me. "What do you have to say for yourself?"

"I came here as requested. I did everything that was asked of me."

"I daresay you did that and more." The councilman narrows his eyes, expressing what he's left unspoken. He knows that I'm responsible for the fates of Mr. Meeks and Mr. Osterman. He knows I broke into the Spire and visited my mother.

I refuse to falter, forcing my posture straighter despite my bindings. "I did what I had control over, and even went so far as to try and ensure my sister's compliance. Her refusal to be present today should bear no weight on either my or my mother's fates."

I'm relieved to see a few nods coming from the jurors.

"So, you would like me to show you and your mother mercy and allow the two of you to go into exile?"

I could say yes. I could say it and this could all be over now. At this point, there's a chance he and the jury will allow us to leave. I almost give in and take the easy route. But there's another path, one I'm already resolved to try. Even if it kills me.

I take a deep breath. "I ask that you leave my sister out of your considerations regarding me and my mother, but I do not ask for our exile."

Gasps erupt from the room.

Mr. Duveau pins me with his cold stare. "Is it death you want then?"

"No," I say. My heart pounds as I deliver my next words. "A new bargain."

Nervous laughter emits from some of the men, but Mr. Duveau does not seem amused. "What kind of a bargain?"

For days I've rehearsed these words, memorized them. That doesn't make them any easier to say. "I want you to let my mother and me remain on the isle and return to Faerwyvae."

More gasps. Mayor Coleman rises from his seat,

expression twisted with malice. "You cannot be serious. The treaty states that any descendants of King Caleos are to be exiled. If we fail to do so, we will break the treaty. Is that what you want? Is this some fae trickery?"

I'm painfully aware of Aspen's eyes burning into me, expression full of shock and hope. I can't meet that hope with my own. Not yet.

Mr. Duveau waves a hand at Mayor Coleman, urging him back into his seat. He returns his attention to me. "Explain yourself, Miss Fairfield."

"I want to save the treaty just as much as anyone in this room," I say. "War is the last thing I want, both for the humans and the fae. I may be both, but as far as I'm concerned, I was human for far longer than I've been fae. I will always have the humans' best interests at the top of my priorities." I force myself not to look at Aspen, knowing I'll find hurt in his eyes if I do.

"How do your *priorities*," Mr. Duveau says the word mockingly, "prevent war when your very presence demands it?"

I dig my nails into the arm of the chair to keep my hands from shaking. "If you allow me to stay and claim the Fire Court throne, I will replace King Ustrin as ruler. From my position as Queen of Fire, I will represent the humans amongst the fae and ensure an ally for you in Faerwyvae. A *true* ally, not a bully with nothing but his crown to care for. Can King Ustrin offer you that? Or does he only offer threats and demands for your obedience? Wouldn't you rather ally yourselves with a true patriot of Eisleigh?"

The councilman takes a step closer. "Your words might be pretty, but they still do nothing to explain how you will claim the throne and stay on the isle without bringing war. Do you not comprehend this simple fact? You taking the throne will break the treaty."

His sentiment is echoed by the council and jury. I wait for their mutterings to subside before I speak again. "I have a solution to that. My taking the throne will not break the treaty, for you will amend it to allow me and any of King Caleos' descendants to stay. Every other term can remain intact. The threat of King Caleos has passed. His violence against humans does not run in my blood."

Mr. Duveau smirks. "Is that so?"

Heat rises to my cheeks, knowing I walked into that one all on my own. I steel my expression. "It is. However, I will defend my life and my honor if forced."

Mayor Coleman speaks again, words heavy with skepticism. "Let me get this straight, Miss Fairfield. You want us to amend the treaty before you so much as challenge King Ustrin? How can we trust you?"

"The fact that I didn't challenge him yet should show you exactly how much you can trust me. I know taking the throne would break the treaty and I'm not willing to do that. I'm not even asking you to change it right this moment. All I'm asking for is time to prove my allegiance and abilities. The treaty may say I must be exiled, but it doesn't say when. If you let me and my mother go today, you won't be breaking the treaty if we agree that you plan on exiling me at a future date. And that's only *if* I fail to prove myself."

"How will you prove yourself?" Mr. Duveau asks.

"I will do anything of reasonable means that supports the peace of the isle. Once I prove myself, only then will you change the treaty. After it is officially changed, I will defeat King Ustrin and claim the throne. I already have followers who support me." That last part is only partially true. Or perhaps it's a full lie. *There are followers I intend on convincing to support me,* would be more accurate. Lucky for me, I'm not full-fae. My lies go undetected.

"We should take a brief recess and then deliberate Miss Fairfield's offer," one of the jurors says.

A wave of hope rises inside me as several other jurors affirm their agreement. They're taking me seriously. They're—

"No." Mr. Duveau's voice silences the room. With slow steps, he approaches me. Once he's in front of my chair, he leans forward and lowers his voice. "You seem to forget something, Miss Fairfield. Changing the treaty to allow you to stay may keep most of the treaty intact, but it will sever the Legacy Bond. Why would I agree to that?"

My shoulders tremble with suppressed rage. "You would put your own love for power over the benefits I offer our people?"

"There's more to it," he says with a malicious grin. "I don't think you have what it takes to beat King Ustrin."

My words come between my gritted teeth. "Then give me a chance. Amend the treaty stating the changes go into effect only if I beat him."

"No," he says again. "The council will not accept. *I* will not accept. You have no right to ask in the first place. You have no right to defy me. You have no right to even beg. As a human, you are nothing but a Chosen, a sacrifice made for the good of the isle. As a fae, you are the illegal ancestor of a criminal."

Fire heats my palms, and it takes all the restraint I

have not to set the arm of my chair ablaze. "It's not for you to decide. The jury—"

"In matters of the treaty, I am the legal judge and executioner. My word is final."

All hope drains from me at once, and with it goes my fire.

He takes a step away, voice rising for all to hear. "Our original terms stand. You, your mother, and your sister were offered exile or execution. Your sister didn't come today, so the punishment is death."

Aspen shudders at my side, chest heaving. I can feel his anger, his helplessness at not truly being here in physical form.

Franco lets out several angry caws, while the jurors exchange furious whispers. The councilmen, on the other hand, seem perfectly composed.

It's over. Mr. Duveau will never let me stay. He's sentenced us to death. There's only one thing left to fight for.

31

"Please," I say, tears springing to my eyes. "Please reconsider. I told you, I tried to get my sister to come. Just...just let us leave the isle. At the very least, let my mother go free."

Mr. Duveau grins. "Oh, now you beg for my mercy? Now you ask me to allow you to take exile?"

Mother tries to speak, but all she can make is a pained moan.

I nod. "Please."

"I want to see you beg." The room returns to silence as Mr. Duveau takes a key from the pocket of his black robe. He places it inside a lock on the arm of my chair. With a turn, the cuffs at my wrists and ankles spring open. He steps back and motions me forward. "I want you to plead on your knees."

Mother's teeth chatter as she says my name, but I pay her no heed. With shaking steps, I rise from my chair and move toward the councilman.

"Don't dare try anything clever," he says, pulling his

robe to the side. A flash of silver catches my eyes. A revolver, like the one Sheriff Bronson had. I swallow hard. Since when do councilmen carry revolvers? "Iron bullets," he says with a smirk.

"Don't do this," Aspen says, voice thick with fury. "Do not beg from this monster. We'll find another way."

I ignore him as I lower to my knees and press my palms together. "Please show us mercy."

"Beg me to exile you."

"Please exile me and my mother." My words are flat, toneless.

The councilman responds with icy silence. "Perhaps I'll consider exiling your mother," he says. "You, however, will serve a different fate before you meet your exile. You made a good point about the treaty. I can exile you without sending you away right now."

I don't know what he's carrying on about, as all words have lost meaning.

He continues. "Before you take your exile, you will serve in the Briar House."

My eyes shoot to his.

"That is the only way I will agree to grant you freedom from execution."

My mouth is too dry to say a word, so I give him a jagged nod.

"Beg," Mr. Duveau says through his teeth. "Beg me to take you to the Briar House. Beg me to be your first patron."

Aspen darts toward the councilman, lips pulling back from his teeth as he roars in his face. Mr. Duveau, of course, can't see him, nor can he feel my mate's antlers making their futile attempts to tear into the man.

I open my mouth to do as told, but this time it's fury that holds me back. Anger builds in my core, snapping me out of my daze. I'm frozen, suspended between words that will condemn my mother and words that will destroy my honor.

An unexpected voice shatters the silence in the room. "You will not beg." Mother's words are said through chattering teeth, but they're stronger than I expected them to be. "You will not utter a single one of those words, Evelyn. You do not plead for this scum to defile you. This ends now. I will end my life myself before I see you on your knees before this filth a minute more."

Mr. Duveau shoots my mother a glare before turning his eyes back to me. "This is your last chance, Miss Fairfield. Beg now or die."

All I hear is my mother's words, her fire sparking with mine, creating an inferno in my heart. My mind becomes clear. My mother is right. I cannot grovel before this man, even if it's for my life or hers. I'm not merely a human Chosen or an illegal fae. I'm so much more. I'm a lover and a daughter and the descendant of a king. I am the Unseelie Queen of Fire.

I turn my head to meet my mother's gaze. Her eyes have grown clear, swimming with flames. We exchange no words, but a silent understanding passes between us. If this is the end, so be it. Mother gives me a subtle nod.

I rise to my feet on strong legs. "No."

"Seize them." Mr. Duveau's shout brings two guards toward me, while the others close in on Mother. A sudden blast of light halts all movement for a split second. I look toward Mother. Despite the icy water soaking her bottom half, fire erupts from her palms, melting the iron cuffs. She yanks them hard, and they break, releasing her. She presses a fiery palm to the chest of the nearest guard, and he shouts in pain.

"Maven Fairfield." My mother's name bursts from Mr. Duveau's lips, carrying the undeniable weight of magic. "Do not move."

To my horror, Mother freezes where she stands, and the guards wrest her arms behind her back. Mr. Duveau retrieves his revolver from beneath his robe and points it at her.

I look from him to Mother, then back again. That's when I remember my final weapon against the councilman. One I didn't want to use unless absolutely necessary.

"Henry Duveau." I say it with the same power I touched when I used Aspen's true name. I await the vision of the bridge, the cliffs, but it doesn't come. Only a flicker of a vast chasm obscured by fog. Perhaps the vision of the bridge is unique to me and Aspen. I refocus on the power of the councilman's name. "You will let my mother go. You will allow us to leave this trial unharmed and will not pursue us for as long as we live."

My eyes lock on Mr. Duveau's, his expression unreadable.

Then, to my horror, his lips pull into a wide grin. "Did you really think I've made my birth name public? Did you honestly believe *you* had the power of my true name?"

He pulls the trigger.

~

My world shatters at the sound of the gun firing, then narrows to the point of a bullet. All sound is hollow in my ears as I watch the bullet strike between my mother's eyes.

There's no moment of hope, no opportunity for Mother to fight against the iron that burrows into her forehead and ends her life.

A scream that is mine yet sounds so far away bursts from my chest as Mother's body topples into the tub, the water quickly running a bright shade of red.

I'm vaguely aware of a raven's caw as Mr. Duveau shields his head, shouting as a black beak seeks to peck out his eyes. A few of the guards leave my mother's lifeless form to charge the bird, while others close in on me.

Anger burns inside my heart, sharpening my mind. The raven shifts into Franco, but he's unlike any version of him I've ever seen. He's tall, lithe, cloaked in shadow, fangs lengthening in his terrifying maw as he intercepts the guards. The guards shrink back with horrified shouts, and I watch as shadows are leeched from them, being pulled in by the prince.

The councilmen and jurors begin to shout, clambering out of their seats.

Mr. Duveau stumbles back from the dark prince, and my eyes lock on him. Heat floods my palms as I pursue his retreat. When his attention meets mine, his composure stiffens. He turns the barrel of his gun on me. "Evelyn Fairfield."

I'm too enraged to fear that he's using my name. All I feel is fire and pain and a burning need for revenge.

"Don't move," Mr. Duveau says, the power of my name heavy in the command.

I freeze, hating the lack of control over my own motor functions. His fingers find the trigger, but before he can pull it, I say his name again. He may have kept his birth name secret, but the Legacy Bond means I should have power over it regardless. So this time, I seek the power of intent. *His true name, his true name.* I repeat it like a mantra, seeking it beneath the fog that blankets the chasm. There's still no bridge, but a thin rope-like tether connects us and is growing clearer by the second. I imagine his hands stiff and immobile, frozen like ice, unable to fire the gun.

The councilman's hand begins to shake, and I can see the effort it's taking him to try and pull the trigger. His gaze intensifies, and I feel his attention on my name. I still can't move, but neither can his trigger finger.

Sweat beads at my brow, but I maintain my focus, gripping that tether with everything inside me. From the corner of my eye, I see Franco still fighting with the guards, most of whom are cowering on the floor, convulsing wildly.

Mr. Duveau blinks a few times, his face growing red. Finally, a gasp escapes his lips and he lowers the gun. In that same moment, an enormous creature barrels between me and the councilman. My heart leaps into my throat. It's Aspen. The real Aspen, not the ethereal version of him that was here before.

In stag form, Aspen charges Mr. Duveau, antlers striking the man's midsection and sending him sprawling across the floor. I'm about to chase after him, my palms yearning to burn his flesh to a crisp, but Aspen steps between us. "Get on," he says.

Mr. Duveau struggles to rise, blood seeping from his

abdomen. Everything inside me wants to finish the job. To do to him what he did to my mother.

"Get on!" Aspen repeats, louder this time. That's when I see the flood of soldiers enter the room. Without a second thought, I pull myself on Aspen's back. He carries us toward the startled soldiers before they can react, swinging his antlers to clear our way. In seconds, we're racing out the front of the building, Aspen's hooves pounding the cobblestones.

"Get Foxglove and meet us at Lunar," Aspen says.

I know he must be talking to Franco, but I don't bother looking for the raven prince. All I see is blood and flames, my mother's lifeless body in a tub of crimson water. Sorrow threatens to unravel me, so I seek my anger instead. It burns easily, searing me from the inside.

I lose all sense of time as we race through the night, Aspen's stag mouth lathering as he carries us from city streets to the quiet forest. Even beneath the cover of trees, he neither slows nor rests. My anger refuses to slacken as well and only seems to grow with every minute, every hour that passes. The heat becomes tangible, uncomfortably warm as sweat drips from every inch of my skin. I'm only half-aware of the bright glow that emanates from my body.

Aspen's voice comes out strained. "Take it to the Twelfth Court."

I don't know what he means, nor can I find words to respond.

Instead, I burn, burn, burn.

32

My next coherent thought is a sudden awareness that I'm surrounded by water from the waist down.

As if waking from a dream, my mind grows sharper, my vision clearer. Up until this moment, all I saw was smoke and flames. Blood. My mother's corpse.

Fire threatens to consume me again, but the water seems to quell it, returning me to neutral.

I blink several times as I take in my surroundings. The domed ceiling overhead is familiar, as is the quality of moonlight streaming into the room and sending the surface of the water glittering.

I'm in the moon baths at the Lunar Court, half-submerged in one of the three pools.

Something soft brushes against my back, a soothing touch. I crane my neck to find Aspen behind me in the pool, a sponge of silky moon moss in his hands as he runs it over my shoulder. I wince, eyes roving to where the sponge made contact. All along my arms are bright patches of raw skin, surrounded by darker charred flesh. The sleeves of my shirt are nearly burned entirely off—or perhaps they were torn by Aspen in order to do what he's doing.

He dips the sponge in the water and returns it to my shoulder, letting the water trail down my arm. Each trickle of water and brush of the moss eases a pain that I'm only just growing aware of.

"What happened?" My throat feels raw, my words coming out hoarse.

"You were burning." His voice is quiet, gentle, although it carries a hint of strain.

"How long?" I'm barely able to finish the sentence as I choke on the last word. My lungs feel like they're filled with smoke.

"Hours. It's just before dawn at Lunar."

I'm surprised it's so quiet, considering this is when the palace is most active. "Where is everyone?"

"Queen Nyxia ordered the moon baths and the hall outside vacated when I brought you here."

"Why?" I wheeze. "Why are we here?"

"In Lunar, or in the bath?"

"Bath."

"Like I said, you were burning. You burned the entire way here."

That explains my scorched skin. I remember how I erupted with fire, how I burned relentlessly until I slipped out of awareness. If it took us several hours to get here, I must have been unconscious for most of the journey. "Why did my fire burn me?"

He dips the sponge in the water again, then trails it lightly over my burns, easing my wounds some more.

"Your powers got out of hand. Fae magic can hurt even its wielder if one knows not how to control it."

"Could it have killed me?"

"Your own fire can never kill you, but when allowed to consume you that way...it's debilitating."

I watch as he dips the moon moss again and returns it to my arm. "I thought water was harmful to fire."

"An attack by water, yes," he says. "However, your fire got out of balance. An opposing element can bring it back to healthy levels without harming you. It's helping you heal."

That much is obvious, but I thought perhaps it had more to do with the moon moss.

"These pools are more than just for daily cleansing," he explains. "They are constantly purified by the light of the moon and stars, charged with energy when the moon is full. This was the only place I could think to take you." His voice sounds pained, expressing an undercurrent of worry beneath his composure.

Aspen pauses, and I realize he's finished soothing my arm. In fact, he must have already tended the first arm, because both seem unmarred save for their deep pink hue. I turn to face him fully but freeze, startled by what I see. He wears no jacket, no waistcoat, and what remains of his shirt is nothing but charred tatters. His chest is covered with what looks like mild burns, and an angry red color marks his neck...as if...

I try to circle behind him, but he's faster. Not so fast that I don't glimpse a flash of red and black puckered skin. I gasp, tears springing to my eyes. "Aspen! Is that from me?"

"I'm fine," he says. "I'm already beginning to heal."

"But I...I did that."

"You didn't know."

"You carried me here on your back in stag form and I burnt you the entire time." This is the first time I've been forced to consider what features fae carry between forms. If even his clothing has been destroyed, then I can only imagine his stag fur and flesh burnt to a crisp.

My stomach churns and I reach for the sponge of moon moss. He lifts his hand over my head, snatching it out of my reach. "You aren't healed yet." His eyes flash over my torso, covered only by the remnants of my burnt blouse.

I try to stretch for the moss, but wince as the motion sears my side. Hoping he didn't notice, I say, "Let me tend to your wounds, damn you."

"No, Evie." His voice is firm yet gentle. "For once in your life, let someone else put your wellbeing above their own."

His expression has me swallowing all argument. Instead, I offer a compromise. "We'll take care of each other then."

He releases a sigh. "Fine."

I glance again at my chest, then start to undo the buttons. Aspen averts his gaze, shifting from foot to foot. It reminds me of how awkward he was before our conversation in the alley. Before our kiss. I hope what's happened since then hasn't pushed us a step back again.

What's happened since. Flames and smoke fill my mind, and the image of my mother falling from an iron bullet. Sorrow washes over me, threatening to drag me into a black void of endless grief. The feeling is so terrifying, I reach for my quickest defense—my fire. Anger ignites, but instead of fueling me, it increases the sharpness of my wounds. I cry out in pain, my legs collapsing beneath me.

Aspen catches me before my head goes beneath the surface of the water. He pulls me close, hand on my cheek as he tilts my head toward his. "Just focus on me right now."

I breathe away my pain, my anger, and focus on his face, the color of his eyes, the angle of his jaw. Facts. Shapes. Logic. It settles me.

"There will be time to grieve and rage after your body is healed," he says.

Once the strength returns to my legs, I pull away from him, but only slightly. This time, he reaches for the buttons of my blouse himself. I shudder as the fabric falls away, then I reach down to slip off my tattered trousers. He brings the moon moss toward me, but I shake my head. "You too."

With a grumble, he allows me to pull the scorched linen off his chest, separate it from the burns on his back. My stomach roils as I examine the full extent of the damage I've caused.

Freed from our clothing, I finally allow Aspen to tend to the burns on my torso. I keep my eyes locked on his, emptying my mind of the terrors that lurk behind every thought, every breath. When all traces of stinging pain leave my chest, Aspen hands me the moss and turns his back to me.

I have to extend my arms to reach the top of his shoulders, but I'm relieved to see the immediate effects of the moss and water taking place. His skin seems to repair even faster than mine, which I'm assuming must have to do with his heritage. Being the son of Queen Melusine gives him an advantage over the water element.

I watch as the charred skin falls away, revealing new pink skin in its place. His golden coloring has yet to emerge, but his healing is promising. Blisters shrink and dissolve, returning the smooth planes of his back, the strong angles of his shoulder blades. A tender feeling stirs inside me, breaking through the chaos that I'm somehow able to keep at bay. Even after Aspen's skin has fully healed, I linger over him, letting my hands trail up and down his back as I study the curve of his spine, the muscles in his arms and shoulders. The silence of our bated breaths speaks louder than any words we can say.

Aspen shudders at my final touch before turning to face me, hand moving to the back of my neck. With gentle fingers, he pulls my damp hair over one shoulder, a wordless signal for me to turn around. As I do, he takes the moss and brings it to my back. With my pains nearly gone, every touch feels like a welcome caress.

My mind begins to wander to the dangerous territory of blood and fire, and I quickly force myself to focus on Aspen's touch. But a memory remains, one neutral enough for me to consider without much harm. I break the silence around us. "When I was burning, I remember you telling me to take it to the Twelfth Court. What did you mean by that?"

Aspen runs the moss over the back of my neck, my upper shoulders. "If you'd taken your rage to the Twelfth Court, you would have been able to more evenly distribute your fire, use it for transformative purposes."

His words do nothing to clear my confusion. "What does that mean?"

"That's how the fae shift into our unseelie forms. It's one way, at least. Most of us can shift at will, but strong emotion or an overuse of our power can shift us without effort. Sometimes, that can be detrimental, but in your case, I think it would have helped."

"You really think I could have...shifted forms?"

"I'm not sure, but I think so."

"How would it have helped? Would I not have felt the same rage?"

"You would have been more in control of it on an instinctual level," Aspen says. "You would have used most of your excess fire in the act of physically shifting. It takes magic to shift forms, and you had a dangerous amount to spare."

I furrow my brow, pondering Aspen's words. Nyxia hadn't told me this when I relayed my doubts about having the ability to shift. From how he describes it, it makes a sort of logical sense.

If magic and logic can ever coexist, that is.

The realization serves to relieve some of the darkness hanging over me. However, there's still so much I know I need to face. That rage I felt on the journey here hasn't diminished. The water is merely keeping it dormant. But now I'm starting to see how I can utilize it in a logical manner. Pieces of a puzzle fall into place before me, and only a blush of anger comes with it.

I return my attention to the feel of Aspen's fingers, the silky moss against my now-soothed skin. Turning my head slightly to the side, I catch Aspen's eyes from my periphery. "You were right," I say.

He pauses his ministrations, then runs the moss down my spine. "About what?"

"The treaty being a broken thing not worth saving. You were right all along."

"I don't revel in being right about this. I never wanted any of that to happen."

I turn to fully face him, shutting out violent images in my mind and replacing them with firm, rational facts. "It has to end," I say. "The treaty, the Reaping, and both councils. I have to take the throne from King Ustrin."

His jaw shifts back and forth, and I remember how little he knows about the plan I tried to enact. "How long were you planning to do what you did at the trial?"

Again, I have to skirt around my pain to seek the facts. "A few days. I'm sorry I didn't tell you. Things were strange between us and I...I couldn't bear the pressure of your hope or mine."

He releases the moss, letting it float away on the surface of the water. "I wish you would have told me. I could have supported you better, long before the trial."

I shake my head. "I can't deal with regrets right now. All I can focus on is what to do next."

He brings a hand to my cheek, moving closer to me until my breasts are a breath away from brushing his chest. I ache to pull him against me as his thumb caresses my jawline. "What will you do?"

"Whatever it takes to make things right," I say. "Not just for one people but for all of them. The fae, both seelie and unseelie. The humans."

His expression brightens, and I realize it's the first time he's heard me voice such care for the fae. Perhaps it's the first time I've admitted it out loud. "You're going to stay?"

I bring one hand to his hip, the other slides up his

torso to rest over his beating heart. I tip my head back and lock our eyes. "I'm staying. Faerwyvae is my home. The Fire Court is my throne. And you are my mate."

He brings his lips to mine and I eagerly receive them, the heat we had to abandon in the alley returning at full force. But before we fall too deep, there are words I need to say. Words I'm no longer willing to hold onto. With so much that can still go wrong, I can no longer keep it to myself.

I separate my lips from his, but our foreheads remain touching. He sinks low into the water, and I wrap my arms around his neck until only our heads are above the surface. I pull away to take in the autumn colors swimming in his hungry eyes. "Aspen, I love you."

He trembles against me, then brushes his lips lightly against mine. Silence stretches between us, and for one terrifying moment I fear I've said the wrong thing. Do the fae even exchange sentiments of love? Then his lips pull into a smile. Not the smirk I adore, or the seductive grin that makes my knees weak. A pure, authentic smile. "I love you too, Evie."

When our kisses return, they are gentler, softer. His tongue caresses mine as a burning need hums at my core. I run my hands through his hair, eliciting a deep moan from him as I bring my fingers to dance along the beam of an antler. He tenses against me. One of his hands grips my bottom while the other explores the crest of my breast. Our breathing rises in tandem, a furious melody playing the tune of our growing desire. I feel weightless as he lifts me off my feet, pulling me close until my hips are pressed against his.

My core burns to deepen the connection, to move

further into my passion. I let it rise to illuminate my entire being. I'm glowing with the need to feel every part of him.

That's when I realize I really am glowing. Like the night of the full moon revel, a violet haze has clouded my vision. Even though I can feel this glow radiating from my inner fire, this kind isn't painful like the one caused by my blazing rage. This one is gentle, glittering, and pleasurable unlike anything has ever been before.

Aspen whispers my name, and I whisper his in turn. Beneath the light of the rising sun shining from the domed ceiling overhead, we move to the tune of our love.

33

Hazy sunlight brushes my eyelids, and the smell of rosemary and cinnamon floods my senses. I open my eyes to find Aspen sleeping next to me. His face is slack, head turned slightly to the side as his antlers hang over the back of his mattress. We're in his bedroom, where the bed is in the middle of the room to accommodate his extra assets.

Speaking of extra assets.

I find my leg is sprawled over his hips, bringing to mind our early morning passions, the moon baths, the way he carried me to his room for us to sleep. Or *try* to sleep for several hours until we finally fell into a heap of exhaustion. It must be midafternoon by now.

I extract an arm from beneath his and bring my fingers to his face. Brushing his golden skin, I drink in the sight of him, so youthful and beautiful in slumber. He stirs at my touch, eyes opening to find mine. The smile that greets me makes my heart flip.

"We managed to sleep in a proper bed for once," he says.

"We did."

He moves closer to me, bringing a hand to my lower back. "Was it better than it was when you visited me in your dreams?"

"It was. In those moments, there's a discrepancy in physical sensation. Is it the same for you?"

His brow wrinkles as he considers. "Yes, I think you're right. That didn't stop me from enjoying it though. I wished so badly that you'd really been there that first night."

His words send a flicker of pain inside me. "I did too."

"And in the dining room at Bircharbor. That's when I knew the visions were more than fantasy. You appeared out of nowhere while I was wide awake." He lets out a light laugh. "You should have seen the terror on that fool girl's face when I roared at her and ordered her back to her room. She hadn't the slightest idea she'd just interrupted a much-desired kiss."

"That kiss was everything I wanted," I say. "Although, at that point, I still thought I was dreaming. In fact, I thought I was having a nightmare, certain that any moment the dream would shift into something I wouldn't want to see. It wasn't until you came to Lunar that I realized those visions had been real." My heart sinks, the words I omitted screaming in my mind. *It wasn't until you caught me kissing Franco.* Now that we've fully reunited, I feel like my apology to him in the alley could have been better.

He moves his hand to my face. "You were right, Evie. You don't owe me an explanation and you are not my property. You are my mate. You are free to seek pleasure with whomever—"

I sit upright, cheeks blazing with indignation. "I only want you, Aspen. You damn well better know that."

Amusement shines in his eyes as he props himself up on his elbows. He quirks a brow. "Only me?"

"Yes. I'm like Lorelei. Monogamous, that is. This is not...this isn't a Nyxia at Beltane situation." Blood drains from my face as I consider something I never have before. Not all fae love the same way I'm used to. Does he love the way I need to be loved? "Wait, do you prefer...taking other lovers?"

A smirk pulls at his lips and I want to slap it off his face. Or kiss it off. No, definitely slap. "I feel the same as you," he finally says, his smirk shifting back to a genuine smile. "It's just us, Evie. You're all I want."

I let out a shaking breath, posture relaxing as I let him pull me to his chest. His heart beats against my ear as his breath stirs my hair.

"You're all I love."

My heart skips a beat, and I lift my eyes to meet his. Love. It's still so new to me, both the feeling and the word. It feels fragile and precious and terrifying all at once. With a soft brush of our lips, we seal our unspoken vow with a kiss.

IT'S ALMOST PAINFUL TO SEPARATE AND FORCE OURSELVES out of bed, but the outside world doesn't stop to cater to my stolen moments of peace. There's still much to attend to. The humans will want retribution for my escape. King Ustrin will want revenge.

And I have a throne to claim.

I return to my room, my body aching with every step —a combination of my leftover strain from the journey and the exhaustion of pleasure. Once dressed, I go to find Lorelei.

She opens her bedroom door and wastes not a moment before throwing her arms around me. "I heard you returned last night, and not in the best state. I was terrified for you."

We pull away, and she looks me over. "I'm all right, I promise. Aspen took care of me."

She raises a brow. "You actually let someone else take care of you for once?"

I roll my eyes. "I know, I know."

Her expression turns serious. "How did it go?"

A shard of glass pierces my heart as an iron bullet shoots through my memory, followed by blood and smoke. Sorrow drags at me, and I feel like I'm being buried beneath mounds of stone. It's so painful, I can hardly breathe, can hardly stand—

I seek my inner fire, transforming my sorrow into rage. This time, the fire doesn't sear me. Instead, it clears my head, my heart, returns my composure.

Tears swim in Lorelei's eyes. Her words are a gentle whisper. "You don't have to say anything. Not until you're ready."

I steel myself and let out a heavy sigh.

"What happens next?" she asks.

"I must meet with the fire fae again to secure their support in claiming Unseelie Queen of Fire."

She bites a corner of her lip. "I won't pressure you to say more than you are ready for, but can I ask...did the humans agree to change the treaty?"

I force the darkness away, keeping my mind trained on facts alone. "No."

"Then you know claiming rule in Faerwyvae will officially break the treaty, right?"

I square my shoulders. "I'm ready to break it."

Her eyes widen, lips pulling into a sad smile.

"However, the bargain I made with King Ustrin keeps war at bay for now," I say. "A fight between the fae council and the rebels will come to pass, but in the meantime, they can do nothing. I think we should use this time to come up with a solid plan."

"Let's do this," she says with a nod. "Have you told Queen Nyxia?"

"No, but I need to speak with her. I want to meet with the fire fae tonight."

She's already moving to the door. "Then let's find her."

We head toward the throne room, plans and ideas buzzing through my head. One question plagues me again and again. I turn to Lorelei. "When I do face King Ustrin, must I make a formal challenge for the throne like Aspen did with Cobalt?"

She shakes her head. "No, those formalities were created by the Council of Eleven Courts. Once the treaty is broken, the rules of the council need no longer apply. With the rebels already claiming a return to the Old Ways, it will be in accordance with the Twelfth Court that you will face him."

"How does it work, exactly?"

She shrugs. "You need to prove you are the alpha blessed by the All of All."

"You say it like it's simple, but I don't understand how that comes to be. Do I engage him in physical combat? Will it be a fight to the death?" My stomach turns at the thought. There's no way I can beat King Ustrin in physical combat. If only I had an iron blade...

"It's impossible to know ahead of time," Lorelei says. "Sometimes it's simply a matter of facing each other in the Twelfth Court, like you did as Aspen's champion. The win may still be shown with a token, like the crown you were given. Other times it's won by submission to the alpha, like with Nyxia and her mother. But yes, there are times when only death can decide the victor. In those cases, the All of All gives their champion strength."

My heart races. It sounds impossible no matter how she puts it. Luckily, my bargain with King Ustrin will give me enough time to prepare.

We are almost at the doors to the throne room when the sound of commotion draws my attention.

Lorelei and I exchange a glance before we take off down the corridor toward the noise. Once we reach the entry hall to the palace, we find dozens of bedraggled fae streaming inside, two of which are Foxglove and Franco. Lorelei runs to Foxglove while Franco offers me a tired wink. Both seem flustered but none the worse for wear. The fae surrounding them, however, look as if they just returned from battle. Their clothing is stained and torn. Those who have hair wear it disheveled, and those with fur appear matted. My heart leaps in my throat when I recognize a figure.

"Gildmar!"

The old fae's bark-like face stretches into a relieved grin as I approach her. "You're here," she says.

"Yes, but what are *you* doing here?"

She extends her arms toward her fellows. "We are who remain of King Aspen's most loyal household. Not everyone chose to come." Her lips twitch into a frown. "And not all made the escape."

My heart sinks at that. I return my attention to the fae continuing to file inside, finding another familiar face—one of Aspen's handsome servants, Vane. The next figure is even more surprising.

Marie Coleman meets my eyes, face crumpling as she rushes to me. The girl wraps her arms around my waist and sobs into my shoulder.

I almost forget how to move. What in the name of iron is Maddie Coleman's little sister doing here?

"Oh, Evelyn, I can't believe I made it. I thought I was going to die."

I'm torn between surprise and utter confusion, flustered at how she says my name with such care. We never were friends before. The most familiarity we ever exchanged was when she wordlessly pleaded with me in Mayor Coleman's parlor. My mouth goes dry, remembering her tears of distress, how her eyes begged me to help her.

I thought I was powerless then.

My arms return the embrace, even though my mind still whirls to comprehend what is happening. She heaves a heavier sob as she pulls away from me, her attention snagging on something she sees over my shoulder.

"Aspen!" Marie runs to my shocked mate, his eyes taking in the swarm of fae and the girl who clings around his waist. He takes a tentative hand and pats her heaving shoulders.

A flicker of jealousy flutters through me, but it dries before it can ignite into something more. There isn't anything sensual in their embrace. The way Marie holds onto Aspen isn't like a lover but a friend. And his consoling touch is more fatherly than anything, although he seems hesitant to give it.

Marie seems to compose herself, pulling away and wiping the tears from her ruddy cheeks. "I'm so sorry, Your Majesty, Miss Fairfield." She gives us each a trembling curtsy. "That was very unbecoming of me. You just have no idea how relieved I am to be here."

"Please don't take this the wrong way," I say, "but why exactly are you here? Is your...sister here too?"

Her expression darkens. "Of course not. Maddie is quite comfortable with her new arrangement, despite the questionable ethics she's embroiled in."

I raise a brow at Aspen, still bewildered.

He takes my hand and gives it a squeeze. "Marie expressed to me her reservations about Faerwyvae from the start."

Marie nods eagerly. "I begged him to send me home. I thought for sure he was going to kill me for my insubordination, but instead, he was kind." She lifts her chin. "He promised I wouldn't have to marry—*ever*—if I didn't want to."

I flash a grin at my mate. "That's quite good of him."

Marie crosses her arms. "It's the first time in my fifteen years of life that option has ever been given to me."

I look away from Marie to take in the rest of the

refugees, seeing the exhaustion tugging their features. "It must have been a difficult journey."

"One I didn't expect any of you to make without aid," Aspen adds. He seems hesitant, anxious almost, before he says more. "The rebels and I had plans to send spies to help you escape."

Then I realize the source of his conflict; he's fighting not to show how touched he is that his household came. They followed him before he even sent anyone to assist them. For a king who keeps his truest, kindest nature behind a mask of stoicism, it must surprise him to find so many loyal to his reign.

It's my turn to give his hand a squeeze, and we exchange a smile.

"We were stuck near the border between Solar and Lunar for two days," Marie explains, oblivious to Aspen's internal struggle. "There were soldiers patrolling the area. It wasn't until Ambassador Foxglove and the Lunar Prince came along that we were able to make it the rest of the way. Some of us were smuggled through the carriage, while the prince flew others across the border one at a time."

That explains why it took Foxglove and Franco so long to arrive.

"Are there more of you?" Queen Nyxia's voice comes from over my shoulder as she approaches us.

Marie pales at the queen's domineering presence. Belatedly, she sinks into a clumsy curtsy. "Yes, Your Majesty. We left Autumn in three separate groups. The second caught up with us when we were stuck in Solar, but the third is still unaccounted for."

"I will inform my owls," Nyxia says. "I'll have them on high alert with orders to allow them safe passage."

"Thank you," Aspen says.

She raises a brow. "I suppose you'll want me to house all your refugees until you get your palace back?"

His jaw shifts back and forth. "Please."

She tuts. "It won't come free. I'm already hosting you and your mate. What will you give me in return?"

I step forward, fingers balled into fists. "We're giving you what you always wanted. A broken treaty."

"*You* are giving me a broken treaty, but what is Aspen providing?" She extends her hands toward the fae cluttering her entry. "A fragmented household? Exhausted soldiers?"

"His household is my household. If you ally with me, you ally with them. Once Aspen and I have our thrones, our people will be out of your way."

Nyxia studies me through slitted lids. After a few tense moments, she says, "You've chosen a side after all."

I maintain my composure beneath her scrutiny. "Will you send word to the fire fae to meet me tonight?"

Her lips pull into a devious grin. "It would be my pleasure."

34

After nightfall, Nyxia, Aspen, and I make our way through the forest toward the same cave I visited before. The waning moon is bright, but the forest is oddly quiet, making the glowing mushrooms and bell-like flowers that light our path seem almost sinister.

It makes me grateful I accepted the presence of my two companions. My first instinct was to refuse. I wanted tonight's meeting with the fire fae to speak volumes, to show them I stand on my own, that I am no one's puppet, and that I don't see them as a threat. However, Nyxia made the compelling point that there are other creatures to fear besides the fire fae. Going to the meeting alone would be foolish.

At least the three of us are under the same agreement. Tonight, I represent myself. Nyxia and Aspen will support me as my allies, not my protectors.

We reach the mouth of the cave. From here, it's black and soundless, giving no hint that anything awaits deep within. A chilling thought comes to mind. What if there really is no one waiting within? What if my first meeting was enough to convince them never to follow me?

Sensing my hesitation, Aspen reaches for my hand. "Are you sure you're ready to do this?"

The touch soothes me. "Yes."

Nyxia lifts her brow. "That...issue...we spoke of last time still stands. Are you prepared to follow through with what I told them?"

I know what she's asking. *Am I ready to show them my unseelie form?* That's an additionally perplexing obstacle, one I've given much thought to but no answer. I tried several times throughout the day to take my anger to the Twelfth Court, like Aspen had described. It did nothing. My anger wasn't nearly as strong as it had been after my mother's death, but that intensity is hard to reach without giving way to sorrow first. And I'm afraid if I give in, not even my rage will be able to save me from it.

I try to put on a convincing face for Nyxia. "I will do what I can."

She flashes me a glare. "I told them you would show them your unseelie form next time you met with them."

A spark of anger stirs within me. "You also told them I'd meet with them when I was ready to make a move against King Ustrin. I'm ready to do that and I'm ready to fight for them. If that isn't enough, then perhaps I'm not enough to be queen. If I'll have their support, I'll have it for who I am. For all I know, this," I wave my hands over the length of my body, "is also my unseelie form."

She rolls her eyes. "Fine. I hope you're ready for this."

"So do I," I mutter. Not an hour has gone by without me questioning whether everything I'm about to do isn't absolute insanity. I escaped the Spire. Eisleigh. Mr. Duveau. I escaped exile. If I wanted, I could lay low, go into hiding. Avoid Mr. Duveau's bounty hunters and the seelie fae who would turn me in.

The very thought ignites my indignation. No matter how many times these doubts creep in, I remind myself why I'm doing this. Because it's the right thing to do. Because the treaty must be broken. Because men like Mr. Duveau and males like Cobalt and Ustrin don't deserve to be in power. Because I deserve a whole life, not one spent in hiding. Because I'm the only one who will fight for both the humans and the fae.

Nyxia enters the cave and I follow behind her. I feel Aspen's steadying hand on my lower back, a silent exchange of his support. His touch lowers my pulse and sends calming warmth through my heart.

After a long stretch of darkness, the glowing mushrooms and luminescent crystals begin to light our way. Soon sounds fall upon my ears, proof that at least someone is waiting within. Finally, we reach the inner chamber.

Like before, a variety of fae are clustered inside, eyes full of scrutiny as I enter. What surprises me is how many more there are this time than the last. There are new kitsune in various colors. Wisps in blues, reds, oranges, and violets float through the air. A second moon dragon with opalescent scales is coiled next to the black one I met last time. There are also several other kinds of fae I've never met before—sprites of dust and ash and odd-looking flames, birds with bright, fiery wings, glittering snakes and salamanders. There are also fae who appear barely different from an average animal, although none

I've seen anywhere but encyclopedic reference—fennec foxes, desert rodents, scorpions. Their keen eyes are all that give their true natures away.

With a deep breath, I walk forward and stand before them. Aspen's hand brushes my back one last time, a gesture hidden from view, before he takes a step away to stand near the wall of the cave. Nyxia does the same, although her resistance is obvious. I can see her struggle not to speak on my behalf written all over her expression.

"You again, and in human form," says the crustacean-mushroom I remember from before. "I thought you'd only come back when you were ready to prove you were one of us."

A rumble of agreement moves through the crowd, and to my disappointment, several fae break away from the group and stream out the cave before I can say a word. The others shuffle, as if eager to follow.

"Wait," I call out, my tone weak and pleading. I take a moment to gather my nerves, reminding myself I'm supposed to be a queen. With a deep breath, I force my voice to ring out with authority. "Give me a chance to speak before you make your decision about me. I will respect your choice, but I will be heard."

The fae go still, and not another tries to exit the cave. Glowing yellow eyes lock on me from the back of the chamber. It's the opalescent moon dragon. "I want to hear what she has to say," says a hissing feminine voice. "I wasn't here last time, if you recall. If we don't like what she offers, she'll make a pretty snack."

Tittering laughter comes from the crowd, but I'm not sure if it's sinister or meant to be cajoling. Whatever the case, I came here for a reason and I can't falter now.

I steel myself, throwing back my shoulders as I try to feign confidence. "Last time we met, Queen Nyxia introduced me as the figure who would fight King Ustrin. Today I come to you as Unseelie Queen of Fire."

Gasps and yips and growls answer. Again, I'm unsure how to translate the sounds. The clamor could be supportive, shocked, or angry for all I can tell. I continue. "I am claiming Unseelie Queen of Fire according to the Old Ways. When the time comes, I will face King Ustrin and the All of All will bless their alpha. I intend to win."

An orange wisp bobs forward, her high, feminine voice floating on the air. "How do you intend to beat him? You are but a human with the blood of a former fae king. King Ustrin has lived much longer than you and he's been king nearly his entire life."

I'm prepared for that question, my voice ringing out clear and strong. "King Ustrin rules without respect for the Old Ways or the All of All. I may not be full-fae and I may not have the experience he has. But I have the heart. I care about the lives of the fae, and that includes the unseelie. King Ustrin cares about his own power and he'll shun your kind to keep it. I believe the All of All cares about the seelie and unseelie in equal measure—the way I do."

"So you believe the All of All will bless you as their alpha?" asks an indigo kitsune with a pale blue flame on its tail. Both his words and expression are heavy with skepticism. "Why you and not another? Why should we support you and not someone else who would fight against him?"

I feel the blood leave my face. That's a question I never considered. Not once have I wondered if there were another eager to take the Fire throne. I exhale a deep breath to steady my nerves and clear my mind. The words that come are from deep within, and I hardly know what I'm saying before I say it. "Because the fire in you is the fire in me. I feel it burning in every vein, in every ounce of my blood. I may not be full-fae but King Caleos' legacy is my legacy. I am the result of his deep love for a human woman. His love should have created unity between the humans and the fae. Instead, it brought war and destruction and ended with a corrupt treaty based on lies. I have every intention of restoring the balance that should have been there from the start."

I see a few nods, but there are just as many hisses. A bright yellow salamander scoots forward. "You speak of love like that should mean something to us. We are unseelie."

"So was King Caleos," I say, "and he fell in love. I know love doesn't always look the same, but its essence is universal. We all love our families, our children, our homes, and our freedoms. We may show it in different ways, but it's the same love."

"How will you fight for us?" asks a swirling dust sprite. "Will you help us eradicate the humans? Will you return the Fair Isle to the fae?"

I'm caught off guard by talk of eradicating humans, but I maintain my composure. All I can offer is the truth. "I don't have all the answers, but I'm committed to hearing all voices and make the decisions that support the highest quality of life for all fae. I may be claiming unseelie queen, but I will not claim to be radical. I will fight for what the unseelie truly represent. Freedom. And that freedom starts by destroying the treaty. My very rule breaks it irreparably."

"What will that even get us?" asks the white dragon. "War will come. The last war wiped out several thousands of fae. Back then, we fought for control over the isle. What will we be fighting for this time?"

"Like I said, I don't have all the answers yet. I don't know what the end result will be. But I do know we'll be fighting for a better world. A better life for all beings on the isle. We'll be fighting for freedom from prejudice and hate amongst fae and humans. We'll be fighting to rid the isle of corrupt leaders and oppressive rules. We'll be fighting for a world where fae aren't captured, experimented on, and sold for parts. Where females aren't sent to brothels."

Fire heats my core, fueling my words. "We will fight for a world where the unseelie are free to be who they wish without sacrificing their ways, their homes, or their land. A world where seelie may keep the lives they cherish without diminishing the rights of the unseelie. We will fight for a world where human girls aren't considered expendable, where they will not be groomed as brides to the fae for a Reaping that never should have been created. We will fight as one. I will fight at your side for all of you. I will defend both humans and fae, and I will fight both humans and fae. Our allies are not those who look like us but those who dream of the same world. I ask you to consider if you want to be part of that vision."

Silence answers. Countless eyes stare back at me, some wide, some hopeful, others narrowed with hostility.

The crustacean scuttles forward. "You'll fight for us,

but are you one of us? How can you understand the unseelie if you can't even show us your form?"

Echoes of agreement rattle through the chamber.

"Yes, show them," a malicious voice hisses from the shadows behind me. I whirl toward it, hearing footsteps echo through the cave walls. Someone followed us. Or found us.

King Ustrin steps into the chamber. In his wake, trails Mr. Duveau.

35

The sight of the councilman hits me like a punch to the gut. He meets my eyes with a stony expression, no remorse, no smile. He's stoic, the way he was when I met him at the mayor's. I can't see his face without imagining the revolver, the bullet, my mother's blood streaming into the water below her. A chasm of sorrow opens beneath me, but my anger burns alongside it, keeping me from falling to my knees. I allow it to grow but keep it at a simmer.

Aspen steps forward with a low growl while shadows curl from Nyxia's fists. The two royals come up beside me, facing our unwelcome guests.

Aspen's gaze burns into Mr. Duveau. "I thought I gutted you."

The councilman shrugs, the hint of a teasing smirk playing over his mouth. His stiff posture is all that betrays the underlying wounds he's hiding. "You tried. Merely got one solid gash in. Better luck next time."

Several guards file in behind Ustrin and Mr. Duveau,

while a small brown rodent, one I'm fairly sure I saw flee the cave when I arrived, circles the Fire King's ankles. Ustrin looks down at it in disgust, then opens his scaly orange palm. A yellow flame ignites over his hand, then disappears. "Your family has been released," he says with a sneer. "Thank you for your service. You may go."

The rodent emits a squeak before scurrying back out.

A violent shudder ripples through my mate as he lowers into a half-crouch, ready to charge.

Ustrin's eyes whip toward him. "I wouldn't do that if I were you. Not if you want your precious refugees to live."

Aspen bares his teeth, chest heaving. "What are you talking about?"

The Fire King takes a casual step closer. "My soldiers stumbled upon them days ago trying to cross Fire in secret. When Mr. Duveau contacted me with the results of Maven Fairfield's trial, I realized the refugees would provide the perfect cover to infiltrate Lunar and coax a meeting from Miss Fairfield."

"Where are they?" I ask. I remember Marie saying one more group remained unaccounted for. If there are even half as many as those who came this morning, there could be dozens.

"They won't be anywhere unless I make it back to them by midnight," Ustrin says. "My guards have orders to kill them if I don't return by then. Therefore, we should hurry on with our business, yes?"

Aspen emits a growl, shoulders trembling. "What's to stop me from torturing you to an inch of your life until you tell me where they are?"

"Do you think I'd give you the chance?" Another ball of flame, orange this time, ignites over his palm. "I can also send a message. With a snap of my fingers, this flame will leave my palm and transport to my guards. Another sign that they may proceed with the execution."

I burn him with a glare. "What do you want?"

"I only want to talk," he says, a false smile plastered over his lipless mouth. He holds out his hands in a sign of surrender, the orange flame shrinking back into his palm until it's nothing.

"What does *he* want?" My eyes flash to the councilman.

"He's here to force your hand should you fail to comply, but I promise we will give you every opportunity to act on your own."

"Then let's talk."

"Tell your mate to either leave or stand down."

Aspen and I exchange a glance. His muscles ripple with agitation, but he gives me a subtle nod.

I return my attention to Ustrin in time to see him close his eyes with a violent tremble. He rolls his neck, then faces Nyxia. "Stop that already."

Nyxia gives him a devious grin, shadows thickening around her. "Why? Afraid of the dark?"

Ustrin continues to tremble as he turns his palm to the ceiling. This time, a blood-red flame emerges. With a snap of his fingers, it disappears.

Nyxia falters, eyes widening. "What was that?"

"That one went to your palace. If it doesn't find you there shortly after it arrives, it will set your home ablaze, starting with wherever your dear brother can be found. I'd hurry if I were you."

Her shadows retreat, eyes locking on mine.

"Go," I whisper.

With a nod, she transforms into her shadow form and streams from the chamber.

King Ustrin lets out a long breath, the tremors gone, and straightens his cravat and jacket. "What about you, King Aspen? Care to leave or stay?"

"I'm staying," he says through his teeth, body pressing close to my side.

"Will you let his people free once we're done talking?" I ask.

"So long as I am unharmed. If I were you, I'd make no move against me." He gestures to his guards. I flinch, but they don't come for me. Instead, they move further into the chamber to form a ring around the fire fae.

Ustrin looks from the crowd to me, a sneer on his lips. "I must say, I was quite affronted when word spread throughout the forest tonight that you sought a meeting with *my* citizens. Did you really think you could steal my people?"

"They are living in Lunar," I say. "They are no longer your people."

"That's where you're wrong. I've been given new rights by the Council of Eleven Courts. It is my duty to bring the fire fae back to the Fire Court. There they will be tamed and taught to free themselves from their savage ways."

Growls rumble through the chamber. A fennec snaps at one of the guards, earning a swift kick. My heart twists as the tiny fox yelps, then falls on its side.

I round on the king. "You're one to talk about savage ways."

He ignores my scorn as well as the increasing growls

and threats and flames coming from the fire fae. "They're armed with iron," he says. The crowd falls into stunned silence. "Each guard carries stone grenades filled with iron shards. Step out of line and I will order their detonation."

Iron grenades. The very thought churns my stomach. I saw what kind of damage explosives can do to the fae, and those didn't contain iron. But wait. The explosion would...

"Won't that hurt you too?" I ask. "And your guards?"

"I will be safe from its radius," King Ustrin says, keeping his voice low.

I don't lower mine to meet his, allowing it to carry. "But you'll sacrifice your guards."

He clenches his jaw. "They understand the risks. They know what they are fighting for."

I cross my arms and take a bold step forward. "So do we."

He lets out a burst of laughter. "Who's this *we*? Do you honestly think you've won their allegiance?"

I purse my lips to keep from saying something foolish. The truth is, he's probably right. The meeting didn't go anywhere near how I wanted it to go.

King Ustrin's posture relaxes. "Speaking of, that's why I came here to speak with you. It's time for you to remove yourself from the isle like you were supposed to. Your presence is a threat to the treaty—"

"You mean a threat to your rule."

His eyes flash dangerously. "—And it prevents the Council of Eleven Courts from engaging the rebels in combat. I can see your bargain with me was far cleverer than I gave you credit for. I should make you pay for your deception. Instead, I offer you a private escort off the isle."

I raise a brow. "A private escort? With Mr. Duveau? Please. I'll take the alternative."

He bares his teeth. "The alternative is he uses the power of your true name to force you to come. What about this don't you understand?"

"What I don't understand is why you're even here. Why go through all this trouble bringing Mr. Duveau to try and get me off the isle yet again? What game are you playing?"

"I'm trying to spare your life."

"Why?"

"I won't kill you." He says it slowly through his teeth, expression twisted as if the statement pains him.

That's when I realize the truth.

"You *can't* kill me. You made a bargain."

He says nothing, confirming my suspicion.

"That's why you've been pushing for my family's exile when you really couldn't care less if we live or die. What was the bargain?"

He lifts his chin. "It was a promise. Before my fool cousin Caleos left for his exile, he made me vow that if it ever came to pass that his progeny found themselves on the isle, I would see that they were treated fairly and given every chance to live well. To avoid stirring suspicion regarding my involvement with his demise, I made the promise. He left it loose enough for me to navigate, but not loose enough to be anything but a thorn in my side since I learned of your existence. He must have known even then what awaited him on the other side of exile. He knew his lover and child had survived."

"Treated fairly?" Aspen growls. "Live well? I don't see how you've fulfilled either of those terms."

"I've fulfilled it enough that I'm still alive, aren't I? Not that every deviation hasn't caused me enough pain to wish for death a time or two. Do you have any idea the suffering Maven Fairfield's death caused me?" He shoots Mr. Duveau a look of contempt.

The councilman, surprisingly, manages not to wither beneath his scorn.

I puzzle over his words, a ripple of shock moving up my spine. Is that what the punishment is for breaking a fae promise? Excruciating pain resulting in eventual death? Before I was willing to accept magic, I thought fae vows and their refusal to lie came from cultural conditioning. Now...I fully believe his punishment is tangible.

Ustrin returns his attention to me. "Let me fulfill my vow and get you off the isle so I can be rid of you once and for all. Not that I'll be truly free until your sister manages to show her face." He says the last part with no small amount of venom.

My heart leaps into my throat at the mention of Amelie. "You don't know where she is?"

His fingers clench into fists. "King Cobalt insists he doesn't know—"

At the words *King Cobalt*, Aspen's growl rumbles in his chest.

"—But he's hiding her from me. I'll deal with him next. He may have the council convinced, but I see through him. Even as an ally, he has much to learn about earning his place."

I take in every word, filing them away in the back of my mind. I'm not sure what it means, but it must be significant that he thinks Cobalt is hiding Amelie from him. While I doubt it suggests noble intentions on Cobalt's behalf, it could mean Amelie's refusal to come to Mother's trial wasn't her choice after all. *Not that it changes anything. Her actions still led to Mother's death.* My simmer of anger rises to a boil. I let it grow, let it burn hotter.

"Let's get this over with," Ustrin says, voice rising an octave. "Otherwise I can hurry your resolve. Mr. Duveau can force you immobile while your ears flood with the haunting melody of the Autumn refugees' dying screams." He turns his gaze to Aspen. "Would you like an invitation to the symphony as well?"

I freeze. His words suggest the refugees are close enough that I'd be able to hear them scream from here. That means we can likely find them without Ustrin's guidance.

"No," I say. Fear floods my body for what I'm about to say, but I call upon my fire to burn it. "We'll get this over with, but I'm not leaving the isle unless you plan on shipping my corpse. We face each other in accordance with the Old Ways. We let the All of All choose their alpha. And we do it now."

Aspen tenses beside me. "Evie, don't—"

Aspen, I say his name in my head, seeking that connection through our Bond. *Please trust me. Make no move against what I'm about to do.*

His eyes search mine, wide with terror. I hear his voice in my mind. *I trust you.*

King Ustrin stares at me for endless moments until a sudden burst of laughter erupts from his lips. "Stupid, stupid girl. You dare challenge me? You dare refuse my offer for mercy? Fine." He shakes his head with bitter amusement. "I gave you your chance. I fulfilled my vow. If you won't come willingly, then you will come by force. And you won't enjoy it."

King Ustrin steps to the side, allowing Mr. Duveau to take his place and face me. Only now does his stoic expression shift into a chilling grin. "Evelyn Fairfield." The name reverberates through my mind, my blood, my bones. "Follow me. Use your mate's true name and order him to remain here until daybreak."

He turns on his heel and takes a few steps away. I stay rooted on the spot, trembling as the command writhes inside me. Ustrin lets out a hiss, making the councilman whirl back around. His face pales, a look of shock in his eyes. He regathers his composure and speaks through gritted teeth. "Evelyn Fairfield."

I hear the name, feel its power, but I'm focusing on something else. Every part of me is fueling my intent—my mind, my heart, my very soul. It grows and grows until it becomes so solid in my mind's eye, I feel like I could touch it.

Mr. Duveau takes a step closer. "Follow me. Now."

I pour my intent into every word. "You have my name wrong."

"Excuse me?"

"My true name isn't Evelyn Fairfield."

"That's a lie. Your mother gave you the name Evelyn Fairfield at birth. It is your true name, and it's a name I've memorized since the day you were born."

"I may have been born with that name, but my name has since changed. It is now Evelyn, Unseelie Queen of Fire."

His face goes blank, but only for a moment. His lips pull into a devious smirk. "Is this your true name you've given me?"

I smile sweetly. "Yes."

Mr. Duveau squares his shoulders. "Evelyn, Unseelie Queen of Fire—"

"No!" King Ustrin's shout roars through the chamber, but it's too late. Mr. Duveau steps back, hand to his forehead as if to stifle a terrible pain.

A roil of nausea washes through me, followed by the feeling of something ripping—something *inside* me. With it comes a searing agony, and I call my fire to combat it. In a flash, it's gone. Like it was never there to begin with.

I open my eyes to find Mr. Duveau panting, face pale and covered with a sheen of sweat.

King Ustrin lunges toward him. "Do you have any idea what you've done? You've broken the treaty!"

The councilman steps back, unsteady on his feet as he shakes his head. "The Legacy Bond should have—"

"The Legacy Bond was destroyed the moment you named her queen," King Ustrin says through his teeth. "The treaty is broken if King Caleos' descendants claim rule. And you, with the breath of the Bond, spoke that very thing into being."

Aspen takes my hand, and we step back from the pair. There's nowhere to go. Behind us are the fire fae and King Ustrin's guards. Ustrin and Mr. Duveau block the exit.

Ustrin's chest heaves as he pins the councilman with a vicious scowl. "Which means our arrangement is over." He lunges for Mr. Duveau, his fingers stretching into claws as he swipes at the man.

Mr. Duveau reaches beneath his jacket and pulls out

his revolver. The movement makes him wince, and he brings his free hand to a place below his ribs. That must be where Aspen wounded him. The arm that holds the gun, however, is steady. Firm. Ready to shoot.

Ustrin recoils at the sight. The two are frozen, eyes locked. Slowly, Mr. Duveau takes a step back. Then another. Ustrin hisses, body shaking as if fighting his instincts to attack the man. When the councilman moves far enough into the tunnel, his form is swallowed entirely by shadows. A moment later, I hear his pounding footsteps fleeing from the cave.

King Ustrin points at two of his guards, nodding his head in the direction of Mr. Duveau's hasty exit. The guards obey, streaming past us.

Aspen and I take another step back.

Ustrin faces me head on, fingers curling and uncurling as flames dance between them. "You get your way. We will fight for the Fire Court throne after all."

36

Ustrin's chest heaves with rage as he storms over to me, fire climbing from his fingers to his shoulders. The blood leaves my face. This is what I asked for, but it doesn't mean I'm ready. Still, I don the bravest face I can, throwing back my shoulders as I take a step closer to him. Aspen's fingers cling to mine, and I can feel his reluctance to let me go. To let me fight. To stand down. But he does.

I'm right here, he whispers in my mind.

King Ustrin burns me with narrowed eyes as he removes his jacket and cravat, throwing each to the ground with force. "You must make the first move," he hisses. "Our bargain keeps me and the council from engaging the fae rebel royals in violence. Even according to the Old Ways, a bid for alpha status is considered an attack. Since you have sided with them, I cannot engage you."

My pulse races, and my mouth goes dry. "Very well."

His fire grows, dancing over the scales of his face and

scalp, creating a blinding shimmering radiance around him. "Come get me."

I make no move as I seek my fire, allowing it to rise from my core and burn down my arms, my hands, my legs. Doubt creeps in, so heavy it threatens to dampen my fire. I hardly know what I'm doing. I'm not ready for this. I can't do this.

What exactly is this anyway? I know we must stand before the All of All. We must prove which of us is the alpha. Do I really have what it takes to do that? I'm not Queen Nyxia, the most powerful lunar alpha in generations. I'm not even close in power to the weakest fae royal I've met.

My mind spins with anxiety. What in the name of iron convinced me I should do this? Shouldn't I have taken death? Exile?

My fire retreats, pulling back from my arms and returning to my core where it remains a white-hot ball of flame.

King Ustrin lets out a hiss of laughter. "You can't do it, can you? You're weak. Nothing more than a pitiful human woman. A girl. A child. You know nothing about rage or warfare. You know nothing about ruling a kingdom or wearing a crown."

A crown. For some reason, the word stills me, my golden crown of flames appearing in my mind's eye. The All of All gave that to me when they could have given anything. They could have given a maple leaf or a robin's feather. Instead, they gave me a crown of fire. That must mean something.

I focus on the arrogance in King Ustrin's face, reminding myself of everything he's responsible for. I remember how it felt to be torn from my mate, to be told we could no longer fulfill the treaty. I think of the burnt apothecary, imagining it as nothing more than a charred husk with all my mother's herbs and jars burnt to ash. Portraits gone and books and spells and recipes lost forever. Then all I see is Mother. Mother. Mother.

Sorrow rips through me, but my rage is hotter. It fills my body in a flash, igniting my skin in a white glow, brighter than King Ustrin's.

The look on King Ustrin's face is priceless. However, the expression is momentary, a flash before he steels it behind a sneer. His glow increases to match mine.

Heat surrounds me, searing my flesh. A jolt of panic racks my core, but I breathe it away. Aspen's voice fills my mind. *Take it to the Twelfth Court.*

I close my eyes.

When I open them, violet covers my vision. My surroundings are like what they were before, but there's no movement, save for the swirling particles of violet light that make up all matter. It's as if time stands frozen.

My mind has gone still, and my only sensations are a calm warmth and the sound and feel of the energy humming through my body. This return to the Twelfth Court feels both new and familiar at once. I feel welcome, yet at the same time, I feel like an invader.

A black tunnel opens beside me, and without hesitation, I enter it. Inside, it's like I'm floating, even as my feet touch what seems like solid ground. I see nothing, hear nothing. Only my body remains, although it's nothing more than violet particles. My observation prompts a memory—no, a reminder. I came here for a reason. To find my unseelie form.

My mind begins to clear, and as it does, the black tunnel reveals shimmering purple far ahead. I run toward it, keeping my goal firmly in my mind so I don't lose track of my awareness. My destination comes into focus the nearer I get, and I find myself standing before a mirror. At least, it seems like a mirror. It's an oval of swirling light with a black void in its middle shaped like a human silhouette. My silhouette.

I squint at it, looking for my features, but they aren't there. Particles of light. A black void. Endless nothingness. Endless everything. Comfort. Terror.

With a shake of my head, I refocus on my mission. *What is my unseelie form?* I think to myself. *How do I shift into it?*

Words float upon my awareness, chilling and ethereal. "You showed us your heart once before. It was a true heart."

I shudder. "I remember," I say, my voice harsh on my ears after the melody spoken by the All of All.

"You will find your unseelie form there."

I stare deeper into the black void that is my silhouette. "What does my heart look like?" I whisper.

The darkness swirls with the shimmering violet. I feel lost in the movement of the particles as they shift and swirl. I see what looks like a blustering wind move in the mirror. Its every move is sharp and quick and effective. A word forms in my mind. *Intellect*. The images in the mirror shift again, showing deep black water, so vast it should be terrifying. Instead, it feels comforting, warm.

Like Mother's arms. Again, a word comes to me. *Love.* The water turns to waves, then form the peaks of trees. At the base of the trees is solid earth, rock, stone. It's strong and steady and calm. *Logic.* The leaves of the trees begin to fall, floating to the ground like heart-shaped jewels. The Autumn Court comes to mind, and thoughts of Aspen follow, making my chest feel light and open. A burning heats my core. *Passion.* As the leaves fall, they grow into beautiful flames. The fire rises higher and higher, and as it grows, I become breathless, enamored with its dangerous beauty. *Rage. Anger.*

The mirror goes still, returning to my silhouette against humming violet particles. I think that might be all it will show me, until the silhouette begins to dissipate and is replaced with golden pinpricks of light piercing through the purple. It reminds me of the sky as seen from Lunar, filling me with that same sense of wonder. Words come to me again. *Mystery. Darkness. Magic. Discovery.*

"You are all of this," the ethereal voice of the All of All says. The mirror returns to stillness. This time, my reflection isn't a black void. It's...something, although I can't see it clearly, like there's a film over my eyes. I blink and stand closer. Colors emerge, and I'm surprised to see something other than violet or indigo. Still, it's difficult for me to understand what I'm looking at. Then finally, I realize it's flames. Beautiful dancing flames. But not like a normal hearth fire. This fire shifts and sways in the most stunning pinks, purples, and aquas. It's like the Aurora Borealis, something I've only read about and seen in paintings.

My heart races as I watch it—watch *me*. I stare deeper into the flames, seeking shape. Two blue eyes look back at me, keen and clever and curious with a hint of darkness in them. A flash of teeth warns me of a quick temper and a fierce determination to protect the ones she loves. Her posture shows me there is logic behind her motivations and that she doesn't react in violence without just cause.

I take a hesitant step back and she does the same. Because she is me. With a small, elongated muzzle, two pointed ears, she—*I*—stand on four tiny paws beneath slender legs.

There's only one word I can think to explain what I've become.

I'm a firefox.

Unlike the lithe kitsune with their slim bodies and their balls of flame hovering near their mouths or tails, my tricolor flames lap over every inch of my fluffy, white fur, rippling around me like waves.

And upon my fox head rests a golden crown of fire.

37

I shudder, torn between terror and awe. I've done it. I've truly shifted forms. And I wear the blessing of the All of All. My crown. The one I left behind at Bircharbor.

A roaring hiss comes from behind me, and the mirror disappears like a violet puff of smoke. I'm back in the cave, although the purple haze remains. Time, however, has unfrozen, revealing King Ustrin towering before me as an enormous orange fire lizard. His beady black eyes are narrowed, nostrils flaring with rage as his tongue lashes out of his mouth.

Gasps and grunts and growls come from the fire fae. I hear whispers uttered, first too quiet to hear. Soon I realize it's one thing repeated. *Unseelie Queen of Fire.*

I meet Aspen's eyes. For a moment I'm scared of what I'll find in them. I've seen him as a stag, but...can he accept me like this? His voice comes through the Bond. *You're beautiful, Evie.*

My heart swells, burning away the remainder of my doubts. I turn my attention to Ustrin.

With slow, slithering steps, he moves toward me until he's positioned between me and the cave's exit. "Fight me," he taunts. "Prove your worth, fool girl."

I know what needs to be done, but I can't do it here. Not where the fire fae—my fae, my people—could get caught in the crossfire. I feel a calm warmth in the back of my mind. Something tells me to turn myself over to it. As I do, my vision becomes clearer, my sense of awareness sharper. Information streams through me at once—every angle of the cave walls, my own weight, size, and shape. But I don't have to think about it or even process it. I just know it in an instant.

I lower into a crouch, springing off all four paws. I soar over Ustrin's scaly shoulder and land on an outcropping of the cave wall next to him. Scrambling to maintain purchase, I feel a weight sliding from my head. The crown. I try to right myself, but the crown clatters to the floor. I look from it to the fire lizard. Before I can make a move, hot orange flame shoots from his mouth, incinerating the crown.

I can do nothing but stare in horror as the gift from the All of All glows red, melting and shifting until what remains is a pile of shapeless molten metal. "No," I gasp.

"There goes your gift from the All of All," Ustrin says. "It was never a sign of their favor. You were never worth their blessing. Now submit to me!"

My heart sinks, eyes still locked on the melted crown. Is this my answer? Am I truly not the alpha blessed by the All of All? How did I ever think I could be?

You are more than that crown. The words shatter my

stupor and I meet Aspen's eyes from over Ustrin's shoulder. *Do not accept defeat, Evie. The crown was gifted to you from an intangible realm. It exists outside physical form.*

I don't think I can beat him, I reply. *He's too strong.*

He isn't stronger than you are. You're the Unseelie Queen of Fire.

His words strengthen me, and I stand firmer on the stone.

"Submit to me," Ustrin says, oblivious to my silent exchange with Aspen.

Wear the crown, Aspen says.

Returning my attention to the cave walls, I launch over the fire lizard to another outcropping that places me behind him. He hisses, whirling around as I launch again, landing on the floor of the tunnel. I take off, my flames lighting my way. Even if they weren't, I have a feeling I'd be able to see in the dark regardless. Ustrin's claws scrape the stone as he tears out of the chamber, hard on my heels.

I know he can't attack me until I attack him first, but I'm not willing to risk him getting too close. As I clear the mouth of the cave, I keep running, my mind processing risk and reward as I seek favorable ground. A clearing ringed by enormous trees comes into view, and I spring toward it, my four paws pounding the earth with ease as if I never had only two legs before. As I reach the other side of the clearing, I skid to a halt and whirl to face the fire lizard.

Grass and earth turn beneath Ustrin's claws as he enters the clearing, flames dancing over every scale. His movements aren't as graceful as mine, his thick limbs slow and lumbering. "Tired of running? Ready to face me?"

I assess the clearing, calculating the arrangement of trees, the grass, the glowing mushrooms. I note every rock and branch, pinpoint which smells belong to which animals lurking nearby. I'm still without much of a plan, but something inside me knows all of this is important. I take in Ustrin's size compared to mine. Even though he's slower than I am, his size makes up for my upper hand in agility. There's no way I can win by dominance of strength. And he'll never concede to me the way Nyxia's mother conceded to her. What other ways can I prove myself the alpha?

Ustrin's voice bellows through the night. "Fight me!"

I shudder at the rage fueling his tone. It's now or never. I may not be able to win by physical attack, but it's the only thing that can start this. Lowering into a crouch, I let my fire curl around me. Then I dart forth, paws pounding the earth as I charge the fire lizard. As I approach, he doesn't so much as flinch. Before I collide with him, I turn to the side and swipe out with my back legs. My claws make contact with his scales, but all they meet is firm resistance. I tear back toward the opposite end of the clearing, spinning to face him in a defensive posture.

Ustrin remains where he is. His tongue flicks in and out of his mouth, then hissing laughter fills the air. "That's all you have? A swipe of your dainty little paws?"

"We're just getting started," I say. It's the first time I've attempted to speak out loud in this form. I'm startled to realize I didn't form the words with my mouth. I've witnessed many unseelie who communicate without the need to move their lips, but it's still jarring to do it myself, no matter how natural it comes. However, the surprise only lasts a moment before my instincts prevail over all else.

"You're right about that." Ustrin opens his maw, and an orange glow surges forth. The ball of flame barrels toward me, almost faster than I can react. I roll to the ground, but the fire skims my side, extinguishing my flames where it touches and replacing them with scorched fur and blackened flesh. The pain feels the same as the burns I caused myself after Mother's trial. At least these wounds seem to quickly subside, as my own flames return, pink, purple, and aqua lapping over my ribs, repairing the flesh and restoring my strength.

I right myself but scramble along the ground to avoid his next blast. This time, the fire skims my fluffy white tail, most of the blast hitting the tree behind me. I speed across the clearing, blasts of heat soaring close enough to feel, one right after the next. I pause behind the wide trunk of a tree. My eyes flash to the clearing, finding patches of burning grass, charred trunks of trees, scorched stone.

Again, that calm warmth pulls me in, and my attention sharpens. I hear several mice burrowing beneath the earth, desperate to flee from what's happening above ground. I hear the fluttering wings of a moth in the tree overhead as it draws near a patch of flame. I hear Ustrin's claws tearing the dirt as he plods toward the tree I'm hiding behind. Even before he opens his mouth, I know what's about to happen, the sound of the fire stirring in his throat now familiar to me.

I try not to flinch as flames lap toward me, burning

the trunk of the tree I'm hiding behind and searing the tips of my ears, my tail, the edges of my fur. With a breath, my fire repairs the damage to my body, and I dart out of my hiding place to another tree. Again, I focus on the sounds, the sights, the smells. A patch of earthy mushrooms glow nearby, but there's a stronger aroma to my left. It's pungent like the mushrooms, but mingling with it is the scent of decay. I look toward the source, finding an enormous tree nearby. From sight alone, it looks just like any other tree. But as my eyes seek the boughs overhead, I see it bears no leaves, no fruit. I hear termites scurrying inside the bark, sense the hollowed patches within the trunk.

Another ball of flame soars my way, but this time I sprint out from behind the tree before it strikes it. I seek the dying tree, circling around it a few times to snag Ustrin's attention. He tears across the clearing, mouth opening wide as he prepares to launch another ball of flame. I skirt around the tree just as the flame hits it. However, he doesn't stop there. Ball after ball strikes the tree, the heat searing me. One misses the tree and sets the grass aflame near my feet. I dance away, then peek around the trunk. Ustrin is now only several feet from the tree, tongue lashing in and out of his mouth.

"Stop hiding," he hisses. "Give me a real challenge, fool girl. Let me show you what a true alpha looks like." Another blast of flame surges forth. When it strikes the trunk, I hear the melody I've been waiting for. A hollow creaking.

I launch onto a large rock and from there leap onto the nearest tree, my paws springing off its trunk as they make contact. The momentum sends me higher, and I soar to an enormous boulder. Once again, I launch away as soon as I touch the surface and find myself even higher now as I leap toward the burning tree. Heat sears my paws as I touch the bark, but I press off with all my strength. As I do, I leave behind a burst of my own fire.

I tumble to the ground, my muscles screaming at the impact as I roll across the dirt. Ustrin tosses his head left and right, seeking where I've gone. Finally, he spots me.

The burning tree creaks louder, then a sound like lightning ripping overhead tears through the night.

Ustrin rushes toward me. But he isn't fast enough.

The rotted tree comes tumbling down, pinning Ustrin beneath its flaming trunk in a tangle of rotting branches. His orange flames burn its base, but where I made contact, my tricolor fire glows and expands, creeping to where Ustrin is trapped.

I stand frozen as I watch, certain I'll see Ustrin rise at any moment.

When I see no movement, I creep forward on silent paws. I find Ustrin in his seelie form, writhing beneath my flames as he tries to combat them with his own. The enormous trunk of the tree crosses his midsection, while his shoulder is speared into the earth below by a thick, sharp branch.

He catches my eye and lets out a laugh. "You think this means you've won? I can heal, remember? You can toss your pretty little flames at me all night, but you'll run out of power long before I do. I'll continue to heal and regenerate, and when I overcome your flames, I'll kill you."

"Submit to me as alpha," I say, voice even.

He laughs again. "You're out of your mind. I just explained I'm stronger than you. I can defeat you."

"Submit to me as alpha," I say again, louder now.

"You aren't the alpha. That was nothing but a clever accident. I am far from defeated."

"Submit."

All amusement flees from his face, and he bares his teeth. "I will never submit to you. Even if you had the upper hand, I would rather die than submit."

I study his face, contorted with effort as he continues to combat my fire lapping upon him from the tree. Just how his flames managed to damage me, my fire seems to do the same to him, blackening his bright scales.

My eyes then fall to his throat, the scales there still unmarred by my fire. In seelie form, I can only imagine his internal anatomy must be humanlike, the same way Aspen's was when I performed his surgery. If that's the case, I know exactly where to find his jugular vein.

I must admit Ustrin is right. He's stronger than me. He'll never submit to me and he will fight so long as he has breath and strength. The truth of what must be done is chilling, but the calm warmth in the back of my mind promises to carry the brunt of the burden. "That leaves me one choice," I say.

With a lunge, I sink my sharp teeth into his scaly throat.

38

Sitting back on my haunches, I stare down into a moonlit stream, eyes locked on the white fox's face staring back at me. Her flames have dissipated to a glow, leaving the blood coating the fur around her neck in clear view. Even her muzzle is smeared with it despite countless attempts to cleanse herself in the rushing waters. At least she managed to wash the taste of blood from inside her mouth.

My mouth, I correct myself. *Me. That fox is me.*

Something large appears on the other side of the stream. I heard it coming minutes ago, knew it was a stag before it appeared from behind the trees. My keen hearing is attuned to my surroundings, yet I can't find it in me to care about a thing.

"Are you all right?" Aspen's voice asks through the stag.

I keep my eyes trained on my reflection. "Did you find the body?"

Silence. Then, "Yes."

Bile rises in my throat. If he found the body, then he saw a fae with its jugular torn out, left to bleed until his heart stopped beating. Bleed as my beautiful flames lapped over him.

"We must find your refugees," I say.

"I already found them." His voice is quiet, careful. Like it's walking on glass.

"You found them?" I allow my eyes to flash up to him, grateful he wears his stag face. I'm not ready to see how his seelie form looks at me.

"When Ustrin's guards took off from the cave, I knew their master must have been defeated. I came to find you straight away. When I saw you here like this, I figured I'd give you some time."

His words make sense. Now that I think about it, I remember a stag coming to this stream half a dozen times before now. A raven visited a time or two as well. I return my gaze to the flowing waters.

He continues. "That's when I sought out the refugees. They weren't far from here. The guards had fled the site there as well. Nyxia joined me after the threat to Selene Palace was extinguished. She brought my people back with her."

"The guards fled? And the flame too? No one put up a fight?"

"The guards likely felt the dissolution of their vows to their king, and the flame he ordered to the palace no longer needed to obey orders either. There was no reason to fight us."

With a single nod, I say, "No reason because Ustrin is dead."

"Yes."

"Because I killed him."

"Yes."

My muzzle twitches, and it reminds me of a human lower lip quivering. "Will he heal from his wounds?"

Aspen hesitates before answering, but I already know what he's going to say. I remember what Gildmar had told me when we treated our patients after the explosion at Bircharbor. If a fae loses too much blood, their bodies can't keep up with the healing. And I left him with more than an open throat. I buried him in my fire.

"He's gone, Evie."

A tremble goes through me. It had been so easy to snap my teeth over Ustrin's throat. My human training told me where to bite. My fox instincts knew exactly how to angle my mouth, how to sink my canines beneath the shingle of scales where I could puncture his flesh. After the deed was done, all I could do was stare. When I could look no longer, I retched, then took off for the nearest source of water.

My stomach turns at the thought, and I try to retrain my focus on my reflection. But now all I can see is the blood still matted in my fur.

From the corner of my eye, I see Aspen shudder, then two legs replace his four. My reflection becomes distorted as feet splash through the stream. When the water returns to its calm flow, I see Aspen at my side in his seelie form. He's gazing at me. Me, the firefox. Me, the killer.

I can't bear to look at him, so I stare at the earth beneath my paws.

A warm, gentle hand falls on my back. I want to pull away from the touch, but I can't find it in me to move.

Aspen brushes his hand along my fur, safe from my flames now that they've diminished to a harmless glow. "I've felt exactly how you feel now," he says, voice thick with emotion. He sounds so different from his stag's voice. I try to remember what my seelie voice sounds like, but I can't. He continues. "This is how I felt after I killed the Holstrom girls. Then again after I slaughtered their animals. It isn't an easy feeling."

"But the act of killing...that part was *too* easy."

"Yes."

I swallow hard, the lump in my throat feeling out of place in my fox's body. "I've killed two people. Torn open two throats without a second thought."

His hand stills, then returns to stroking my fur. "It won't get any easier. But what you did was necessary. Unlike me, you didn't fall victim to your rage. You protected yourself. Stood up for what needed to be done."

"How do you know? You weren't there when I left Mr. Meeks to burn alive. You weren't there when I sank my teeth into King Ustrin's neck."

He angles himself closer to me, but I still won't meet his gaze. "I know because I know you. I know how calculated you are. How calm under pressure. How precious you consider life."

"You are one of us." A new voice fills the air, one I only half-noticed in my distracted emotional state. It's the crustacean from the cave, and he's scuttling toward me from between the trees.

In fact, several dozens of figures stream from the shadows, lighting the night with their balls of flame, their bright bodies, their glowing eyes and fiery wings. "You're one of us," the fire fae echo.

A white kitsune steps forward and lowers down on its front paws, eyes closed. "Unseelie Queen of Fire."

A blue wisp bobs at the kitsune's side. "No. Ustrin is defeated. There is but one ruler of Fire now." She flourishes a glowing, blue hand and bends into her version of a bow. "Queen of Fire."

The rest of the fire fae perform their own bows, echoing the wisp. "Queen of Fire."

I stare wide-eyed at the fae surrounding me. My fae. My people. The daunting task of ruling them falls heavy on my shoulders.

After what feels like an endless silence, the fire fae rise. Some stream off into the night, but a few step closer to me, as if awaiting instruction. The kitsune who first bowed taps anxiously from paw to paw. "Can I eat him?" he finally says.

I'm caught off guard. "Eat him?"

"The dead king."

The other kitsune nod, pleading to join the feast. A fire sprite flies overhead. "Can I burn him?" she asks. "That is, if Your Most Gracious Majesty hasn't consumed all of him with your flame."

A firebird swoops down from the trees. "May I harvest any remaining scales? They will insulate my nests and keep my young warm."

My stomach churns at the eagerness in the eyes around me. My human side shouts from the back of my mind, *No, absolutely not. This is not how we treat our dead.* But a new part of me admits the chilling realization that I know very little about the unseelie.

Both sides confess I'm in way over my head.

Finally, I turn to Aspen. Without reading his expression, I give him a questioning glance. In return, he offers a subtle nod.

"Do what you will," I say, hoping my voice doesn't quaver. "Harvest him, burn him, and consume him as you wish, but do so without argument amongst each other. You may have your requests in the order I received them, and not one fight will break out amongst you. When you are finished, I want no sign of him remaining."

Another round of bows follow, and after thanking me, the fire fae disappear into the night. A few remain close; some retreat to the boughs overhead, others burrow in holes nearby, and a few sprites and wisps float about the trees.

Aspen and I are left mostly alone in silence.

After a while, he asks, "Do you know how to turn back?"

I shake my head. "I'm afraid to."

"Why?"

The lump rises in my throat again. I can't give voice to my feelings, my fears. In truth, I'm afraid that once my fox side falls away, I'll crumble. I'm afraid I'll taste blood in my mouth, feel it on my flesh and never be able to face myself again. And I'm afraid how Aspen will look at me. He seems to accept the vicious firefox. Can he accept the violent woman?

"You can't stay in this form too long," he says. "At best, you'll be putting off the inevitable. At worst, you'll forget who you really are."

"What's the inevitable?"

"You must face what you've done and accept yourself.

You must feel. For one with human blood, I can only imagine it's going to be far more painful than anything I've experienced. But it's the only way."

I'm pulled between two terrors: the fear of emotions that will surely cripple me, and the fear that I could lose myself completely. "How do I do it?"

"Someday it will be effortless to shift between forms," he explains. "For now, strong emotion is the easiest. What helps me find my seelie side when I'm trapped in a rage is tender feelings. Anything sad or painful or joyful. Do you remember when you stopped me in my stag form when I was on my way to your village? You helped me remember. You made me feel."

I nod, recalling how he'd calmed and returned to his seelie form. "But you were stuck in a rage. I'm stuck in...I don't know what this is."

"You're in between," he says. "You're trying not to feel one way or another, but you must give in at least a little. You must let yourself feel something."

The resistance is like a solid wall. Fiery anger stands on one side while debilitating sorrow stands on the other. I'm perched on the top of the wall, balance tenuous as I teeter on a blade's edge.

Aspen's hand rests on my shoulder. "You can fall, Evie," he whispers. "I'll catch you."

With that, I close my eyes, a sob lurching over the lump in my throat, tears streaming from beneath my eyelids. I shudder, again and again. Then a ripple of pain tears through me from my head to my toes. My body feels like it's grown unwieldy, heavy, lumbering, enormous hands where dainty paws just were, clawing into the dirt.

My eyes catch those looking back at me in the stream. Wide and wild, auburn hair like a tangled nest around my head, blood splattering my cheeks. I slap the water with my hand, disrupting the reflection, then take my damp fingers and smear them across my face, furiously rubbing.

Hands grab my shoulders, warm and strong. I freeze, finding Aspen's eyes. I'm locked in his gaze, unable to move or look away. It's the moment of truth. The woman in the reflection was more of a crazed animal than my firefox form was. Is that what he sees too?

He studies my face, and I study his. I've never been more aware of our contrast. His golden skin is pure and flawless, his eyes swimming with color. The angles of his jaw and cheekbones look as if they were carved by a master craftsman. And his hair; even in disarray, his blue-black tresses fall in elegant waves around his antlers. But me? I'm...I'm...

"You're so beautiful, Evie." A hand leaves my shoulder and lights on my cheek, thumb brushing away the dampness of tears and water from the stream. "In every form, you're beautiful. In every form, I'm here for you. In every form, I love you."

His face swims before me as more tears obscure my vision. My shoulders slump, and Aspen pulls me close. I nestle into his chest, clinging to his shirt as his warm arms wrap around my back. The dam breaks from within me, unleashing the sorrow I held back after my mother's death, releasing my agony over the two lives I've taken. I let it all out, let myself break and crumble, break and crumble.

Throughout it all, Aspen maintains his silent vigil, holding me like a vessel for the pieces of my shattered soul.

39

A warm light touches my face, and I turn away from it, burrowing my head into Aspen's chest. I inhale his scent deeply, his rosemary and cinnamon helping to clear my mind. We must have slept by the stream last night after I sobbed for hours. I don't remember falling asleep, but my body feels rested. Invigorated. A buzzing sound flutters by my ear along with an odd warmth.

I turn my head and open my eyes, expecting to find the light of dawn. Hazy morning sunlight has fallen over the woods, but that isn't the light that first woke me. A fire sprite hovers over my face, head turning one way then another as she smiles.

My eyes widen, and she darts a few feet back. "Forgive me, Your Majesty," she begs, her tiny voice quavering. "I came to thank you for your gracious gift last night. Then when I saw you, I couldn't help but look upon my queen. You're so..." she lets out a dreamy sigh, "pretty."

Aspen stirs next to me, and he lifts himself onto his elbows, brow furrowed as he takes in our little interloper.

I pull myself to sitting, and the sprite dances in the air before me.

"I didn't realize how pretty you were before," she says. "Truly, I didn't like you much at all, but then you were a firefox with those lovely flames, and then you defeated Ustrin. Then you let me burn him." She lets out another sigh, this one contented. "I feel quite invigorated this morning. I've never burned a royal before."

"He was delicious." I whirl toward the voice, finding a kitsune sitting on the other side of the stream. He runs his tongue over the side of his muzzle as if savoring the memory.

My stomach churns, and I suppress a shudder. I've yet to utter a word and am still befuddled over what I could possibly say.

Before I can come up with a coherent reply, a firebird lands nearby. "His scales will keep my hatchlings warm. Thank you, Your Majesty." She bows, and the other two fae follow suit.

I manage to find my voice. "You're welcome."

"Will you be taking us home?" the kitsune asks.

"Home?" I echo.

The sprite clasps her hands together, expression wistful. "To Fire. I haven't been since I was a wee spriteling. Now that Ustrin is gone, you can have his palace!"

I'm overwhelmed by their forward nature, by thoughts of going to the Fire Court and claiming a palace. But these are my people. These strange, unsettling creatures that feed off carrion and harvest the dead are whom I now rule. They are whom I must care and advocate for. I plaster a forced smile over my lips. "Yes, we will return once I have settled the details of my travels."

The sprite flutters closer, head tilted to the side. "Might I travel at your side? I can light your reading materials and I promise not to burn your gowns."

"I'll consider it," I say.

"And may my tribe light your travels at night?" the kitsune asks. "Do not allow these duties to fall on the wisps. They will take us miles off course each night. They have no sense of direction, despite what they will tell you."

"Another thing I'll keep in mind."

The firebird flaps her wings. "And will you—"

I hold up my hand to silence her. Squaring my shoulders, I adopt a regal bearing. "Let us discuss travel once I am prepared to hold a formal audience. You may petition me then."

The three fae bow, uttering, "Most Esteemed Queen of Fire."

When they make no move to leave, eyes still trained on me, I rise to my feet and extend a hand with a nod. "You may go."

Once they're out of sight, I hear Aspen snickering behind me. I round on him. "Stop that. I have no idea what I'm doing, and you know it."

His lips pull into a smirk. "You're doing fine."

I try to match his grin, but my lips falter. All at once, the crushing sorrow I felt last night returns in a rush. My knees buckle beneath me, but I clench my fingers into fists to steady myself. Sorrow and rage go to war within, but I neither fight them nor encourage them to grow.

Aspen's face softens as he offers me a hand. "It will get better."

I'm tempted to follow my rage, to take it all to the Twelfth Court and shift back into my firefox form. I could run free, with only a fraction of the burden I feel now. Perhaps it would be easier to rule the unseelie in that form as well.

I shake the thought from my head, reminding myself I have more than the unseelie to fight for. There's a war coming. Two, most likely. The seelie council will discover what I've done and they'll come for me. They'll come for all the rebels. We'll be forced to fight, fae against fae. The humans will come next. Without a treaty, what's to stop violence from breaking out? What's to stop the humans from crossing the faewall with iron swords, guns, and grenades? What's to stop the fae from crossing the wall to slaughter innocents in an attempt to reclaim their land?

Me. I'm the only one who can temper the destruction. I'm the only one who cares enough about both sides to fight this war without letting the Fair Isle fall into chaos.

War will come. It's already here.

I sparked it. I'll fight it. And I'll end it.

I don't know how, but I know that I will.

With a sigh, I take Aspen's outstretched hand, and we make our way through the forest together.

~

By the time Selene Palace comes into view, an imposing figure is halfway between us and the front doors. Queen Nyxia closes the distance, expression twisted with irritation. "Look who finally decided to show up. The good Queen Evelyn."

I furrow my brow, taken aback by her scorn.

She puts her hands on her hips. "As if I didn't already have enough unwelcome guests."

My mouth falls open and snaps shut as I search for words. "If I'm no longer welcome—"

"Not you." She flutters a dismissive hand. "Your...*sister*." The last words come out more like a hiss.

The blood leaves my face. "My sister? She's here?"

"Yes. She claimed the protection of a peaceful exchange of words and said she'd speak to no one but you."

"Did she come alone?"

Nyxia nods. "Thankfully, otherwise I wouldn't have spared the girl's life."

"Where is she?"

She lifts her chin and purses her lips, as if preparing for reproach. "The dungeon."

I start off toward the palace again. "Take me to her."

My heart pounds in my chest as Nyxia leads me through the front door, then down a hall I've never been to. We descend a flight of stairs that end in a corridor carved from obsidian. My mind is whirling to comprehend what Amelie's arrival must mean.

I feel Aspen's hand graze my elbow. "Be careful," he whispers. "We don't know what to expect."

I nod. Every part of me assumes this is some sort of trick, and I don't fault Nyxia for choosing to lock her up.

The dark corridor widens, and two wraiths in flowing black translucent robes stand guard before what must be the dungeon. Nyxia nods to the guards, and they stand apart, allowing us to enter. Beyond, everything is carved from the same glossy, black stone as the corridor, and the bars of the cells are blanketed in writhing shadows. The only light comes from a few sparse orbs along the walls, keeping the occupants hidden from view.

Nyxia stops before a cell, gesturing toward it before she steps away. Arms remaining crossed, she takes up post along the empty wall opposite the cells. Aspen does the same.

Only I approach the cell. I step closer, squinting into the dark. A figure shifts inside, but I can't see clearly. I lift my hand.

"Don't touch the bars," Nyxia says, making me jump.

I look back at her, taking in the warning her eyes are trying to convey.

"The shadows will incapacitate you," she explains.

I swallow hard and return my attention to the cell. Hand still raised, I turn my palm upward. My motions are almost automatic, as is my intention for light. As soon as I think it, a blue flame ignites above my hand. Only then does a wave of shock move through me.

"Evie." The voice comes from within the cell. The figure steps closer to the bars, as do I. My fire illuminates my sister.

Rage and tenderness and sorrow fight for dominance as I take in her haggard appearance. She looks worse than I did last night—than I likely still do now. Her copper hair is matted with dirt, tangled around her shoulders. There's no sign of her selkie skin, only filthy flesh and a thin, torn dress that ends above her knees.

She smiles, eyes swimming with tears. "You're making fire," she says with a gasp. "Are you queen now?"

My eyes narrow, suspicion creeping over me. Is that why she's here? To fight me for my throne? She's the eldest. It never occurred to me that she would fight me for the crown. That she might have a stronger claim to it than I do. I lower my hand, extinguishing the flame as my fingers clench into fists. "Why are you here?"

She takes a step back, as if surprised by my cold tone. "I escaped him. I finally did it, Evie."

I steel myself to voice my next words. "Our mother is dead."

Her hands fly to her lips. "No."

"They killed her because you refused to attend her trial." I know I'm omitting more than I'm saying, but in this moment, I want to wound her. I want to punish her for everything she's done and for everything she intends to do now.

She slides to her knees, wailing. Her hands reach for the bars but flinch away before they make contact with the writhing shadows. "He did this," she cries through her teeth, slamming her fists on the obsidian floor.

"Who?"

"Cobalt." The name escapes her lips with more wrath than I've ever witnessed her demonstrate. "He...he destroyed me. You have no idea the things he made me do. The things he made me say and suffer through."

My heart squeezes, but I refuse to fall for her words. He could have sent her here, could have planted every reaction and every word into her. He could be lurking near the border, waiting for some sign from Amelie that he and the council can make their move against us. She could be here to poison me, to take my crown. "Why are you here?" I say again, more forceful this time.

She looks at me through glazed eyes, cheeks wet with tears. "I came to see you."

"What do you want from me?"

"Your protection."

I let out a bitter laugh. "You had your chance and you refused my help. Why should I protect you now? After everything you've done—"

"I want to kill him." She says it like a growl, face twisting into a hateful mask I've never seen her wear. "I want your protection. Then I want to help you kill Cobalt."

I study her, seeking signs of Cobalt's manipulation. "How would you help me do that?"

"I have the power of his name," she whispers.

"You're Bonded, so he has the same power over yours as well," I argue. "He could be ordering you to do this, to be here and say everything you're saying at this very moment."

She shakes her head. "I made sure I waited until all his orders that could possibly harm you faded. He had to give me new orders daily to ensure he always covered all his bases with me. But with his new wife," she says this with clear disdain, "he became easily distracted. Stopped renewing my orders as often. Left me alone in the undersea palace for longer and longer. When I felt no current command to keep me there, I fled. I crossed lakes, rivers, and streams to get here. Ran until my feet bled."

I can feel my resolve to hate her beginning to lessen, a sure sign I need to cling to it more. "How can I trust you?"

She rises to her feet on trembling legs. Tears continue to stream down her cheeks. "Evelyn Fairfield," she says, voice quavering. "I give you my name. I give you the power of my true name."

A hum of energy buzzes toward me, feeling like both a lightness and a weight at the same time. It isn't like the mutual hum between me and Aspen. This one only moves one way. Rage soars through me, revulsion at this one-sided power she's bestowed. I never asked for this burden. All I ever wanted to do was protect her. Now I control her.

Angry tears swim in my eyes, but I blink them away. I square my shoulders to hide how shaken I am and burn Amelie with a glare. My voice comes out cold. "Thank you, dear sister."

Without another word, I turn on my heel and march from the dungeon, letting my sister's sobs follow me long after the sound of them is gone.

ABOUT THE AUTHOR

Tessonja Odette is a fantasy author living in Seattle with her family, her pets, and ample amounts of chocolate. When she isn't writing, she's watching cat videos, petting dogs, having dance parties in the kitchen with her daughter, or pursuing her many creative hobbies. Read more about Tessonja at www.tessonjaodette.com

ALSO BY TESSONJA ODETTE

THE LELA TRILOGY - YA EPIC FANTASY

Shadows of Lela

Veil of Mist

Shades of Prophecy

YA DYSTOPIAN PSYCHOLOGICAL THRILLER

Twisting Minds

CPSIA information can be obtained
at www.ICGtesting.com
Printed in the USA
LVHW031152131221
706054LV00001B/87